Dead Letter

Dead Letter

Jane Waterhouse

WHEELeR
PUBLISHING, INC.
ROCKLAND, MA

★ AN AMERICAN COMPANY ★

Published in Large Print by arrangement with G.P. Putnam's Sons, a division of Penguin Putnam Inc. in the United States and Canada

Wheeler Large Print Book Series.

Set in 16 pt Plantin.

Library of Congress Cataloging-in-Publication Data

Waterhouse, Jane.
    Dead letter / Jane Waterhouse.
        p. (large print) cm.(Wheeler large print book series)
    ISBN 1-56895-953-2 (softcover)
    1. Quinn, Garner (Fictitious Character)—Fiction. 2. Women journalists—Fiction. 3. Stalking victims—Fiction. 4. New Jersey—Fiction.
5. Large type books. I. Title. II. Series

[PS3573.A812 D43   2000]

813'.54—dc21

00-062056
CIP

Acknowledgements

I'm grateful to the following people for providing me with information that helped in the writing of this book: Special Agent Robert E. Booth, Hélène Blanton, Inge Nuss, Ann Hartig, and Jason, Matt and Missy at Jack's Music Shop.

I'd also like to thank Christine Pepe, Carol Clayton, Carol Tvrdik, Kim Schapman, my friends at Fair Haven Books, and the entire Lotano clan for thier encouragement and support. Last but not least are the earthbound angels in my life: Joyce Evans, Icilda Fields, my wonderful parents, my sister, Amy and my son, Baylen—who managed to be sensitive and patient throughout my wanderings in what he calls "Garnerworld."

For Michele

*"Fear death?—to feel the
fog in my throat,
The mist in my face."*

ROBERT BROWNING

PROLOGUE

On summer nights, back in the sixties, a fleet of yellow trucks would travel up and down streets along the Jersey shore, driving with funereal solemnity, trailing white plumes of mosquito spray. Errant children often slipped out of doors just to run through the perfumed mist. I know because I was one of them.

The insecticide was like a cool kiss blown into the heat, an ether that made your limbs go heavy, and the inside of your mouth prickly and thick. Those nights, I went to bed early, impelled into a sudden, deep sleep—and oh, the dreams I dreamt!—bucking kinescopes dipped in Easter egg dye, then swirled to a runny blur. Dreams so fragile they shattered into nightmares under the weight of the chemical fog sifting through the window screens, leaving me gasping in a straitjacket of twisted sheets.

That's when, from down the hall, I'd hear the sound of padded footsteps, and the door opening, and Cilda Fields would appear in a whoosh of fresh air. "Shussh, Ga'ner Quinn," she'd say, untangling the bedclothes with crooked fingers. "It's just one of your dreams. Go back to sleep."

"I can't. Tell me a story."

And Cilda lowered herself against the headboard with a sigh, her nightgown giving off little sparks in the dark. "Once upon a time," she began, "there was a beautiful princess wit' fiery red 'air and skin white and smooth like a satin pillow."

I closed my eyes, free-falling into the black velvet holes of her island woman oohs and ahhs. "The princess, she lived in a big castle by the sea. And 'er father, the king, 'e was a great, important man, rich and 'andsome! And 'er mother—though far away—kept watch over the girl, like an angel. And everybody loved that young princess. Ev'ry-body, far and wide..."

"Who?" I asked, for I wanted to hear her say the names.

"Well, there's Kathianne did, and Camillia. And Annalee, and Deon, and pretty little Mercedes too." Cilda went on in a singsong lullaby voice: "And Deshon, Debbie, and Deena, and Akila, and Kadean, and Kahlil, and Kaleesha..." They were real people, members of Cilda's family, who lived on the island of Jamaica.

Snuggled up in my pink and white bedroom, blinking away a fleece-edged sleep, I had to remind myself that the rest of the story was just a fairy tale. I knew that Cilda Fields's shoulder came with a paycheck attached. She'd been hired to care for and comfort me, because my father, a famous attorney, and my mother, an infamous drunk, somehow could not.

But I was tough. They couldn't pull the fleecy wool over my eyes—not any of them. At a tender age, I mastered the first three commandments. People lied. Looks deceived. And truth never came easy. Like the glow of

2

taillights glimpsed through a mist of mosquito spray, truth was something you had to fight your way toward, with your eyes wide open, no matter how much it stung.

Years passed. I became a true crime-writer. My early cynicism served me well. I sold a lot of books, made a name for myself, added a few more commandments to the stone tablet. Thou shalt not marry a lawyer. Thou shalt not get emotionally involved with a subject. Remember the deadline date and keep it holy.

I'd proven my original hypothesis a million times over. In real life there were no princesses, no kings or angelic queens. Not only were there skeletons in the closets of every castle, there was liable to be a corpse in the keep as well. I'd seen so much, so many awful things, that fear no longer held sway over me. One by one, my childish nightmares evaporated like an insecticide-laced fog—mysterious and sweet, with the aftertaste of distant poisons.

At thirty-nine, I was still an innocent, blissfully unaware of the terror to come.

PART ONE

The first letter arrived in early August—just a plain white envelope addressed to my home. Local postmark, no return.

We were less than forty-eight hours away from embarking on this big-deal family vacation I'd planned, and there were a million loose ends left to tie; but it was one of those mornings that scribble poetry on your senses and draw you out of doors, so I stuffed the mail into a tote bag, poured some coffee into my portable mug, and said, "Think I'll head over to the office for a while."

My daughter, Temple, shrugged up from the table with bleary-eyed disinterest. Over at the sink, Cilda Fields was scraping the last of the scrambled eggs into the garbage disposal. We'd known each other for so long that any given inanimate object had become a fair medium of communication between us. *Give it up, Ga'ner Quinn,* the drain gurgled now. *Won't be not'ing from that man Blackmoor in the post today.*

"I have some calls to make," I said.

Touchy, aren't we? Cilda telegraphed with a swish of sponge over the tile counter. I let the screen door slap shut on its hinges behind me, glad to have had the final word.

Outside, in the bright, unflinching sun, I stopped pretending. I never could fool Cilda Fields anyway. How many mornings had she witnessed my hopeful pilgrimage up the drive to meet the mail truck? Watched me thumb through each delivery, my fingers itching to tear into every tissuey envelope stamped <PAR AVION>, my heart aching for the sight of one name nibbed in India ink? And yet a year had gone by without so much as a word from Dane Blackmoor.

If I closed my eyes and held my breath, I could still remember the slow, soft progression of his mouth along the underside of my jaw, upward to my ear, how he'd whispered his parting shots in a hoarse, raspy voice, calling me "relentless" and "difficult," "maddening." "How come," I asked, coming up for air between kisses, "it doesn't feel like I'm getting dumped?"

Blackmoor had laughed sadly, but he was already backing his way out the door. "So what are you telling me—" I said grabbing the lapels of his jacket. "I'm never going to see you again?"

"I don't know." He spent a long moment gently extricating my fingers. "That's something I have to figure out."

"How will I know when you've figured it out?"

"You'll know." Blackmoor's eyes were solemn. "I'll send you a sign."

But month after month passed, and no sign had come yet. I ran my palm down the side of the canvas bag. Today, I knew, would not be any different. Without any sense of anticipation or relish, I hefted the tote onto my shoulder and continued down the path.

My office stood less than five hundred feet away, connected to the main house and the guest quarters by a maze of herringboned cobbles. All the architecture is dark, Gothic, with steeply pitched gables, slanting roofs, weathered shingles. One might think, by looking at them, that these buildings have been here forever. Actually, when I bought the land, there was nothing on it but a thatch of pines, a strip of sand, and an old seawall. Sandwiched between the banks of a river and the raging Atlantic, this place became my refuge and sanctuary—not to mention, when nor'easters hit, my very own flood zone.

Today, though, the sky was a guileless delft blue, with no wind. My office, on the other hand, looked locked up and defensive, jutting out from the pitch pines like a set of clenched teeth. The outer door stuck, so I had to kick it, sloshing my coffee around the rim where the lid wasn't tight. Once inside the reception room, I flicked on the lights. The sight of the desk where my assistant once sat always surprised me. I still expected to see Jack there, swiveled back on the castors, juggling the phone on his shoulder.

"Any messages?" I asked the empty chair. The answering machine winked back at me craftily.

I hit the play button, walked into my office, and dumped the mail out onto the blotter, riffling through it as I listened. Max Shroner called to say the contracts had arrived, and please God, it looked like the film deal would go through in time for him to pay for his daughter's wedding. Our handyman, Ben Snow, wanted to let me know that he'd picked up the garage doors I ordered. The last call came from Peggy Boyle, the realtor who was listing my father's estate in Spring Lake. She wanted to have an open house while we were on vacation—there was already *such a lot* of interest, oh, and would I mind *terribly* if she catered breakfast? She'd be out of the office today, so could I *please* call her at home.

Except for the new garage doors, I didn't give a damn about any of it one way or the other; I figured I'd better call Peg, though, or she'd have a fit. When I went to the machine to get her home number, I mistakenly hit fast-forward instead of rewind.

"Hey, Snowbear," my daughter's voice said. "Pick me up at the sports shed behind the school as soon as you can." It was an old message, but it made me smile. Snowbear was the name of the tattered stuffed animal Temple had slept with when she was a baby. It was our secret code, the password that prevented her from going off with strangers. But in Temple's vernacular it had also come to mean, *Come as soon as you can,* or, when friends were listening in, *Hey, Mom, I love you.*

I love you too, kiddo, I thought to myself, picking up the mail. A quick once-through produced nothing from *that man* Blackmoor. I pushed the pile aside. For the next hour I took care of business, returning calls that couldn't wait until I got back from Maine. It must've been nearly eleven when I finally turned my attention to the mail again. This go-around a plain white envelope caught my eye. Using my letter opener, I sliced through the flap. The note had been handprinted on a standard leaf of copy paper. I began to read:

DEAR MS. QUINN,
SAW YOU ON NIGHTLINE AND WAS FRANKLY AMAZED THAT A WOMAN SO FEMININE & PHYSICALLY ATTRACTIVE COULD WRITE SUCH GRAPHIC ACCOUNTS OF SEXUAL PER-VERSION & VIOLENCE... INTRIGUED...WENT OUT & BOUGHT EVERYTHING WITH YOUR NAME ON IT....THE DEGENERATE NATURE OF YOUR SUBJECTS SIDLED UP TO THAT CLEAN, HIGH SOCIETY PROFILE, NOT TO MENTION YOUR EYES AND HAIR AND SEXY LITTLE PERSONAL ASIDES (YEAH, I GOT THEM) ON THOSE COOL WHITE PAGES. GOOD BAD GIRL, *YOU ROCK MY WORLD.*
XXXXXXXXXXXXXXXXXXXXXXXXXXXXXXXXX XXXXXXXXXXXXXXXX
       ALWAYS,   CHAZ

I fought a cresting wave of nausea. After the physical response subsided, I forced myself to turn a cold, analytical eye back to the page.

The print, though handwritten, looked as though it could have come out of a comic book, all uppercase letters, distinctive, yet at the same time oddly *generic*. I picked up the envelope. How had this guy managed to get my home address? The personal tone, the implied sex-uality, the row of X's—everything about it creeped me out. But then I've never been comfortable with the concept of having fans, let alone getting mail from them.

11

Notoriety had ambushed me at a time in my life when I was least prepared for it. I didn't seek the attention; I sought justice. My first book was written in a state of moral indignation—"a childish snit," according to my father. Dudley and I seldom saw things the same way.

I was thirteen years old when he took on what would become his most challenging case: the defense of Dulcie Mariah, a rock star accused of killing her baby son. Not only did the great Dudley Quinn win an acquittal, he also fell in love with his client. Many years later, I uncovered what I believed to be irrefutable proof of Dulcie's guilt. The result was *Rock-a-Bye Baby.* The book's astonishing success... Dudley's subsequent lawsuit... the *Time* and *Newsweek* covers, our photo profiles pasted, nose to nose—

QUINN VS. QUINN:
Legendary Defense Attorney Retaliates After Being Hit with "ROCK"

—I don't think anyone could've predicted all that. In one fell swoop, I became rich, sought after, and most bewildering of all, *a celebrity.*

I'll admit I haven't always been a completely passive participant in my own rise to fame. During the early years, it was quite a rush—playing confidence games with serial killers; figuring out the twists and turns of their minds; slipping into their shoes, and walking the dark side awhile. I've gotten myself into some dicey situations, made some mistakes, and quite a few headlines. But all the media hype about Garner Quinn the hotshot, someone who plays it fast and loose—that's just myth.

I don't take chances unless they're absolutely necessary. After all, I'm a single mother with a teenage daughter. I have responsibilities. *Exercise caution*, that's my latest commandment. Which is why I wasn't about to just dismiss this Chaz.

"Watcha doin'?"

I spun around in my chair so fast the letter fell to the floor. "Holy Mother—what're *you* doing, sneaking in here like that?"

Temple grinned. "I'm not sneaking. We're shopping for bathing suits today, remember? Get with the program, Mother." Only someone with a sixteen-year-old body could smile at the prospect of trying on six inches of string and spandex in a poorly lit stall filled with carny mirrors and mounted cameras.

"All right, all right," I groused, leaning over, trying to pocket the note.

Temple's antennae shot up. "What's that?"

"Just another nut."

She opened the mini refrigerator and took out a Coke. "What's this one want?"

Her nonchalance disheartened me. That nutty people wrote to her mother was nothing new to Temple. Letters poured into my agent's office daily—convicted killers wanting Garner Quinn to prove their innocence; parents, out of their minds with grief, begging me to write about murdered sons and daughters; the confused, the besieged, the wounded, who'd somehow wandered onto violent terrain, wanting me to help them find their way back to safe ground.

"What's he want?" Temple repeated.

"I don't know," I said. "Maybe nothing."

She perched on the edge of the desk. It seemed odd, almost intrusive, her being here like this. School had been out for six weeks, but we hadn't yet found our summer rhythm. That was why this family vacation was so important.

Temple's gaze followed mine to the letter in my lap. "What're you gonna do?"

"I'm going to take us shopping for bathing suits," I told her, stuffing Chaz's note into the top drawer of my desk. And that's where it stayed, in my private office, near the story-book house I'd built, on a remote finger of land pointing out to the sea.

Two days later another letter came. This one was thick—fourteen pages, front and back, of the same cheerful, uppercase printing. Scanning it, I found that Chaz had transcribed long passages from my books, underlining certain words and rearranging them to form new sentences.

For instance, in *All Through the Night* I'd quoted a detective as saying, *"Soon as we come in we saw the girl, and there are gashes all over her body, and a deep one across her neck."* Chaz wrote:

"SOON AS WE COME IN WE SAW THE GIRL, AND THERE ARE GASHES ALL OVER HER BODY, AND A DEEP ONE ACROSS HER NECK."

Then, under it, he put the words:

SOON AS WE COME
WE ARE ONE

Once again, I fought a tide of nausea. A line from the first note came to mind, something about the "sexy personal asides" in my writing. My eyes skittered to the final paragraphs:

BY THE WAY, SENT FOR A TAPE OF THAT INTERVIEW YOU DID WITH CHARLIE ROSE. SHAME ON YOU, GARNER, LETTING HIM FLIRT WITH YOU THAT WAY!!! PLAYING IT OVER, I SAW 11 EXAMPLES OF ROSE'S PERSISTENT HAND TOUCHING... 6 TOUCHES 2 TO 3 SECONDS IN DURATION. & YOU LAUGHING LIKE IT'S SOME BIG PRIVATE JOKE. WELL, IT'S NO JOKE.

PROVOCATIVE BEHAVIOR CAN BE DANGEROUS, GARNER. YOU OF ALL PEOPLE SHOULD KNOW THAT. IT'S UNDERSTANDABLE THAT YOU NEED TO PRESENT A SOCIABLE DEMEANOR FOR THE PURPOSES OF P.R. & BOOK PROMOTION, ETC., BUT PUTTING YOUR FINGERS UP NEAR YOUR MOUTH AND CERTAIN BRAZEN EYE CONTACT CAN BE MISCONSTRUED. SORRY IF THAT SOUNDS HARSH, BUT OUR RELATIONSHIP IS BASED ON HONESTY.

ALSO, IT'S ABOUT TIME FOR YOU TO START GROWING YOUR HAIR AGAIN. DON'T YOU AGREE?

The signature, LOVE, CHAZ, was offset by another row of X's. I stared at it for a long

15

moment, trying to ignore the roiling in my gut. Then I spun my chair around and picked up a leatherbound book from the shelf behind me. One of the perks of my job is having such a book, an alphabetized compilation of the phone numbers and addresses of cops, FBI agents, and private detectives all over the country. From A to Z, I was extremely well connected.

I leafed through a few pages, then stopped. *What're you going to say, Garner? That some fruitcake thinks you're writing him secret love notes in your books? That he caught you flirting with Charlie Rose, and P.S., doesn't much like the new haircut?* It took me years to burrow into the old-boy crime-fighter network and I hadn't done it by acting like a wuss.

The boldly printed words—

<u>SOON AS WE COME</u>
<u>WE ARE ONE</u>

—stared insolently back from the page. *You didn't do it by ignoring your instincts either,* I reminded myself. The name I wanted was buried among a dozen other H's. J. Emmett Hogan, Special Agent, FBI.

Before I could reach for the receiver the phone rang, startling me. "Hello?"

"Yes, 'ello." Cilda sounded harried. "We got the man up 'ere with the doors for the garage, Temple wants to know can she go hover to Jamie's 'ouse, and Mercedes says should she take a taxi from the train?"

"Tell Ben's guy to go ahead with the doors.

16

Keep Temple home, and let Mercedes know we'll pick her up at the station." The day was starting to spiral out of control. We were leaving for Maine in the morning. I had suitcases to pack, the car to get organized. "On second thought..." I sighed, "Tell them all I'm on my way."

I closed the book on Hogan's number. Folded Chaz's thick letter and put it in the drawer next to the first one. *He hasn't threatened you, it's probably nothing,* I told myself. *You can handle it once you get back.*

TWO

I'd never been on a family vacation before. Dudley—my only parent to speak of—preferred willowy blond travel companions, and my ex-husband hadn't stuck around long enough to take that Big Red Boat to Disney World. I'd spent most of my daughter's childhood in courtrooms and at crime scenes. There were long weekends, of course, and holiday getaways; but Temple and I seemed such a small, precariously balanced unit—too *two* to be considered something as all-encompassing as Family with a capital F.

This time, though, I told myself, things would be different. Cilda was coming with us. Cilda, and her daughter Mercedes.

Admittedly, the Mercedes part made me nervous. Temple had brought up the subject of our trip at Cilda's birthday dinner. The next thing I knew, I was blurting, *"Hey, you're welcome to join us if you can get time off from the show,"* thinking, like, *Fat chance.* Never in a million years would I have imagined she'd say yes.

Mercedes Fields was a producer for one of the local New York news broadcasts. Only slightly less driven than I, she made up for it by being far more ambitious. I knew how hard she worked; I also knew that when she played, her idea of a vacation ran along tropical lines—Martinique, Barbados, Acapulco, the south of France. Not some Podunk town on the coast of Maine. With me.

You could've knocked me over with a feather when, without skipping a beat, Mercedes accepted my invitation. "All right," she said. "I'd like that."

"You'll come?" Temple—who adored her—cried in delight. "Really, Auntie Merce? You really will?"

"I really will." She caught my daughter up in her arms, and they spun across the kitchen tiles together. Such spontaneous displays of affection were the norm for them. "We'll have a nice long holiday together, Temple my girl. You and your mama. Me and mine."

Coming to a dizzy halt, Mercedes smiled at me. "One big happy family, right?" In the electricity of her smile, I caught a sudden flare—a meteoric trace of the tension between us, the tension that had been there from the very beginning.

Mercedes was seven years old, the youngest of five, when her mother left for America, to work in my father's house. I remember the day Cilda arrived in Spring Lake—remarkable in itself, because at that point she was just one in a long stream of white and black faces. Nannies, governesses, tutors, help, hired by the hour and the week, people I called "the Keepers."

"I don't like you," I told her outright.

"And who are you, please?" she demanded sternly.

"Garner Quinn," I said.

"Well, Ga'ner Quinn." She drew her arms across her chest. "What is about me you don't like?"

"You're too black," I replied with five-year-old candor.

Cilda Fields shrugged. "Yes, well, God put too much dye on me, just like 'e put too much vinegar in you."

"The last girl who came to take care of me left in the middle of the night." I smacked my lips with satisfaction.

"The last girl wasn't Jamaican?" I shook my head. "Because, in Jamaica, girls 'ave a *way*," Cilda said in a low voice. "We know 'ow to keep our men true, and to make nasty little girls behave. You know about the *way*?"

"No." I shook my head again, edging closer, reeled in by this woman's aura of magic and mystery. Five minutes flat, and Cilda Fields had already beguiled me.

Some mornings her voice would be ragged and harsh, the whites of her eyes shot through with blood like a startled horse's. I knew at those times she'd been up all night, crying for

19

her children. The money Cilda sent home every week put clothes on her kids' backs and shoes on their feet. It paid for private schools and college tuition. Once a year she went home for a visit, her suitcase stuffed with photographs of me, birthday cards signed by Garner Quinn, snatches of poems I'd written.

I don't think Mercedes ever forgave either of us for that.

These days her mother no longer had to work for a living. When my father died, he left his former housekeeper a large inheritance. Cilda could've spent the remainder of her days as a woman of leisure; instead she chose to stay with me, cooking when she felt like it, bossing around the cleaning lady who came every week, and watching over my teenage daughter like a hawk.

I loved the old woman deeply, and she loved me; yet twice a month I deposited a check into her bank account—money she never used, payment for services that didn't have to be rendered. It was the great equalizer, an acknowledgment that no matter how entwined our lives and hearts had become, Mrs. Fields still retained the power to stay or go. But if I understood and accepted this arrangement, her daughter Mercedes clearly did not.

Several neat piles of clothes sat on my bed, waiting to be packed. What had I gotten myself into? The prospect of spending two weeks in a rustic cottage with the combined combative forces of Cilda and Mercedes Fields was far more daunting to me than a one-on-one interview with Charlie Manson. I picked up a stack of maps and stuffed it into my leather satchel. A brochure fell onto the floor—"COME TO CAMDEN," it said. I thumbed through the pages of rosy, backlit photographs.

This could be us, I thought. Climbing barefoot down these wet, mossy rocks. Eating lobsters out of soggy newspapers. Sitting on the porch at night, spooning sugared blueberries in our matching sweatshirts from L.L. Bean. I wanted to do all these hokey things. Suddenly I felt incredibly jazzed by the possibilities. I wanted to write postcards, and wear ill-fitting shorts, and buy a snow globe with a pink plastic lobster inside that said *Maine*.

It'll be great, I told myself. The turning point in our relationships. A chance for Cilda to bond with her daughter, and me to bond with mine. An opportunity to heal the hurts which had prevented Mercedes and me from becoming friends.

The reality check came early on.

"Would you raise the window, Mama? We're getting blown away back here," complained Mercedes from the backseat.

"The fresh air won't 'urt you," sniffed Cilda.

"It's *'urting* me plenty," Mercedes mimicked back. She'd worked hard to lose any trace of a Jamaican accent, and it annoyed her that Cilda's dialect had remained *t'ick as molasses* after all these years.

"Ooh-ee. It's stuffy." Cilda fanned herself with a map.

"Turn on the air conditioner," Mercedes suggested through gritted teeth.

"And 'ave that blowing on me?" Her mother shivered. "No t'ank you."

"The wind's messing up my hair."

"Maybe that big Fift' Avenue 'airdresser you got don't know enough about black 'air to make it stick." Cilda stared straight ahead. "Kathianne, now, *she* know about black 'air." Kathianne, the eldest of Cilda's grown children, owned a beauty shop in Brooklyn.

"I don't have time to travel all that way, Mama." Mercedes sighed.

"Hall t'at way," Cilda grumbled under her breath. "Well, Kathianne don't need your business. Friday nights you can't get a seat under t'ose nine dryers. They're walkin' around the block waiting on 'er."

"That's great," Mercedes said out the window.

"Kathianne's smart." Cilda made a show of talking to me, but loudly. "I told 'er when she was lookin' for that shop—stay away from t'ose Fift' Avenue places. Go where the poor people is. And look! Nine dryers, and they're walkin' round the block!"

"You go girl, Kath." In the rearview mirror I watched Mercedes smooth an Hermès scarf over her windblown hair.

"I can put the vent blower on. Then maybe

we can roll up the front window, okay?" I shot Cilda a glance. She punched the controls as though she were launching a Stealth missile.

"What's that game we used to play?" I called over my shoulder to Temple. "The one where you have to count Volkswagens?"

"That's so lame, Mom," she groaned.

The mirror reflected a miniature Mercedes—jaw set, scarf on. "How's it feel back there now?" I asked.

"Fantastic," said Mercedes.

"Because I can crank it up a notch if it's—"

"Chill, Garner." Mercedes cut me off with a wave of crimson nail tips. "Things are just fine back here in the cheap seats." Her sleek, scarved head dipped toward Temple. "Aren't they, sugar?" And the two of them started to giggle.

Postcard to my agent:

Dear Max, *Well, here I am in lovely Maine. I'd like to tell you that the harbor is as pretty as this picture, but it's been socked in with fog since we arrived. They say it may stop raining tomorrow.* *Wish you were here,* *Garner*	MR. MAX SHRONER SHRONER LITERARY ASSOCIATES 708 THIRD AVENUE NEW YORK, NY 10017

"What a beautiful blouse," I complimented Cilda as she passed me the dinner rolls. "Isn't that the one Mercedes gave you for your birthday?"

"Yes," she replied. "See where it don't 'ang right."

"The draping is what makes it special." Mercedes dismissed the bread basket with that characteristic wave of her hand. "It's an Emanuel Ungaro."

"Hemanuel Hungro," Cilda grumbled. "Still don't 'ang the way 'e should."

Steam rose from a bowl of chowder, appearing to come out of Mercedes's ears. "It's a two-hundred-dollar shirt, Mother," she said pointedly.

Cilda Fields sniffed. "Ooh-eee—'ow hextravagant you are! And you on your own wit'out a man or even an automobile to drive."

"I live in Manhattan," Mercedes explained to Temple. "I don't need a car."

"And men are vastly overrated," I chipped in brightly. They all looked at me. "So I hear," I amended, stirring a packet of oyster crackers into my soup.

"Why don't you say it?" Mercedes dared her mother. "Kathianne is married. And Camillia and Annalee."

"That's right." Cilda smiled smugly. "Yes, they h'are."

"What about Deon? He's single."

"Deon's just a boy yet."

"He's forty-five, Mother. Four years older than me," Mercedes said. "He's a forty-five-year-old security guard."

"Not everybody got one of t'em big, glamorous jobs with the TV, you know. Some of us got to work."

"*I* work," said Mercedes.

The waiter came over to pour more wine. "Well..." I turned to Cilda, hoping to change the subject. "I think the blouse looks great on you."

"I *work*," Mercedes repeated as if I hadn't spoken. "And I could have a car, Mama, anytime, if I wanted to."

Postcard to a colleague:

Hi! *Finally taking that long-deserved vacation. The Maine coast is breathtaking, and so peaceful.* *Almost called you about a professional matter before I left—no biggie, though, so don't worry.* *Well, take care, Hoge—* *Garner Quinn* *P.S. Regards to Sue and the kids...*	MR. J. EMMETT HOGAN 1107 SILVERBROOK ROAD MCLEAN, VIRGINIA 29702

I glanced up from the morning paper, trying to catch the fresh source of laughter in the next room. Apparently Mercedes was teaching my daughter a new dance step.

It had been raining for a week now, but the weather hadn't dampened their spirits. They shopped, and went to movies, and gave themselves pedicures. Nights were reserved for endless rounds of pool, Pictionary, or a particularly raucous card game called Egyptian Rat Screw. It turned out that, among her many talents, Mercedes had an uncanny knack for zoning in on hot spots frequented by cute local boys. They'd walk into one of these places and a sea of Eddie Bauer would part for them—this stunning black woman, and the girl with the Audrey Hepburn face.

Cilda objected to "tramping around town h'all wet," and three was a crowd, so we usually stayed at the cottage while the kids went off on their forays. When I wasn't reading, or writing postcards, I spent an inordinate amount of time trying to convince myself how great this was, being able to relax in such a safe haven, far away from the pressures of deadlines and career.

I pored thirstily through all the newspapers. Recent headlines were blazing about real estate tycoon Warren Petty, who'd been killed when his jet exploded in the sky. Authorities suspected terrorism. *"No one is safe from this kind of thing,"* the billionaire's grieving fourth wife had been quoted as saying. The world was becoming an increasingly dangerous place to live while I sat doing nothing, and Mercedes and Temple shagged barefoot in the next room.

Watching them through the open doorway, I remarked to Cilda, "You'd never know she's old enough to be Temple's mother."

"Mercedes," she replied, without looking up from her knitting. "That girl won't ever grow up."

Postcard to my ex-husband and his new wife:

Dear Candace and Andy, *Just a line to let you know* *that we made it up okay.* *Now that the weather's* *finally cleared I'd like to* *take some day trips, if I* *can tear Temple away—* *she's having a ball! We'll* *be back by the 26th—* *Tem's looking forward to* *Labor Day weekend with* *you—* *Best, G.*	MR. & MRS. ANDREW MATERA 360 EAST 62ND STREET PENTHOUSE E NEW YORK, NY 10022

On the tenth day, the two of them came back to the cottage with purple hair.

"Can I speak to you a moment?" I said to Temple. "Alone?"

"I've got to check in at the office anyway." Mercedes smiled.

"It washes out," my daughter announced the minute she had gone.

"You look like an eggplant," I told her. "You look like a potted kale."

"Mercedes says it brings out my eyes," she replied, as if that were the end of the subject.

I motioned her to sit. "Listen, Tem." I lowered my voice. "I want you to cool it with Mercedes for a while."

"I'll wash it out."

"It's not the hair," I said, leaning forward and touching her hand, girl to girl, the way Mercedes always did. "Listen, honey. I asked

27

Aunt Mercedes to come with us because I was hoping it would give her and Cilda a chance to... to, well... bond." The word I'd used in my head seemed so trite, once said out loud.

Temple looked at me blankly. I tried again. "You know, sometimes there're things that come between mothers and daughters..." *Things like leaving them to go off and take care of little white girls, or spending one's life chasing down the murderer of the month.* "And when that happens, well, they need time to work it out together, you know, time to knock away whatever it is that's keeping them apart. Just the two of them..."

Temple brushed a strand of purple hair off her forehead. "Get over it, Mom," she said.

Postcard to my handyman:

Hey Ben, *Cilda's daughter got called back to New York so we're coming home early. Any chance the roof will be finished by the 19th? Tell Ruth I'm bringing her some blueberry preserves to die for...* *Love to you both* *Garn*	MR. BEN SNOW 54 WASHINGTON STREET RUMSON, NJ 07760

"So," I said, trying to keep pace with Mercedes Fields as we walked along the beach. "That's great news, about the job offer." For years Mercedes had been paying her dues as a behind-the-scenes producer, but now a syndicated show called *Front Cover* wanted to feature her as an on-camera investigative reporter.

"Yes." She swung her arms with every stride. "I'm just sorry it means having to cut short your holiday."

"Don't sweat it. Personally, I'm pretty Maine'd out."

After twelve days the sun had finally come out. We stopped for a moment to watch it set, tipping like a paint can, splashing red and gold light into the crevasses of the rocks. Tomorrow we'd get back in the car and head home. The family renting the place opposite ours had invited Temple into town for pizza, and since they had two daughters, and a handsome teenage son, she'd jumped at the chance to go. Cilda—determined to leave the rented cottage more spotless than we'd found it—had switched into whirling-dervish cleaning mode.

It was just Mercedes and me, at sunset, in this splendid Kodak moment on the beach. I decided to try to end the vacation on a note of friendship. "I'm just glad," I said, "that after all your hard work, you're finally getting the recognition you deserve."

"At least," she replied stiffly, "I haven't proven an embarrassment to you."

"An embarrassment?" It took a moment to realize what she was talking about; then it hit me: Mercedes felt she owed her job to me.

"Hey, Merce, wait up!" I called. She was moving fast now, bounding along the sand in her neon-green sports bra top and running

29

shorts. "Mercedes, stop!" I shouted again, before I managed to catch up with her. "Nobody got you where you are today. Not me, not anyone else. You did it yourself—"

She stopped short, standing with her hands on her hips, huffing and puffing. "Tell that... to my mother..."

It always boiled down to the same thing. Mercedes would forever be Cilda's wild child—smart as a whip, flamboyant and headstrong. Her other daughters had taken conventional paths—Kathianne and her beauty parlor, Camillia teaching high school, Annalee becoming a nurse. They'd married, settled down, given Cilda grandkids.

But Mercedes envisioned a loftier future for herself. Despite her mother's threats and protestations, she'd dropped out of college after two years. For brief periods she worked as a fashion model, a dancer, even a clothing designer, and began short-lived careers in advertising and sales. By age thirty, Mercedes was on a track to everywhere in general, heading nowhere in particular, fast.

Cilda insisted that the key to happiness could be summed up in two words: *cosmetology school*. Mercedes could get a job in Kathianne's beauty salon, she said, then live with her sister and brother-in-law until the right man came along.

Running out of time, money, and options, Mercedes had turned to me. She told me she wanted to be a journalist; then she took a gulp and asked, "Could you help me, Garner?" I remember her gulping, specifically, remember thinking that here was a woman swallowing her pride. I'd put an arm around her, awkwardly, and assured her that I'd be happy to do what I could.

I'd given lectures at NYU, and one well-placed call was enough to get Mercedes enrolled in the broadcast journalism program there. Three years later she graduated, cum laude. I made a few introductions to people I knew at the networks. It was no big deal. At least, for me.

"You know, once you're a big TV personality plenty of people will be asking *you* for favors," I remarked. "I might, myself."

Mercedes's face softened. "Well, I owe you one or two," she said.

"We don't have to keep score." A young couple and three towheaded kids were sailing kites on the sand a few feet from us. I watched them for a moment. *So that's what a family vacation looks like,* I thought, and my shoulders sagged with a sense of loss.

Mercedes took off her sunglasses. "You have a wonderful daughter, you know." She nudged me.

"I know."

"She loves you very much." It was probably the kindest thing she had ever said to me, but then she went and ruined it. "If you want my opinion, though, you should let go a little."

"Let *go*? I'm just getting her *back*!" Immediately, I became defensive. "I've been off running around on one project after another for most of her life—"

Mercedes smiled as if I just didn't get it.

31

"The attachment is *here,* Garner." She put a hand to her heart. "It doesn't matter how many miles apart you are, or whoever else is in her life."

Her sincerity was touching, but to be honest, I found it annoying, the way Mercedes always seemed to be trying to teach me something.

One of the towheaded kids was bringing his kite in. It swiped at us as it buckled to shore. We ducked and started walking again. "So," I said, trying to change the subject, "I guess you'll take the offer, huh?"

"Probably," Mercedes said. "I'd have a lot more autonomy." "Autonomy" was another word for "control," which was definitely one of Mercedes's issues; we were alike that way.

"What about you? Will you start on the Sea Bright story when we get back?"

For months now I had been "between books"; recently, I'd been considering writing about an unsolved case, the torching of a halfway house in a small Jersey shore town which had resulted in the deaths of five mentally handicapped men. "Nope," I told Mercedes. "I've decided to pass on that."

"Yes." Her laugh was low and bitter. "After all, just a bunch of retards and colored people burned up, right? Nobody important enough to sell a lot of books."

I stopped short. "What's that supposed to mean?"

"Well, you have to admit it, Garner. You write about crimes committed against upper-middle-class white people."

I was outraged. "Are you calling me a *racist*?"

"Not exactly."

"Well, good," I said. "Because I'm not."

"Uh-huh," she muttered under her breath as she moved away. "Some of your best domestics are black."

"I can't believe you said that." I ran to catch up to her. "Cilda's a member of my family." A flood of bottled-up emotion caught in my throat. "She raised me! She was more a mother to me than my own mother was—"

"How nice for you." Mercedes pumped her arms vigorously. "Because she *is* my mother, and she didn't raise *me*." Always, always, it came back to this.

"I can't help that, Merce," I said. "That's just the way things turned out."

The cottage was only fifty yards away. Mercedes began sprinting toward it. I followed at a clumsy gallop. By the time I got there she was already sitting on the porch step, knocking sand out of her Nikes. "Go ahead," she challenged. "Name one real friend you have who's black."

In my mind, I ran down the list—a couple of cops, a defense attorney, a journalist. Colleagues, criminals. Business acquaintances. "I don't have any real friends," I sputtered finally.

This time Mercedes's laughter was soft as silk. "You know, Garner," she said. "I can believe that."

On the ride home, conversation was polite, but strained. Mercedes talked a little about

33

the new job on *Front Cover.* It would give her an opportunity to cover some big stories, she said, like the terrorist bomb that had just blown up Warren Petty's Lear jet.

"Wow." Temple sighed. "After college I want to go into broadcast journalism just like you, Auntie Merce."

In the rearview mirror, I saw Mercedes put her arm around my daughter. "Tell you what, baby girl. Next time you have a vacation from school, you can come work for me, as an intern."

"Get out—really?" Temple was ecstatic. "Can I, Mom? Can I work for Mercedes's TV show during my vacations?"

"We'll see," I said.

Cilda just scowled and put the front window down.

Late that night as I was unpacking, I found a small package in the bottom of my suitcase. I tore away the tissue.

It was a snow globe. When the tiny snowflakes settled you could see a wooden cage with a pink lobster inside. The cage was stamped *Maine.*

"Thanks for the memory. Love, Mercedes," read the accompanying note.

THREE

"Hey Rich, what's doing?"

"Nothin' much, Garner," said the man behind the postal desk. "What, you just get back from one of your book things?"

"Nah. Family vacation."

"Oh, yeah, sure." He snickered as if this explanation was a cover for a far more intriguing story. "Come to pick up your mail?"

No, Rich, I just drove all the way into town to chat with you. "If you've got it," I said sweetly.

He ducked behind a partition decked with posters of collector stamps. "Jeesh, Garner," I heard him say. "You holding some kinda contest?"

"What?"

"For your fans or something?" Rich appeared holding up two canvas sacks. "An offer to give away free books?"

"No." My heart started to pound. "Look, I need—" I gestured to the desk near the door. "Mind if I dump them out over there?"

"Don't bother me." Rich shrugged genially. "How long you been gone, anyway?"

"Couple of weeks," I murmured, running my hands through the pile of plain white envelopes—hundreds of them—addressed in cheerful comic book print, with a blank space for the return.

The door opened and I spun around defensively, startling the little old lady who'd entered. "Could I buy some stamps?" she asked in a timid voice. I pointed to Rich at the postal desk.

My legs were shaking, but I went back to the mountain of letters, pawing and sorting, separating the plain white envelopes from others in the pile. "Would it be okay if I returned these duffels tomorrow?" I called over my shoulder to Rich.

"No problem," he replied. As I pushed my way out of the heavy glass door, I heard him tell the old woman, "That's Garner Quinn. The famous writer."

The hot August sun hit my clammy skin and made me shiver. I walked past the big blue mailboxes and the bike racks. The sacks weighed a ton. Next to the post office was a stationery store with an outdoor trash receptacle. I put down the lighter of the two bags, the one with the regular mail; then I picked up the one with Chaz's letters, and tipped it into the garbage can, watching with satisfaction as the flood of white paper spewed into the dark hole. When the bag was empty, I myself felt lighter, almost buoyant.

"See ya, Chaz," I said. Tossing the bags over my shoulder, I headed across the parking lot to my car.

It took only twelve minutes to reach the stone gates on the outermost edge of my property, but every bump and pothole punctured a hole in my euphoria, so that by the time I pulled up in front of the house, I felt as flat and deflated as the canvas sack by my side.

Temple was eating breakfast at the kitchen table. Cilda had the counter television tuned to *Front Cover.* "What's new?" I asked, all upbeat and breezy.

Cilda shrugged toward the screen. "Planes blowin' up. A lot of bombs and killing. The whole world's going straight to 'ell."

"Switch the channel," Temple suggested with a mouth full of Cheerios. "They have *Bewitched* re-runs on Nickelodeon." She trained her spoon at the duffel bags. "What're they for?"

"The mail." I tucked the paper under my arm. "I'm going over to the office."

"I thought we were going to Dad's."

When my ex-husband and his new wife discovered we'd cut our vacation short, they asked if Temple could spend the extra week with them, at their beach house in Southampton. I lost the coin toss and got stuck with driving out. "Give me an hour," I told Temple. "It'll take you at least that long to get dressed."

I jogged down the footpath without so much as glancing toward the beach. The office door stuck as usual and I kicked it, viciously. It was dark inside, but instead of opening the vertical blinds, I switched on the lights in both rooms. I took my address book from its place on the shelf and began to dial.

No one answered at Special Agent Hogan's house in McLean, Virginia. *It's the end of summer,* I reminded myself. Hoge and Sue were probably traveling with the kids. The five of them, on a family vacation. *But why would he leave the machine off?* asked the niggling voice in my head. I glanced at the newspaper I'd tossed on my desk, and started reading the front-page story:

TERRORIST GROUP LINKED TO BOMBING

Sources at the FBI say that a Middle Eastern terrorist cell with links to Hamas and the Islamic Jihad may be responsible for the downing of a private Lear jet owned by business tycoon Warren Petty over the Atlantic last week...

I stopped.

My sometime partner-in-crime J. Emmett Hogan (affectionately known by his colleagues at the Bureau as J. Edgar) had retired months ago, but with a big case like this in the works, I knew he'd find it difficult to stay away. On a hunch, I tried his old office number.

"Noose," said an unfamiliar voice.

"I'm sorry," I said. "I was hoping to reach Emmett Hogan."

"Special Agent Hogan is retired, ma'am," the voice said. "This is Special Agent Noose. May I help you?"

"No thanks—uh, I'll try him at home." I wondered whether anybody ever chose to stay on the line to be helped by an FBI agent named Noose.

"The secretary forwards Mr, Hogan's messages on a regular basis," Noose said. "If you hold on, I'll switch you over."

"No thanks," I demurred. "It's nothing urgent."

• • •

The ride out to Southampton was a nightmare. For three and a half hours my valiant little Volvo 120 plugged along, inching and idling in traffic. I sat behind the wheel, praying it wouldn't overheat; when it didn't, I added a prayer of thanks for all these crazy New Yorkers who'd never heard of the Jersey shore. *Dear Lord, keep them from finding out about our beaches. Amen.*

By the time we reached Andy and Candace's place, the sun was poised to set. It was that golden hour when the privileged took their glasses out onto terraces and watched the sky slide into night, while someone less fortunate prepared them dinner. Having had a drunk for a mother, I always made it a point to steer away from that scene, but the day had left me feeling as drained and delicate as empty crystal; I found myself saying yes to Andy's offer of a cocktail. We sat down on the patio overlooking the pool—my ex-husband, our daughter, his new wife, and me. With the first rush of alcohol whooshing through me, and the sun melting in a striped magenta sky, it had all the makings of a genuine out-of-body experience.

"So, Temple." Candace broke the silence. "How did you like Maine?"

"It was awesome," she replied, and I found myself wondering, *Was it really? Where was I?* "I'm going to be a production assistant on Mercedes's new TV show over Thanksgiving vacation."

"That's still under consideration," I said.

"Who's Mercedes?" Candace asked.

"The housekeeper's daughter," Andy replied.

I wanted to smack him, but instead I lifted my empty glass. "Please, sir, can I have some more?"

After the second martini, Candace's invitation to stay for supper seemed like a neat idea. The once and future Mrs. Andrew Materas walked arm in arm through the French doors, giggling. Behind us, I could sense Andy's dismay. This house, purchased by him after our divorce, was classic Early Bachelor Pad—sparse furnishings, glass and chrome, lots of squishy black leather. A LeRoy Neiman hung over the stucco fireplace, in a questionable obeisance to fine art.

"Isn't it awful?" Candace sighed. "I'm planning to redo the whole thing."

"You should start with him," I suggested, hooking my thumb toward Andy, who was trailing behind us with the tray of empty glasses. We all laughed as though I'd meant it as a joke.

The meal itself was a blur, except for Temple, who sat in the imaginary chasm between me and her father. Her need for us to get along together was so palpable, I could taste it, like a piquant sauce on my food. *Okay,* I thought, *I can do this.* Let Andy sit there glowering, pouring glass after glass of wine. I'd rise to the occasion. I'd pour on the charm.

"Speaking of house-lifts," I said, "you

wouldn't believe what I just went through, renovating my father's house—" It was hard to miss with a good unreliable-contractor story; I figured I could do fifteen minutes on electricians alone. By embellishing detail, I was able to carry on through the main course, by which time Candace was laughing, Temple was beaming, and Andy and I had polished off a bottle of Merlot.

"I can't believe you want to sell it," he said when the gaiety subsided.

"What would I want it for?"

"Well, for one thing, you'd do a helluva lot better living in Spring Lake than out on the edge of nowhere."

"It's not nowhere," I said. "It's my home."

"S'too goddam dangerous if you ask me," Andy muttered. "Christ, Garner, you'd think after that last close call you had—"

"That's enough, Andy." Candace shot him a formidable glance; then she turned to me and asked, "Who's ready for dessert?"

At the word my stomach took a dive and the room began to spin. Despite a buffer of solid food, I realized I was in no condition to stand, let alone get in the car and drive back home. It seemed, like everything else, to be Andy's fault. Here I'd been trying so hard to be nice, for Temple's sake, chattering along, while he plied me with fine wine and liquor. Suddenly, I felt angry and pit bull mean.

Andy leaned forward on his elbows. "Whatcha working on these days, Garner?"

"I'm between projects at the moment."

He caught my eye, with a little smirk. "Hey,

41

I'm sure it won't be long before another one of your sociopaths comes along."

"Like they say, Andy." I held his gaze. "Stick with what you know."

He steepled his palms under his chin. "Funny, from what Temple says, we understood you were trying to break away from true crime." It was an offhand comment, but drunk as I was, it smacked of betrayal to me.

Temple opened her mouth to explain. Just then Candace returned, carrying a big cheesecake dripping with strawberry compote and runny whipped cream.

"Excuse me." I struggled to my feet. "I'm going to be sick."

Candace was characteristically kind. By the time my head was out of the toilet, she'd already turned down the comforter in the spare bedroom and raised the windows to let in fresh air. I crawled atop the clean white sheets, fighting a swooning sleep. From outside came the familiar lulling sound of surf slapping sand. Long Island beaches smelled different, somehow—high and salty, not the rich, swampy musk of coastal Jersey.

Temple appeared in the doorway. "You okay?"

"Humiliated," I said, "but breathing."

She came in and sat down at the foot of the bed. "Dad has this way of asking questions that, like, point out his own personal agenda."

"He's a lawyer."

"He's a jerk." She said this affectionately; then she added, "I like where we live."

"You like your grandfather's house too."

"Yes, but I've only been there a few times," my daughter said, wisely. "It doesn't hold any memories for me."

I reached out and took her hand. "You know I'd do anything to keep you safe."

Temple curled up like a cat beside me. "I know," she said.

When I got home I found Cilda on the phone in the kitchen, talking to her daughter Kathianne. She acknowledged me with an impatient wave. "You can't let 'er do that," she was saying vehemently. "Tell 'er she 'ave to pay the 'ole fee." Cilda was forever instructing Kathy on how to run her beauty parlor.

The morning mail was on the table. I shuffled through it, breathing a sigh of relief when there were no plain white envelopes from Chaz. *Hey,* I needled myself, *do you realize what just happened? That was the first time you forgot to look for a letter from Dane Blackmoor.* An emotional milestone—and I owed it all to a nutty fan.

I poured coffee into my mug and walked my fingers in front of Cilda's nose, pantomiming that I was headed over to the office. Outside, the hot wind hit me with the force of a low-speed blow-dryer. Sunlight streamed through the clouds over the ocean, but to the west, the sky looked threatening.

The path veered away from the seawall, toward a small stand of scrub pines. My stomach was still queasy from last night's drinking binge, so I stopped a moment to gulp down some coffee. Then I saw the package—a cardboard box about eighteen inches high—under the protective overhang of the front door. It might've been a parcel post delivery, except that UPS never came back here. The typed label was addressed to me.

I nudged it with the toe of my shoe. It was heavy enough to offer resistance. I jogged a few feet down the fieldstone walk, scouring the open area between the guest quarters and the beach. No one in sight.

I went back to the office, unlocked the door, and used my instep to push the box inside. Before opening it, I buzzed Cilda at the house. "Did you have any visitors while I was gone yesterday?" I asked.

"Yes. Ben Snow and 'is wife stop by. She said tell you she ate up hall that good jam you brought."

"Did Ben leave something for me at my office?"

"I don't know. He went down that way, to look at the roof."

"Thanks."

I picked up a letter opener and jabbed the side of the box a few times. My Pandora-sharp curiosity was screaming, *Open it, open it,* while a small voice in my head warned me to proceed with caution. What broke this psychic tie was a surge of anger at being intimidated by a four-square of corrugated cardboard. I took a breath and sliced through the packing tape.

A putrid smell overtook me the second I parted the cardboard flaps—the gummy stink of stale food and wet paper. *Oh God, what is this?* Corners of Chaz's white envelopes poked out of the filthy mess like origami sailboats. He'd written a note in permanent black marker. It said:

I WILL NOT BE TREATED LIKE GARBAGE

FOUR

"For crying out loud, Garner." Max's voice rose to such a pitch that I had to move the receiver away from my ear. "What on earth possessed you to open the box? It could've been a bomb." It was exactly what the detective from the local police force had said to me.

"A stink bomb's more like it." I laughed off my agent's concern. "The office still reeks." *Is that really why you've spent the morning making calls on the kitchen phone?* the voice in my head needled. *Or is it because the thought of walking down that lonely path, past the clump of trees, toward the door scares the bejeezus out of you?*

On the other end of the line, there was a tiny click, then a slow exhalation of breath. Max Shroner had just lit up a cigarette. "Who've you called?" he asked.

"I tried to reach Hogan."

"So what's he going to do, leave his wife and kids to come camp out on your lawn?" Max scoffed. "You don't need the FBI, you need somebody who specializes in fruitcakes like this. A client of mine's daughter had some creep

45

boyfriend wouldn't leave her alone. They hired a security firm and that ended it, fast. You ever hear of Reed Corbin?"

Not only had I heard of him, I'd met Corbin once at a televised discussion forum on violence. I said, "Bodyguard to the stars? Forget it, Max. I'm not Madonna."

"No." His irritation crackled over the line. "You're a high-profile, single woman who writes books about serial killers, you live with a teenage girl and an old woman, all the way out in *farkakte* New Jersey, and you're getting care packages full of garbage from a stalker. Lemme tell you, sweetie—Madonna's got nothing on you."

"Well, if you put it that way." I leaned back in my chair wearily. During my agent's tirade, I was thinking about Reed Corbin. We'd been seated next to each other at the panel discussion. He seemed shy and ill at ease with me, but once the camera started rolling, he spoke with a calm, cool authority that I found, well, attractive. "You wouldn't happen to have a number?" I asked.

"It's on file. Hold on a second." Max was delighted at my change of heart. "I'll have Stacy get it for you."

Reed Corbin was out of the office, so I left a message with the receptionist, put on a fresh pot of coffee, and prepared to wait. The phone rang five minutes later.

"As much as it's a pleasure to hear from you, Ms. Quinn"—Corbin wasted no time after the initial hellos—"I understand you wanted to speak to me about a professional matter."

We established that he could drop the Ms. Quinn and call me Garner, and I gave him the Cliff Notes version of my situation. Corbin interrupted only once to ask, "And you *opened* the box?"

"I'm a hands-on type person," I replied defensively. "I open all the mail myself."

"But this one had no postal or courier marks." His tone was perplexed, not accusatory. "And it was delivered, not to your front gate, but to a place well within your property bounds, is that right?"

"Yes," I conceded.

From the other end I heard soft tapping on a computer keyboard. "Could you spell the name of the detective who came out to see you?"

I glanced at the card on my counter. "Lehnert. L-E-H-N-E-R-T."

Again, the typing sound. "That's all I need for now," Corbin said finally. "If it's all right with you, I'm going to ask your local police to send me the letter and the other evidence for assessment. At the same time I'll arrange for a surveillance team to watch your premises. Do you have an alarm system?"

"Yes."

"Use it. Better yet, go stay with a friend until we get a handle on this guy."

Butterflies fluttered against my rib cage. Corbin was scaring me. "Wait a second," I broke in. "Aren't you overreacting a little?"

"Maybe. Or maybe you're underreacting. It's safer my way, for the moment." Corbin added, more deferentially, "It would also be extremely helpful if we could sit down together as soon as possible to discuss your options." He asked what would be the most convenient arrangement for me.

I told him I would come to him.

While I was on the phone it had begun to rain. It started as a soft, slurring grayness, then sharpened into long, glistening needles that jabbed the windowpanes and pricked the roof. I walked aimlessly into the great room.

With Temple at her father's, the house seemed empty. I curled up on the sofa, straining my ears to hear past the downpour outside. When Cilda padded up behind me in her bedroom slippers, I almost jumped out of my skin.

"You know, I was thinking," I said. "Why don't you take the rest of the week off? Go visit Kathianne."

The old woman's eyes narrowed. "What're you going to do?"

"I have to be in upstate New York tomorrow morning. I could drive you to Brooklyn, camp out on Kathy's sofa tonight, and leave from there."

Cilda flip-flopped away without another word. I heard the low hum of her voice talking on the kitchen phone; then, just the rain. A few minutes later she reappeared in the doorway, dressed to go out. "Kathy's down wit' flu. She says yes, please, drop me to 'er 'ouse, but that you should spend the night wit' Mercedes in town."

Now wouldn't that be the perfect capper to the day? I said, "That's okay. I'll just stay in a hotel."

"Kathianne already called 'er at the TV station." Cilda brushed some lint from the shoulder of her jacket. It was a brisk, no-nonsense motion, one that told me, *It's a done deal, Ga'ner Quinn. Might as well give up.*

By the time I reached Mercedes's Upper West Side apartment building it was nine o'clock and only drizzling. The doorman handed me an envelope with a key. I read the enclosed note as I went up in the elevator.

Garner,
I have a dinner date. There's Chinese in the refrigerator and fresh sheets on the sofa. Enjoy!—
Mercedes
P.S. Don't wait up.

I ate leftover moo shu pork out of the carton and watched television. *Nightline* had a special report on the death of Warren Petty. The footage showing investigators collecting evidence particularly interested me—I kept expecting to see my pal Hogan. It must've been after midnight when I drifted off to sleep.

I awoke in a total panic. Someone was at the door. *He was coming to get me. Chaz was here.* Only thing—at the moment, I had no idea where *here* was. The door swung open, and the sudden spill of light from the corridor blinded me.

"Sorry," came Mercedes's whisper. "Did I wake you?"

"What time is it?" I croaked.

She moved past me, across the dark room,

a swoosh of silk and leather and spicy perfume. "After two, I think," she said, still whispering. She put her purse down on the coffee table and stepped out of her high-heeled shoes. "Did you have something to eat?"

"Um-hum." Mercedes snapped on a small overhead light. She stood in front of the mirrored hallstand, taking off her earrings. Her face was flushed and shining; I thought to myself, *I bet she's just had sex.*

"Mama told me about the creep who's been sending you letters."

"Yeah." My mouth felt dry as cotton. "Bummer."

"You need to make major adjustments to your life, girl." Mercedes's voice purred softly in the darkness. "You're attracting altogether the *wrong* element."

FIVE

Since I'd been informed that the Manhattan office of Corbin, Incorporated, only handled clients from the federal government and major law enforcement agencies, I'd agreed to meet Reed Corbin at the firm's training facility, a thirty-acre compound called Forked Brook just outside of Tarrytown, New York. I'd pictured something along the lines of a prison, with barbed wire spooling off windowless buildings, but Forked Brook looked more like a swank country club.

The guard at the gatehouse wore khakis, a

cotton shirt and tie, and a security pass clipped to his breast pocket which said, *Mr. William Mallet, Corbin, Inc.* "Straight ahead, Ms. Quinn." He checked my name off on a clipboard. "When you come to the fork, take a left. A and M is a quarter of a mile down on your right. You can park in the guest lot."

Whispering his instructions to myself, I drove to the fork. At the precise quarter-mile mark stood a large pagoda-style building. The sign out front read:

CORBIN, INCORPORATED
ASSESSMENT AND MANAGEMENT

A&M. I pulled into one of the visitor spaces in the parking lot. It seemed redundant to lock up. If the car wasn't safe here, I really was in the wrong place.

The walkway curved toward the front entrance under a canopy of Japanese maples. In a grove just off the path, a bowl-shaped fountain dripped languidly into a pool of koi. I wondered how many prospective clients had been lulled into a false sense of security by this scene of landscaped tranquillity. But of course, I was more resourceful, smarter than the average bear. I'd handled sickos scarier than Chaz, and on my own too.

So what was I doing here?

I caught a glimpse of myself in the plate glass of the front door, and with a pang, realized I was smaller than I pictured myself to be. *Must be the damn sweater.* This morning, as I was getting ready to leave her apartment, Mercedes had stopped me. "You're not going to wear that blazer are you?"

"Yes. Why not?"

"It's two, three sizes too big, that's why." She went to her closet and came out with a little slippy knit thing in a bright, bright turquoise.

"It looks like one of those old Howard Johnson signs," I told her.

"You need something short and colorful to offset that long dark skirt." With the skill of a professional dresser, Mercedes peeled off my jacket and blouse. Rather than stand there in my underwear, I took the sweater.

"Look, Garner." Mercedes smiled once I'd pulled it on. "You have boobs."

Now, in the plate glass reflection, my new-found chest seemed to dominate all other features like a pronounced overbite. I tugged at the top, adjusted my bra, then opened the door to Corbin, Incorporated.

"Ms. Quinn, it's an honor," said the young Asian woman at the reception desk. She wore a black dress with a white collar and very red lipstick, which happened to match the color scheme of the modern painting on the wall behind her. As she stood to shake my hand, I noted the name on her badge, *Ms. Tamara Ma*. "Reed's been expecting you," she said with a smile. "Come right this way."

I followed her down a well-lit corridor, past several well-appointed conference rooms and a separate wing of offices. The walls were covered in nubby, linen fabric, which didn't mute the steady hum of activity.

Corbin, Inc., seemed to be quite the happening place. We crossed a small bridge over another pool of fish-filled water. "This is A-Wing, where Reed and Matt Raice work," she explained. "When they're here. Reed is on the Coast a lot, and Matt usually operates out of the Manhattan office, which handles our international clients." Tamara slid open a rice paper door.

Reed Corbin was on his feet, ready to greet me, by the time I hit the threshold. On another man, the name might've been a pretension, but it suited him well. Tall and slim, with thinning blond hair and gold-rimmed glasses, there was a deceptive frailty about him. He made me think of a very expensive fishing rod my father had when I was a child. It was whip slender and it bent at the lightest touch, but I'd once seen Dudley haul in a six-hundred-pound mako without it breaking.

"Garner." Corbin pressed my hand, then quickly let it go. "Wonderful to see you. Did you have any trouble finding us?"

"No."

"Can I get you anything, Ms. Quinn?" asked Tamara Ma. "Coffee, tea? A mineral water?"

"I'm fine, thank you."

"Buzz me when Matt gets back from Manhattan, will you, Tamara?" Corbin called as his secretary closed the door.

I took a quick look around. Honorary plaques, celebrity photographs, and letters of commendation covered the walls—all professional stuff, no studio portraits of the

53

wife and kids. I couldn't help noticing Corbin wasn't wearing a wedding band either. An immense cherrywood desk was flanked by the requisite number of armchairs. But instead of inviting me to sit in one of these, he gestured toward the cozy leather sofa by the window. I took a seat on the far left. He sat on the right.

"Just so you know," Corbin said, "we've already begun a threat assessment on the material we received from your local police."

"A threat assessment," I repeated.

He picked up on the sarcasm in my voice. "Is something wrong, Garner?" he searched my face with his sharp, kind eyes.

"No. Well, yes, actually," I admitted. "It's just, I'm not really sure why I'm here. I'm not exactly your run-of-the-mill client." My eyes drifted toward the framed photos. Ballplayers and actresses, politicians and corporate giants—what the hell did *they* know about dealing with the dark side?

Corbin waited for me to continue.

"I come into contact with potentially violent characters all the time. It's what I do." Perched on the edge of the leather cushion, I was poised for flight. "So it seems ridiculous, involving you. Especially when there's no reason to believe this guy Chaz poses any real danger."

Corbin nodded in agreement. "You may be right."

Something inside me went limp; I hadn't realized how tense I'd been. "There's certainly nothing run-of-the-mill about you, Garner.

But have you considered"—above his glasses, Corbin's brows drew into a line—"what makes the man who's writing you these letters different from the ones you encounter in your work?"

I looked away from him.

"When you meet them in the professional arena, it's a whole other ball game, isn't it?" Corbin leaned across the sofa until we were almost nose to nose. "This guy's been sniffing around on your home ground. He's invaded your space, Garner."

For a moment he stayed that way; then he stood up. "It's up to you, though. The best advice I can give is, go with your gut."

I remembered the wave of nausea I'd felt after reading Chaz's first letter. My gut had known, from the beginning. Something was wrong. I said, softly, "So what happens now?"

Just then a buzzer sounded and Tamara Ma's voice came over the intercom. "Excuse me, Reed, but Matt just got back."

Corbin walked over to his desk and hit the two-way button. "Thanks, Tam. Send him in, will you?" He turned to me. "My partner, Matt Raice, is already up to speed on your case. He's a good man, very thorough. Cut his teeth in covert ops for the Secret Service. Nobody understands the criminal mind better than Matt. He has an uncanny feel for the way these predators work. You'll be in good hands."

Good hands? "But I'd assumed—" I broke off, not wanting to say, what? That I'd assumed I'd be in *his* hands, that *his* would be the hands doing the handling?

Before Reed could reply, the rice paper door slid open and a man stepped inside. He was younger-looking than Corbin, well built and black Irish handsome. A stubble of beard ruggedly darkened his milk white skin. "Hullo, hullo." He clicked his heels and bowed. "Matthew Raice here, reporting for duty as ordered."

A look passed between the two men—a sort of mental tug-of-war which Reed Corbin somehow won. That's when the penny dropped: *Corbin had asked his partner to take on my case as a personal favor.* I'd been palmed off on Matt Raice, and Raice wasn't overly thrilled with the arrangement.

Reed said, "I was just telling Garner about you."

"I'm in the nick of time then." He held a hand out to me. "Whatever Reed said was colored by a deep-seated—and I might add, understandable—jealousy."

For a moment the three of us stood appraising each other, separately and together—Corbin in his conservative summer suit; Raice in his denim shirt, dark tie, and khakis; me in my borrowed turquoise sweater set. The ensuing silence was fraught with a subtext I couldn't quite read.

"How'd the meeting go?" Corbin asked, finally.

"Fucking Bureau of Investigation." Matt shrugged. "What do you expect?"

Corbin explained, "We're sharing a case. The late Warren Petty was a client."

"Christ, Reed, what kind of thing is that to

say?" Raice feigned a cringe. "Let me assure you, Garner. Not everyone who hires us blows up midair. Stalkers—bless their shiftless black souls—are infinitely easier to control than terrorists."

The intercom buzzer rang. "Intech is on the line, Reed," Tamara's voice said.

"Thanks. I'll take it in here," he replied. Corbin glanced up at me. "Matt can walk you through the threat evaluation process and answer any questions you might have."

"Yeah," I said, angry to be hurried out the door this way. "Thanks a bunch."

"It's been great seeing you," Corbin said, but he did not extend his hand.

SIX

There were no celebrity photographs in Matthew Raice's office. The furnishings were stark and utilitarian—a desk, some bookshelves, a wide-screen television monitor, and a computer. On one wall was a display of Venetian masks; on another, a dark, brooding oil painting which immediately drew my attention.

It was a desert scene. An oil lamp flickered seductively inside a tent. Under the canopy of gauze, a handsome man in a safari suit and pith helmet waited for a harem girl to begin to dance. But there was no romance here. The soldier was slumped back in his chair, a riding crop propped against his boots—half watching the girl, his eyes hooded with cruelty, and boredom.

"Who painted it?" I asked.

"Guy named Dean Cornwell, an illustrator back the twenties. I picked it up for a song at a gallery in New York." Raice swallowed the *r* in New York, and spooned his vowels like a native Bostonian. "Perhaps it's my latently imperialistic nature, but somehow the picture speaks to me.

"Of course, you haven't come all this way to talk about my taste in art—or lack thereof." He sat, and motioned for me to do the same.

"I'm beginning to think"—I remained standing—"that this has been a mistake. The letters from this guy are nothing I can't handle, and you," I added pointedly, "probably have more pressing cases to attend to."

"Am I being so obvious?" Raice's standard-issue grin softened into the genuine article. "I'm really sorry. Please, sit down for a minute and let me explain." I lowered myself to the edge of a chair.

"Warren Petty was our first big client. Fifteen years of providing security for someone, a thing like this happens, you tend to take it personally." He shook his head. "Warren wasn't just a name on my Rolodex. I'd been around the world with him. Saw him through two divorces, three marriages, and a merger. When that jet went down, I lost a friend."

"Any closer to finding out who's responsible?"

"Middle East terrorist, middle-American militia man." Raice spat out the words in frustration. "Neither would surprise me. But like my corporate better half says, I'm so close to it now, I can't see the forest for the trees."

He propped both elbows on the leather blotter. "I'll admit when Reed suggested I take you on, I had a hissy fit. But he's got several good points." He ticked off reasons on his fingertips. "One, I need time away from the Petty case to regroup. Two, this squirrel Chaz of yours is highly volatile. And three"—his Irish eyes twinkled—"nobody's better at handling volatile squirrels than me.

"So why don't you sit back a little," Matt Raice said. "Let me bring you up to speed on what we've done so far. Okay?"

"Okay." I nodded.

Raice opened the file folder on his desk. "As you know, we have a team of men watching your house. According to their report, no one came on or near the property last night, and there were no letters from Chaz this morning."

"That's good." I sighed with relief. "Maybe that's the end."

"We can hope," Matt said. "But we shouldn't count on it. In my experience, people who exhibit this kind of obsessive behavior don't give up easily. Here, I want to show you something."

He rolled his chair over to the computer monitor and typed in a command. A list of names appeared on the screen. Raice scrolled down. "If you've got a day or two, I'll go through all thirty thousand. Their victims

59

range from the girl next door to the President of the United States. Of course, only a fraction of these cases ever become public."

"And they're all stalkers?"

"Uh-huh. We keep terrorists and assassins in another part of the system." He clicked on a name at random. A picture of an attractive blond woman appeared on the screen. "Ah, yes. I remember her well," Matt chuckled as he read. "Kerry Anise. Brookline, Massachussetts. Age forty-two. Worked as a nurse in an abortion clinic. After the guy she'd been dating broke up with her and took up with someone else, sweet Kerry sent him a dead fetus in the mail. Things escalated from there."

"You keep track of all these nuts?"

"Track 'em and rate 'em." He closed the file and spun around to face me. "We know more about what makes them tick than their own mothers do. Reed designed this whole system of artificial intelligence. He calls it PREDICT, which stands for—well, don't ask me what it stands for." Matt laughed. "Reed's the one with a hard-on for abbreviations. A and M... TQI... INT... The only one I'm known to use on occasion is the WC."

Raice leaned back in his chair, hands folded on his chest. "Anyhow, PREDICT is like this huge cyberpsychological threshing machine, separating, if you will, the threats from the chaff. With PREDICT, we're actually able to tell which of these nutsy fagins will ultimately become violent. That brings us to Chaz."

My mouth suddenly went dry. "You've located him in the system?"

"I'm afraid not," Matt said kindly. "The bad news is, we fed his writing samples through our information banks and couldn't find a match. The good news is, I'm sure it won't be long before we're able to add his name to our list."

"How do you know?"

"He follows a recognizable pattern. Out of the twelve predictors of violence we use to assess correspondence, Chaz exhibits eleven."

"What does that mean?"

"There's a rhetoric of violence, Garner, that goes beyond simple words. It's a feeling *behind* the words—an attachment that the stalker *feels* for which there's no basis in reality." Matt Raice spoke earnestly now. "A sense that he shares some common destiny with the object of his obsession, which *entitles* him. Confusion as to his own personal identity, apart from the person he's stalking."

Matt leafed through the file on his desk and began to read, "*Saw you on Nightline.*" He scanned to another quote. "*Sent for a tape of that interview,* and here, *Read the whole book in less than a day.*" He looked up at me. "Notice anything unusual about his writing?"

"He never uses the word 'I,'" I said. I'd realized that, on a subconscious level. It had bothered me.

"He uses it once," Matthew Raice corrected. "When he sent you the box. He said, *I will not be treated like garbage.* It's in the implied threat that he becomes a separate entity, you see, a fully realized person. That's who he is, Garner. And my instincts tell me that now that he's found himself, he could pose a real danger."

Don't let this tight little sweater fool you, buster, I wanted to tell him. *I'm Garner Quinn— danger is my middle name.*

Then, in my mind's eye I saw myself, alone on the path. Emerging from the stand of trees, seeing the package. *It's like going to a doctor,* my wiser self whispered. *Just give up control, and let the specialist do his job.* I said, "So what do you propose to do?"

"The first step is to defuse his connection with you."

"Other than in his head," I pointed out, "he has no connection with me."

"That's where you're wrong." Matt Raice leaned toward me. "The very fact that you go to the mailbox each day, that your fingers touch the letters he's written, has intimate implications for him. That's why one of our men will be picking up your mail from now on. We'll forward your normal correspondence. Anything from Chaz will be sent here to be evaluated. Is your voice on the outgoing message on your answering machine?"

"Yes."

"We'll tape over it with a male voice. It's important to limit his access to you in every way we can," Matt continued, "which will be difficult, I realize, considering your high-profile career. I'll need to know what your daily routine is, work-related travel, if you've scheduled any public appearances."

"Actually, I expect to be spending most of my time at home," I said, "doing preliminary research for my next book." Ever since my talk with Mercedes on the beach that day, I'd been mentally tinkering with the idea of tackling the unsolved arson of that halfway house in Sea Bright.

Matt jotted something down in my file. "We'd also like to send a team over to your ex-husband's place on Long Island to keep an eye on your daughter," he said.

My heart thudded to a stop. "You don't think he'd come after Temple?"

"Just a precaution," Matthew Raice said. "You're our major concern, Garner. According to Reed's notes, your daughter is gone through Labor Day anyway, right?"

"Right."

"That gives us ten days to wait and see. I understand where you live is quite remote."

"It's secluded," I admitted.

"The bad news is, that makes it a little scary for you. The good news is, if Chaz wanders in on our watch, we'll see him. You think you and your housekeeper could find another place to stay in the meantime?"

"Cilda's in Brooklyn with family."

"What about you?" Raice's quick eyes drifted back to the file. "You stayed at a friend's place in Manhattan last night, didn't you? Couldn't you hang out there again?"

She isn't my friend, I wanted to tell him. *I don't have any friends. Black or white.* I said, "I'll figure something out."

"Fine. But don't go back home. We don't

want to take the chance that Chaz could follow you to another location. If you need clothes or personal items, we'll get them to you."

"Gotcha." I checked my watch as though I might be late for an appointment; in truth, I just had to get out of there. "Well, sounds like you've got all the bases covered."

"For the moment." From his expression I could tell there was something he wasn't telling me.

"Let me guess," I ventured. "You've got some more good news, bad news?"

"You're making fun of me." Matt sounded hurt, but his blue eyes crinkled merrily. "I like that in a client. Actually, I think we're in good shape as long as Chaz hasn't been lying to us."

"How do you mean, lying?"

"Well, what if he isn't who he says he is— a guy who just happened to see you on television and was smitten?" Raice said. "I think you should face the possibility, however slight... that this fellow calling himself Chaz might be someone you know."

After a brief business discussion about the firm's contracts and fees, Matt accompanied me out to the reception area. We passed Reed Corbin's office on the way. Through the open door I saw Corbin, at his desk, talking on the phone. "That restraining order isn't worth the paper it's printed on," he was saying; then he glanced up, and our eyes met. He waved—a tentative gesture that may or may not have meant, *Come in.* But I was in no mood for Reed Corbin's tidal shifts of interest, so I pretended not to notice.

Tamara Ma went all aflutter at the sight of Matthew Raice. "I found those accounts you were looking for on the Petty case, Matt," she cooed.

"Thanks, Tam." Raice turned to me. "You'll let us know where you're staying?"

"Of course," I said, adding, "If you have any news before then, you can call me on my cellular."

He took my hand and gave it a reassuring squeeze. "It's going to be all right, Garner."

"Yeah," I said.

I walked to the parking lot in a funk. *Splush-splush,* trickled the fountain. The koi made shimmery ripples in the pond. A red leaf fluttered down from the Japanese maple and landed at my feet. The Zen-by-landscape quietude seemed to mock my inner turmoil.

That the letters could be coming from someone I knew had never occurred to me. "As a precaution," Matthew Raice had said, "I'd like you to make a list of all the people you've encountered—personally and professionally—who might be capable of this type of behavior." I'd promised him I would try.

The Volvo was like an oven. I slid behind the wheel, rolled down the windows and put on the air. He wanted a list. What, alphabetical? By geographical location? Chapter and verse from first book to last, or numbered according to case the way they'd appeared in court? A majority of the subjects I wrote about—"my sociopaths," as Andy called them—were dead or behind bars; but along the way were others who'd fallen in between the cracks. Vengeful and manipulative men who spent their lives playing dangerous mindgames.

And the hard-core criminals were just the tip of the iceberg.

As I exited the gates of Corbin, Incorporated, I went through a preliminary roster—seedy lawyers; one of the cops I'd pissed off; spurned suitors; jealous colleagues; ordinary joes who felt they'd been misquoted or misrepresented in one of my books. My former assistant, Jack, who'd quit in a blind rage.

Would the list of suspects be so widespread if I wrote, say, romantic fiction instead of true crime? The answer was obvious, but I'd been over that a million times before. A year short of turning forty seemed too late to make a major career change. I was who I was.

Three solid lanes of traffic clogged the length of Highway 287. It didn't matter. I wasn't even sure where I was heading. The sun had burned off the morning clouds, offering a million-dollar view of the shoreline from the Tappan Zee. Halfway across the bridge, it suddenly became clear—there *was* a place I could go.

I put on my sunglasses and picked up the cellular phone.

SEVEN

The aftermath of an accident made it slow going on the Garden State Parkway, so I pulled off at the Red Bank exit. It would take longer to get to Spring Lake this way, but at least the drive along Ocean Avenue would be scenic.

Peggy Boyle had been less than enthusiastic about my proposal. "You're going to st...ay there?" her voice had wavered.

Despite the poor connection, I got the gist. "It'll only be for a few days," I said. *Like maybe ten to fourteen.*

"Oh dear. You know, I...ve that one young couple who're extreme...terested." She sighed. "They wanted to...ring their parents to see it...s week."

"That's no problem," I assured her. "I promise I'll make myself scarce."

Again, Peggy sighed—or maybe it was just the static. "You'll be alone you said? Your daught...r isn't..."

I filled in the blank. We'd met at the house once to check on the renovations, and I'd brought Temple with me. She'd spent the whole time running through the upstairs hallway and sliding down the mahogany banister. "No. She's with her dad."

"Oh." Peggy Boyle sounded relieved. "I supp...that'll be okay, Mrs. Quinn." Big of her, I thought, considering I still owned the place. She asked if I needed the key and I told her no, I was carrying one on me. I always did, even though the last time I spent a night in my father's home, I was eighteen.

Trafficwise, Ocean Avenue wasn't much better than the Parkway. Uniformed rent-a-cops, sweat-stained and cranky, stood in front of the beach clubs, directing members in and out of the crowded parking lots. Weekday or not, it was hot and sunny, and there were only two more weeks of summer left—which translated into high times at the Jersey shore.

I kept driving, past Seven Presidents—where busloads of kids from Newark and Jersey City came to swim—through West End, into the posh communities of Deal and Avon by the Sea. Avon's stately graciousness spilled onto the edges of Asbury Park, but in the center of town, the fun house that Bruce Springsteen had made famous in *Tunnel of Love* was dark, the carousel gone, and the business district had a desperate, going-out-of-business pallor.

I took Route 70, skirting the eccentric little community of Ocean Grove, where blue laws had prohibited driving on Sundays well into the seventies. The bridge was up in Bradley Beach and I waited in a line of cars for twenty minutes while a single fishing boat drifted through.

Belmar, the college town, was in full party mode. Rollerbladers streaked by in spandex shorts and bikinis. Fraternity boys hung out of the oceanfront rentals, catcalling to pretty girls, toasting them with cans of beer. One house sported a life-size figure of Spider-

68

Man on its roof in a rubbery clinch with a blow-up sex doll.

"Hey, Red!" one guy called to me. I had to laugh.

Belmar's raucousness dead-ended at a pair of brick gates topped with graceful stone finials. This was Spring Lake, affectionately called "the Irish Riviera." Since the turn of the century it had been a watering hole for the wealthy elite. My father kept a summer house on Ocean Avenue, and after he divorced my mother, he kept me in it.

I slowed down in front of the low wall, pleased with what I saw. It had always been a showplace, but the renovated exterior, with its fresh paint and smart new windows made it seem less intimidating—welcoming almost. The For Sale sign was pleasing too. Dudley had died over two years ago. It would be a relief, once it sold, to finally unload the past.

Instead of pulling into the drive, I continued toward the center of town. Spring Lake was crowded, but there was a high-toned unhurriedness to this bustle. I even found a parking space near my favorite lunch spot on Third.

A local cop I knew was finishing up a piece of Snickers pie at the counter. Gerald T. Donovan, Lord of the Diet. "Garner," he said, sheepishly. "Caught me red-handed with the goods."

"This seat taken?" I slid onto the stool next to him.

"Always room for you, Garn," he said.

I ordered a turkey on rye and two Diet

69

Cokes to go. "On the lam as usual," Donovan commented good-naturedly. "What's up? You sell the house?"

"Not yet," I said. "As a matter of fact, I'm going be staying there for a week or two. I'd appreciate you telling the boys at the precinct that if they see some activity, nothing hinky's going on."

"Sure thing," Gerry said. Static came from his squawk box. "Gotta run. It'll go this way till Labor Day I guess." He slapped a buck down for the tip. "Hey, if you're around, why don't you come by some night for dinner? My wife'd be thrilled. You know, she's your biggest fan."

She's only an amateur, I thought grimly. *I'm hiding from my biggest fan.* Out loud I said, "That would be great."

I parked the Volvo in the garage, disengaged the security alarm, and let myself in through the back entrance. The immense kitchen was a glacial white, spare and modern, nothing like the way it looked when I was a child. I'd made sure of that.

Tossing the bag with the sandwich and sodas on the counter, along with the afternoon paper I'd bought, I did a quick inspection of my surroundings. The phone had been disconnected after Dudley died, so it was good I had my cellular.

Reed Corbin and Matt Raice were in a meeting, but Tamara Ma promised she'd let them know my whereabouts as soon as they emerged. Cilda seemed happy that I was staying in Spring Lake. Only Temple was suspicious.

"What's wrong?" she asked.

"Nothing," I told her. "I just wanted a change of scenery, that's all."

"Mother..." She wasn't buying it. "Your face turns all red and sweaty every time you go into that house."

"It does not." But of course, she was right. Already I could feel the beads of perspiration dripping down my forehead, the flush creeping over my cheeks. "The point is, there's still a lot of stuff in the attic I need to go through. And what better time than while you're with Daddy and Cilda's in Brooklyn with Kathi-anne?" It sounded so reasonable I almost believed it myself.

"I guess." Temple sighed. "As long as you're sure you'll be all right."

"I'll be fine," I assured my daughter. "It's going to be fun. Like camping out."

I hung up before she remembered how I hated camping out. Fortunately the water, gas, and electric service had never been discontinued, so there was no need to rough it. I opened the refrigerator and twisted the dial to "Initial Cool." Tonight, I promised myself, I would take a long, hot shower and go to sleep at some absurdly early hour.

A set of swinging double doors once sectioned off the kitchen from the rest of the first floor. The architect I'd hired opened up the floor plan to create one huge space out of what had been the cooking area, and the dining and drawing rooms.

At the suggestion of my realtor, the house was kept partially furnished. "It's a little spooky, coming into huge rooms like these when they're empty," Peg Boyle had said. "Prospective buyers want to be able to picture it as a home."

That was a stretch for me. I'd spent a ton of money on the renovations. The place had been modernized. Sunlight now poured through windows that had been heavily masked by damask drapes. The smell of tobacco and Dudley's bourbon, and the lingering ether of mosquito spray no longer hung in the air. And yet, the place seemed to me anything but homey. Still, I'd agreed to leave some of the best pieces—the matching velvet settees, the baby grand, the sideboard, the liquor cabinet, the hallstand.

I walked through the near-empty rooms, into the foyer. The front door was securely locked. *Chaz doesn't know you're here,* I reminded myself, and for the second time in one day my shoulders sagged as the tension left them; the first time it happened was early this morning, sitting on the leather sofa, next to Reed Corbin.

There were no tables or chairs. When Kathianne bought her place in Brooklyn, I sent the Duncan Fife dining set as a housewarming present. I ate my sandwich, standing up at the kitchen counter. After I'd finished, I scooped the crumbs back into the bag, picked up my suitcase, the paper, and a can of soda, and started toward the mahogany staircase.

I was halfway up the steps when a sudden,

urgent pealing froze me in my tracks. My phone was ringing. With shaking hands, I pulled it out of my shoulder tote. "Hello?" I whispered.

"Garner," a man's voice said. "It's Reed Corbin."

Corbin. My stomach lurched. "What's happened? Have you found him?"

"No, I'm afraid there isn't any news on that front."

"Oh God," I lowered myself on the banister until I was sitting on the carpeted step. "For a minute I thought—"

"Sorry if I frightened you." He sounded dismayed. "I was just checking to see how you were settling in."

"Everything's fine." I pressed my forehead against the staircase spindle. The way it hurt felt good.

"Is there anything you need?" Corbin asked. "Clothes? Personal items? I can have stuff sent down from the other house."

I did a quick mental rundown of the contents of my suitcase: jeans, a white T-shirt, the blazer that Mercedes had refused to let me wear, a pajama top for sleeping, another change of underwear, a pair of sneakers, a toothbrush, make-up, soap, and baby shampoo. Plus the skimpy turquoise sweater set I had on. The thought of telling Reed Corbin that I could use a bathing suit and a half-dozen pairs of panties was out of the question. "I'm okay for now," I replied, primly.

"Well, just let us know," he said.

"I will."

There was a silence on the line. I pulled myself to my feet, dusting the rear of my one and only skirt. "Is there anything else?"

"No." Corbin's voice suddenly sounded far away and wavery. "Well, actually, yes. The reason that I called—I wanted to explain why I asked Matt to handle your case—"

"You don't owe me an explanation."

"Yes, I do. You see, there was a conflict of interest." The line broke up; when it cleared again, he was saying, "...didn't want to blur the boundaries. Providing you with complete protection should be an entirely separate thing, but considering the way that I..." more static. "...I thought it would be best, from a purely psychological point of view, if we kept any personal relationship compartmentalized—"

Once again the connection cut out. Then I heard Reed say, "...perhaps we could go to dinner."

There was a long silence. "I'm having some trouble hearing," I said. "Did you just ask me out?"

"I have an early day tomorrow. I could be in Spring Lake by late afternoon."

"I don't—" The line crackled, and I thought, *I don't what? I don't want to? I don't date nice men? I don't think you could ever measure up to some overly romanticized image I have of Dane Blackmoor? I don't know why—in spite of all that—I'm standing here on the staircase in my father's house with a big, shit-eating grin on my face?*

"Sorry, Garner." Reed's apology came in

loud and clear. "I should never have...Please know that you can expect nothing but absolute professionalism—"

"Dinner would be nice," I cut in. "Just bring a battery pack. I need to recharge my phone."

EIGHT

I tried sleeping in the master suite that night, but couldn't. No matter that the walls had been repainted, that new carpeting had been laid, and the massive walnut bedstead replaced with a dainty four-poster; it was still the place where Dudley had once slept. After an hour of tossing and turning, I crept down to the room at the end of the hall.

My old bedroom was now an upstairs study. I myself chose the color scheme: dark brown and deep red—the antithesis of all the white wicker and pink roses of my childhood. The new windows slid open easily on their sashes. No perfumed fog would drift through them tonight. A pregnant moon sat over the water. Even after I curled up on the sofa it stayed with me, a luminous circle behind my eyelids.

The next thing I knew, it was after nine in the morning. My body felt like it had been run over by a truck. I dressed quickly and drove into town for a huge breakfast of fried eggs, bacon, home fries and coffee.

As I was coming out of the luncheonette, something in the shop window across the street caught my eye. I strolled over to the opposite sidewalk for a better look. It was a khaki-green jumper in a rumpled cotton, with a plunging back crisscrossed by shoulder straps. I went inside.

"I'd like to buy the dress in the window," I announced to the woman behind the counter, "and a pair of sandals, if you sell them, and some underwear."

All summer footwear was fifty percent off, she told me. She had one jumper left in a size petite, and no undies, but I could buy a pack of Hanes panties at the variety store down the block. I did, stopping off for a bottle of wine and, while I was at it, a bag of potato chips, a box of crackers, and a liter of Diet Coke.

Reed Corbin called shortly after noon to say he expected to be in Spring Lake by three. At two-thirty I put on the jumper and finger-combed my hair. I'd cut off my long, curly mane a year before, and while the act had been strangely freeing, I still wasn't used to the low-maintenance routine.

I decided it would be nice if when Reed pulled in the drive, I was out in the yard. Not by the pool, which was covered. In the garden. A landscaping company came twice a week to tend the grounds, and there was an automatic sprinkler system, but I figured I could pick the dead blooms off of geraniums without doing much harm. It would make me appear to be all those things I was not—casual chic, earthy and nurturing, at one with my surroundings.

I picked shriveled stems for twenty minutes.

For fifteen more I plucked off blossoms that had barely begun to fade. Under the light cotton jumper, my skin was soaked with perspiration, and my cheeks and shoulders had begun to burn. Each time a car passed on the other side of the wall, I wiped the sweat away with the back of my hand and shook out my hair.

At three forty-five, Reed still hadn't come. An irrational fear seized me. What if something was wrong? Except in the first split second upon waking, I hadn't even thought about Chaz; now it occurred to me that I might've been dangerously naive. Not only had Chaz read all my books, he'd pored over interviews I'd given, articles written about me. Surely somewhere was a mention that I'd grown up in a small town called Spring Lake. Would he make the connection? If he did, it would be easy enough to find me. Any local could tell a body where the Quinn estate was.

Despite the heat, I started to shiver. The house and grounds were protected by a security system, but I'd turned the alarm off when I came back from town. Tossing my fistful of plucked stems aside, I raced toward the rear entranceway. The door was open. Inside, the sudden absence of sun momentarily blinded me. I palmed the wall until I found the alarm pad, punching in the code.

Once my sight returned and my breathing slowed to normal, I checked all the rooms, upstairs and down, to prove to myself that no one had managed to sneak in while I was outside playing Martha Stewart. I'd just completed my patrol when I heard the sound of a car turning into the drive.

From the window I saw Corbin, pulling through the gate in a black Volvo sedan.

The second I opened the door, all hell broke loose. A wailing siren propelled me into the garden. Then hundreds of in-ground sprinklers went off, spurting tiny fountains of water into the air. Reed got out of the car and ran toward the rear entrance. Moments later the sprinklers dribbled to a stop and the noise subsided.

"Somebody must've fiddled with the panel in here," Reed called.

I was soaking wet. "You think?" I called back. "How can you tell?"

He walked across the damp lawn. "Sorry I'm late," he said. "The traffic."

"Summer." I nodded; a bead of water ran down my nose.

"You should probably change, before you catch a cold," he suggested.

Why the hell was he always so considerate? *And so goddam neat.* I glared at his lightweight summer suit, pale shirt, and striped tie. A few damp spots marred his crisply pressed trousers from when he'd touched the wet grass.

I began walking toward the house. My sandals made slappy, squishy sounds with every step. "Just a minute." Reed jogged over to his car, and came back with a large white shopping bag. He followed me inside.

"This is nice," he said, in the kitchen.

"Can I get you anything?" I gestured toward the empty cabinets. "Coke? Some saltines?"

For the first time he smiled. "Thanks. I'm fine." He took a seat on the velvet settee. I could sense him watching me as I squished my way upstairs.

The suitcase with my few meager possessions was in the master bedroom. I shut the door and locked it. In the antique mirror over Dudley's dresser I saw a wavery reflection—a mop of wet hair...a bad sunburn...a rumpled, splotchy bag of a shift. Could it get any worse than this?

Certainly, a dark voice in my head taunted. *The night is still young.* If I locked the door and just stayed in here, I figured sooner or later he'd get the message and leave.

"You all right?" Corbin called from the downstairs landing.

I sighed. This guy was definitely not a leaver. "Yeah, yeah," I shouted back, ending with a whispered, "Hold your horses." I put on my jeans, T-shirt, and sneakers, and unlocked the door.

He stood up as I entered the room. "You look beautiful," he said.

"Sure." I pointed to the bag on the settee. "What've you got?"

"I brought glad tidings." He pulled a small cardboard box out of the bag. "A battery charger." With a flourish he dug into the bag again. "And one...two...yes, there it is—*three* cellular phones with pagers."

It was my turn to smile. "What do I need three for?"

"One for you, one for Mrs. Fields, and one for Temple." It pleased me to hear my daughter's name roll off his tongue so naturally.

"Do you think that's necessary?"

"Maybe not at the moment," he conceded. "But they could come in handy once you all move back home."

"Have there been any more letters? Or am I not supposed to ask you that"—I flashed him an insolent grin—"since you're not actually handling my case?"

Corbin looked perplexed. "I hope you don't—"

This will never work, I thought. *The man is way too serious.* I said, "I'm kidding, Reed."

"Oh." He adjusted his glasses. "I was afraid you might've felt I pawned you off on Matt. Without good reason."

"No. I don't think that."

"Because if you were my wife"—he blushed at the word—"or my sister... and someone was sending you threatening letters, I'd make the same call. Matt's got an incredible instinct when it comes to these predators."

"So you've said." I nodded. "You shouldn't worry. I like him very much."

Corbin frowned. "Well, I'm glad," he said.

"Me too." We fell into an awkward silence. Once again my eyes fastened on the bag. "What else?" I asked.

"Excuse me?"

"Don't you have something else in there?"

"Oh, it's"—Corbin hedged—"really nothing." I snatched the bag away from him and peeked inside. "Just a thing I wrote, a sort of survival guide to help people react in potentially dangerous situations. My editor sent me a couple advance copies, so I thought, if you got bored one day, you might..." His voice trailed off.

I studied the book cover. It was eye-catching—big silver print on a shiny field of black, and one of those in-your-face titles:

THE FEAR FACTOR
by
Reed Corbin

---

*How Your PFQ (Personal Fear Quotient)
Can Save Your Life*

I remembered Matthew Raice's comment about Corbin's hard-on for abbreviations. Stifling a giggle, I turned the book over.

The back was filled with glowing endorsements from well-known clients of Corbin, Incorporated. One name popped off the page like flashing neon. Dane Blackmoor, *sculptor.* *"Corbin gives striking proof,"* read Blackmoor's quote, *"that violence may be the only thing that isn't perfectly random in this cold, cruel world."*

Reed must've noticed my pained expression. "I'm afraid I don't take a very good picture," he said, self-consciously. I followed his gaze to the bottom corner of the jacket. The author photograph wasn't bad, for a driver's license or a passport.

"You should smile next time," I said. My

voice was raspy. How could the mere sight of Blackmoor's name in typeset make me feel this way? It seemed so unfair—that he was also one of Reed Corbin's clients was yet another invisible tie lashing us together. The book on my lap suddenly felt hot, juiced with its own electricity.

"Can't wait to read it," I said, putting it down on the velvet cushion between us.

"Who knows?" Reed pushed back the ridge of his glasses jauntily. "Maybe the famous author Garner Quinn will give me an endorsement for the next one."

"Maybe," I said. I didn't tell him that the back cover wasn't big enough for both Dane Blackmoor and me.

NINE

It was such a beautiful day, Reed said, it would be nice to get out, maybe walk along the beach.

I looked at him doubtfully. "Dressed like that?"

He said, "With a few minor alterations." Taking off his jacket and tie, he folded them precisely, then draped them over the back of the settee. "Ready." He smiled.

We went out through the kitchen. I let Corbin set the alarm and close up the house. "Sure you wouldn't rather drive?" I asked.

"Nope," he said, but halfway to the gate he jogged back to his sensible Volvo, zapped the automatic lock, and leaned into the back seat. "For your sunburn." He tossed me a baseball cap with the letters IAD embroidered over the brim.

"What's IAD stand for?" I asked, tugging it on. It was several sizes too big.

"Oh, that's our protective security group." Corbin took off the hat and went to work realigning its plastic snaps. "We call it our Invisible Armor Division."

"Catchy," I said.

Very gently, he replaced the cap on my head. "Perfect," he said, and for some reason I knew he wasn't talking about the fit.

In one of those states of agitation that I'm prone to when a man pays me too much attention, I simultaneously triggered the remote to the electronic gate and started walking and talking. "So those are the guys who're watching my house and keeping an eye on Temple—the Invisible Armor?"

The gate closed noisily behind us. "Yes." Reed seemed about to say something else, then he stopped, his face turning serious. "Who else has entry to this place?"

"The realtor," I said. "And the landscape company. A cleaning lady comes every Monday. Oh, and my handyman, Ben Snow. I think that's probably it."

Reed snapped a pair of sun visors down over his glasses. "I'll need a complete list, with addresses and phone numbers. The firm will coordinate their comings and goings while you're here."

We stood on the corner of Ocean Avenue,

waiting to cross. The sun was on a slant now. Families had begun to pull up stakes, returning from the beach with fold-up chairs and furled umbrellas, empty coolers, wet towels, and boogie boards. Young kids horsed around under the public shower spigots, the bottoms of their bathing suits weighted down with sand, their skin sticky with Popsicle goo, suntan lotion, and salt. From this vantage point, Spring Lake boardwalk seemed to go on forever—a child's toy seaside village under a painted backdrop of sea and sky.

"You don't think he'd come here?" I asked. Despite the attack of paranoia I'd had only an hour ago, it seemed out of the question to me. There was something inviolate about this town.

"I doubt it," said Reed. "But if he does, we'll be ready for him." He nodded his head toward an unmarked beige van parked on a side street across from the property, then, in an uncharacteristically confident manner, he tweaked my cap. "Invisible Armor," he said.

"You never answered my question," I shouted into the wind as we dodged the traffic on the avenue.

"Which one?"

"Was there a letter in the mail this morning?"

Reed stopped at the foot of the boardwalk ramp and turned to me. "Under normal circumstances, I don't discuss that sort of information with clients. You have to understand, my job is to keep as much distance—both geographical and psychological—between you and your stalker as humanly possible. For your own protection—"

I cut him off. "There was a letter, wasn't there?" Corbin started to walk away. I caught the back of his shirtsleeve. "You have no right to withhold information from me. I want to know. What did he say?"

"Garner," Reed implored. "It's being dealt with."

I sat down on a bench. "Tell me what he said."

"A note came via the regular mail." Corbin sat down next to me. "Same handwriting. One line. It read, *They can't keep you from me.* It wasn't signed."

I pulled the cap down over my nose. "Shit," I muttered. "Shit, shit, shit."

Corbin patted my knee and then took his hand away and put it in his lap. "We're going to find him, Garner. I promise."

We sat on the bench in silence. After a few minutes, we climbed down to the beach and continued along the sand. Reed took off his socks and shoes and rolled up his trousers. His shins and feet were very white. A couple of kids were piling buckets of wet sand around a boy of about ten, who was already buried up to his neck.

Reed strode over to them. "Hey, guys," he said in a friendly voice. "Let me give you a hand and we'll get your buddy out."

"No way," protested a chubby boy with a baggy swimsuit and a crew cut. "It took us an hour to get him this deep."

"All that sand is too heavy for someone so small," Reed said. "It could crush his chest."

"Who're you anyway, mister?" the little

kid in the hole scoffed. "The *sand* police?"

The other boys laughed, but Corbin didn't even crack a smile. "As a matter of fact"—he pulled an official-looking badge out of his hip pocket—"I am. Could I see some identification, boys?"

The chubby one tried to act cool, but his eyes were scared. "Gee, I musta left my wallet in my other bathing trunks, Officer."

"I wanna get out anyway," piped the kid in the sand. "I got an itch."

Corbin and I helped them open up the hole. As we walked away from them, one of the older kids shouted, "Hey, lady—is he *really* the sand police?"

I pointed to my baseball cap. "IAD," I yelled back, putting a finger to my lips to signal it was hush-hush. Then I turned to Reed. "You really get off on this saving people stuff, don't you?"

He looked embarrassed. "Sorry. Hazard of the trade." He stopped, flipping his polarized lenses up to show me how sincere he was. "Matt calls me 'the self-righteous stiff.'" Reed laughed as though it hurt. "I'm trying to loosen up, though. I think if I could retrain myself to stop seeing the potential danger in every moment, then I could start appreciating—" He broke off, lamely. "—the moment itself, you know?"

Just then I happened to glance down at his pale, slender feet. The hair on his narrow calves was speckled with sand. I don't know why, but it made me feel sad. "Have you ever had a frozen custard?" I asked.

"Pardon me?"

"A custard," I repeated. "It's like eating ice cream on a cloud."

He shook his head. "Can't say that I've tried that."

"Well, jeez louise, Officer Corbin," I said. "You haven't lived."

We bought custards and ate them as we strolled through town. Corbin had put his socks and shoes on and smoothed out his pants, so he looked less vulnerable. "This is much tastier than ice cream," he commented. He held a paper napkin around the cone and had a methodical way of licking, so that all the sides were even, like a beehive that just got smaller and smaller. Me, I nuzzled, and swallowed, and slurped, unmindful when he warned my cone had begun to drip down one side.

A walk through the local playground near the lake turned out to be a mistake. While I pointed out the sights—the copper dome of St. Catharine's, the picturesque bridge, the family of swans—Reed kept one eye out for unattended toddlers, strange men lurking in the bushes, and potentially dangerous monkey bars.

"Relax," I told him. "This is Spring Lake. Nothing bad happens here."

"Seems like a great place to grow up in," Reed said, a little wistfully.

"Yes," I agreed, content for the moment to bask in the glow of an imaginary happy childhood. "Where are you from?"

"San Diego."

"Beautiful city."

Reed shrugged. "Not the section I lived in." We paused at the center of the bridge, leaning on our elbows to look down at the clear water of the lake. "Where I lived was a real pit. Of course, that was more than geography—it was the chaotic nature of my family."

He turned around, his back resting against one of the wooden supports. I knew he was going to tell me the story of his life. For some reason, people always did. "My father was a Navy man. Chief bosun's mate. Big, barrel-chested guy. Not as tall as me, but built like a fireplug, with these huge Popeye arms covered in tattoos. Poor bastard. He could never understand how his kids turned out so puny. My baby brother and I..." Corbin removed the shades from his glasses and put them into his breast pocket. "We took after our mom—rangy, but tough.

"We had to be." He laughed ruefully. "You need to be quick and hard when you're a human punching bag."

"He beat you?"

"On a regular basis," said Reed. "My mother got the worst. Broken ribs, broken wrist. A fractured skull. One time he pummeled her so bad her cheekbone caved in. After that, the left side of her face just kind of hung there, like somebody who had a stroke."

"That must've been hard for you," I said. "It certainly explains a lot about your choice of careers."

"Yeah." He picked up a leaf and threw it into the air. It danced on the breeze for a long moment before landing on the water. "People talk about definitive moments in their lives," he said. Behind the gold-rimmed glasses, Corbin's eyes were fixed on some faraway horizon point. "Well, my definitive moment came when I was ten years old.

"It was an ordinary night. My father came home, drunk and belligerent, as usual. As usual, something about the dinner wasn't right, the meat was cold, the potatoes were lumpy, it didn't matter. It always ended up on the floor, or splattered on the walls, anyway. And as usual, he sat there at the kitchen table, bellowing for my mother to clean up the mess he'd made. Only this night—instead of dropping to her knees with a scrub bucket, cowering and crying, trying to dodge his savage kicks, his big fists and filthy insults—she went over to the cupboard, took out a gun, and shot my old man dead."

"You saw it happen?"

Reed Corbin nodded. "For years I played that scene over and over in my head. I mean, just about every night of my life I'd heard my father threaten to kill my mom. A couple of times, it looked as if he might succeed. But it was my mother who calmly opened that drawer, picked up the revolver, and aimed it at his heart. And the more I thought about it, the more I realized"—he looked earnestly into my eyes—"*I wasn't surprised.* Growing up around all that violence had given me a sort of second sense, an instinct. Like, just before it happened, I remember taking my little brother by the hand and shutting him in our bedroom. I remember knowing ahead of time, when my mother pointed the gun, that she would shoot. That it was going to go off.

"I learned two valuable lessons at an early age," Reed said. "One, the person who makes the biggest threats doesn't necessarily pose the greatest danger. And two—and this is the really crucial one—it's possible to predict violence." His voice rose passionately. "And if you can predict it, that means you can also prevent it."

Now that he'd finished, some of his old self-consciousness returned. "Which concludes our lecture for today." He pushed his glasses back on the ridge of his nose and smiled. "Sorry if I bored you."

"You didn't."

We fell into step together. "You know," Reed said, "you're a very good listener."

I did know. I was a professional. Like a priest or a shrink, people told me their innermost secrets, only not being bound by laws of confidentiality or the confessional, I was at liberty to turn their shared confidences into bestselling works of nonfiction. The whole process amazed and, quite often, repelled me. Listening to Reed Corbin's story was different, though; this was not fodder for an upcoming book. It was, for the first time in a long while, *personal.*

"What happened to your mother?" I asked.

"I wish I could say there was a happy ending," Reed said. "She spent four years in prison. My brother and I went into foster care. By the time she got us back, she was involved with another abusive man. She died about eight years ago."

"I'm sorry. What about your brother?"

"Unfortunately, he got into drugs. We don't see each other much."

We walked through the playground on our way back to the center of town. It was after six o'clock. Most of the kids had gone home for dinner. My stomach was starting to growl. "I'm hungry," I said, "but I don't feel like sitting in a restaurant."

"We could go back to the house," Reed suggested. "Share a box of saltines and a Coke."

I told him we might be able to do better than that.

We laid our picnic out atop a satin comforter on the floor of the empty dining room. I'd found candles in the utility closet, but there were no candleholders, so instead I took a couple of flashlights and stood them on end at either side of the blanket. Their small weak beams cast yellow cutouts on the ceiling.

"Is there a corkscrew around here?" I heard Reed rattling around in the kitchen cabinets.

I'd bought wine, but forgotten the damn screw. "Sorry," I called. "And there's nothing to cut the cheese with either."

He entered with the bottle and some paper cups. "We can use our hands. You have a coat hanger?"

"A what?"

"A wire hanger, like for coats?"

"I'll check." There was one in the closet in the foyer.

Reed took the hook and straightened it. "A little trick from my college days." He inserted the hanger end into the cork. "Matt and I used to be able to do this, half in the bag, with our eyes closed."

"Is that where you two met?" I was already divvying up the sandwiches. "At school?"

"Harvard." Reed nodded. The cork slid out on the tip of the wire coat hanger.

"My," I said, "you did pull yourself up by your bootstraps, didn't you?"

"I had help," he said modestly, bending at the waist to pour wine into our paper cups. "I always did well in school, but the emotional baggage I was carrying pretty much weighed me down. My first year at college I floundered, partied too much with Matt and the guys. Acted stupid."

I tried to picture Corbin acting anything but smart, but couldn't. "Then I started to get to know Matt's dad. Dr. Raice was a university legend—an early pioneer in the field of child advocacy and domestic violence. I took every one of his classes. Became his protégé. He helped me articulate all the things I'd experienced in dumb silence. Without him, I would've never had the confidence—or the means—to come up with a tracking system like PREDICT. He's still the person I call on when something's got me stumped."

Corbin lowered himself awkwardly to the floor. I'd only known one man who could do that with any kind of grace, but I was determined not to think about Dane Blackmoor anymore tonight. Reed said, "I haven't stopped talking about myself since I got here. And you've said nearly nothing about yourself."

It was a comfortable ratio for me. Chalking up points for the childhood and college years, it now stood Corbin: 2, Quinn: 0. But the wine had already gone to my head. I decided to raise the stakes a bit. "What do you want to know?" I asked.

"Well, for one thing"—he broke off a piece of French bread—"I know you're divorced—"

"Isn't everybody?"

"Actually, no." Corbin shrugged sheepishly. "Some of us are married to the job."

"You mean like you and Matt?"

"Matt's got a girl in every port," Reed said. "I've got a cellular phone and a fax machine."

"I can relate to that," I said.

"Can I assume you're presently unattached, then?"

"Is that a personal question, or is it just something else for the file?"

Reed did the push-back thing with his glasses. "I guess if you tell me you're unattached, it's personal. But if there is someone in your life, he goes down in the file."

"There's no one to be concerned about," I said. The words left me with a sinking feeling. I felt as if, in saying them, I'd snipped one of my invisible ties to Blackmoor. Which was good, I reminded myself, very good.

"Good." Reed Corbin smiled at me. "Very good."

TEN

I stayed in my father's house for eleven days. During that period Reed Corbin drove down from his firm at Forked Brook five times. Max had told me that Corbin had a reputation for hand-holding important clients, but even I could see that this went way beyond the call of duty. Still, his manner toward me remained restrained and formal. He took me to dinner, and once, to a movie. We walked along the boardwalk at night, when the beach was dark and deserted. We had lively conversations about nothing much important—books we both liked, people we knew in common. Dane Blackmoor's name never came up. Reed talked some more about his family. He told me he'd never visited his father's grave, that he didn't even know for sure if his brother, Mark, was still alive; the last he'd heard, he was in Amsterdam, strung out on drugs.

I heard myself say that, apart from Temple and Cilda, I was alone too. And when I brought up the subject of Dudley I could tell by the kindness in his eyes that he already knew. It pissed me off each time I was reminded of the humiliating public spectacle Dudley made of our differences, but that's the way these newsworthy stories go, I suppose. It isn't every day a father sues his own daughter for ten million dollars.

On our third evening together, as we were walking barefoot along the beach, Reed asked, "Who did you want to be when you were little?"

"Hayley Mills," I said without a moment's thought, "up until the time I was twelve. After that I wanted to be Vincent Bugliosi." Reed's mouth dropped open. "You know, the prosecutor from the Manson trial?"

"I *know*." He shook his head. "Man, you must've been some kind of kid."

"Oh yeah?" I poked a finger into his chest. "Who did you want to be, huh?"

Reed adjusted his glasses. "Batman," he said, quite seriously.

I howled. He laughed. The waves crashed. The stars shone. We were getting beyond that initial sniffing stuff, the mating rites you see on The Discovery Channel; I was actually starting to like him. And yet, on that evening, like the others preceding it, when I walked him to his car, Reed Corbin simply took my hand, pressed it gently, and said goodnight.

The days between Corbin's visits went by swiftly. I decided to give the master bedroom another try, and to my surprise, I slept there like a rock. Every morning on my way out to breakfast, I passed the unmarked beige van. I made no attempt to speak to the men inside. I didn't want to get to know them. They were the IAD, my invisible armor, and it seemed important to keep them that way. Sometimes, though, I caught a glimpse of them from an upstairs window as they were changing shifts—well-built men in button-downed shirts, ties, and khakis, the vigilant protectors from Corbin, Inc.—and, inexplicably, Chaz's words would spring to mind. *They can't keep you from me.* And despite the well-regulated central air, I felt chilled to the bone.

I spoke with Matthew Raice every morning. He took my calls right away and always made it sound as if I were his top priority. No other letters had appeared. They were following up a few promising leads, and he promised he'd let me know the minute something clicked. "He'll trip himself up," Matt insisted, "and when he does, we'll be there with the nets. You can count on it, Garner." I wondered whether this was trickle-down enthusiasm, coming from his partner's office, or whether Matt had truly overcome his initial reluctance about taking on my case.

"In the meantime," he told me, "our men are there to serve. Anything makes you nervous, you just call them." I promised I would.

If Corbin, Inc.'s Invisible Armor Division was a welcome presence to me, it totally unnerved my ex-husband. "Do you realize they carry *guns*?" Andy whispered frantically, after grabbing the phone from Temple.

"They're a protective security team," I retorted. "What do you want them to carry, sharpened sticks?"

I heard familiar little popping sounds over the line: Andy was a finger snapper. He snapped when he wanted his secretary to bring coffee, he snapped when he wanted privacy or silence, and now he was snapping for Temple to leave the room.

Once she did, he breathed deeply into the receiver. "What have you gotten yourself into this time, Garner?"

"Just another man who can't get enough of me, Andy," I replied. "You know how it is."

"This isn't funny." I could picture him scowling into the phone. "Men with guns sitting around in armored vans..."

"The vans aren't armored," I said. "That's just what the division's called."

"Whatever." Andy snapped. "In any event, it's a totally inappropriate environment for you to raise our daughter."

"Thank you for your concern," I said haughtily, "but it's a little late, don't you think? I raised our daughter for sixteen years without any input from you—"

"Do we have to go over that again?" Andy whined.

In truth, I didn't want to any more than he did. I brought up the past as a weapon because the words "inappropriate environment" scared me. Now that he'd resurfaced after all this time, with a sweet, smart, responsible adult wife in tow, I was afraid he might be deemed by some to be the better parent. After all, strangers didn't send Andy cardboard boxes of garbage, and as far as I knew, I was the only person who wanted to hurt him.

I said, "Let's drop the whole thing. Forget about the van. Pretend it's not there. The situation is under control, I promise."

Later, Temple got back on the phone. "I told him everything was okay," she said in a low voice. "He's such a stooge."

"Don't talk about your father that way," I said, but inwardly my heart sang.

I found a trunkful of old papers in the attic. Under the eaves it was so hot the dust had a burned smell to it. The metal hasp felt warm in my hand when I touched it, and inside, the photo albums and folders were flimsy and flat, like things that had for years been pressed under glass. A stack of old report cards was wound with an ink-stained rubber band. I took one out of its manila envelope.

"Garner is a bright, imaginative child who does not play well with others. She refuses to engage in kickball during recess, and despite constant reminders, continues to neglect cleaning out her desk." Under this condemnation my third-grade teacher, Sister Virginia Michaela, wrote in beautiful, flowing script, *"How could such a neat little bird have such a messy nest?"*

The albums were the old-fashioned kind, rectangular, with shoelace strings on the binding, and thick black pages inside. Paper triangles had once bracketed the pictures, but the glue had dried up and they spilled out of the books like little yellow hats. I didn't know many of the people in the photographs, although I did recognize a few faces—one or two of Dudley's blond girlfriends; his partner, Geoffrey; a baseball player client. Besides these photographs, the albums contained newspaper clippings of the important cases my father had brought to trial. There was always a picture of him, smiling broadly for the camera, waving an outstretched hand or striking some other confident pose. I tried to remember whether it was I who had cut out these articles in such precise, scissored lines, or whether Cilda had.

In one album someone had stuck a bunch of snapshots, probably in the hope of coming back to paste them on the page one day. The pictures were very small, with perforated edges. I'd taken them with a camera I'd gotten for my thirteenth birthday—a zippy red teenager thing called a Swinger. Most of them were of Cilda Fields (young, beautiful, and a dead ringer for Mercedes), who was clearly annoyed at having the camera pointed at her face. There were several candids of Dudley's friends larking around the pool, and one of Dane Blackmoor.

I dropped it like a hot potato.

The picture fluttered for a moment in midair, then disappeared back into the recesses of the trunk. I pawed through the leatherbound albums, shuffling the report card envelopes like cards. The singed dust flew into my eyes and up my nostrils. From somewhere far away I thought I heard a bell ringing, but I didn't pay any attention. I kept searching through the trunk until I found it, wedged between a wooden cross-support, this small, faded image of an astonishingly beautiful young man in a light colored shirt with a stand-up collar, snapped unawares, at a distance. Turning it over, I saw my own childish writing: *"Dane. Aug. 31, 1969."*

A noise came from downstairs—the front door being pushed open. Someone was in the house. With the pictures still in my hand, I slid on my rear end, backing as far as I could under the slant of the eaves.

"Hello?" a voice called. "Mrs. Quinn, are you there?"

Only one person persisted in calling me Mrs. Quinn in spite of all efforts to set her straight. "Peg?" I stood so suddenly, I bumped my head. "Peg Boyle, is that you?"

It took me several minutes to climb down the narrow attic steps. All the while Peggy shouted her manifold apologies—she'd been trying to reach me on my cellular for hours but nobody answered...she'd even checked with that nice man, Mr. Raice, the way she was supposed to...and just to make sure, she'd rung the bell three times...

"Don't worry about it," I said, making my final descent into the foyer.

The realtor turned an imploring face up to me. In her pink linen dress and wide-brimmed hat, she looked like a hothouse flower craning toward artificial light. To her right, under the crystal chandelier, stood a well-dressed couple in their early thirties. The man came to the foot of the stairs to greet me. "Ms. Quinn, this is truly a pleasure," he said, extending his hand.

I had to stuff the snapshot into the pocket of my T-shirt before I could properly shake. "Hello," I managed. I realized what a shock I must be to him—dripping sweat, streaked in dirt, with a full moon of dust on my behind. Bestselling author Garner Quinn.

"Mr. and Mrs. McCarthy are meeting their parents here." Peggy Boyle placed particular emphasis on the name. "They wanted to show them the house." Her eyes busily telegraphed, *Don't you remember?*

"Of course," I said. "Well, I'll get out of your way—"

"Oh." Mr. McCarthy looked crestfallen. "You don't have to leave on our account."

Over his shoulder, I could see Peggy Boyle holding her breath under the wide-brimmed hat. "I'm afraid I have to. I was upstairs, sorting through a pile of junk, when I suddenly remembered there was some stuff I needed to do," I said. I imagined the McCarthys describing their encounter with me to friends. *She's oddly inarticulate,* they would say. *Perhaps she drinks.*

"I'll lock up when we're done," Peg said.

"Take your time," I told her.

"We just love your house." Mrs. McCarthy spoke up as I was leaving. She had a long, drawn face and sad eyes that seemed to fasten on things as though they might contain that little shred of happiness she was looking for.

"Take your time," I said again.

I walked briskly to my car, rolled down the windows, and turned on the radio. The local oldies station was having another Beatles marathon. When I pulled my old Volvo out of the gate, the IAD guy sitting behind the driver's wheel of the van gave me a friendly nod. I nodded back, then turned onto Ocean Avenue.

About a block away from the pavilion, a

101

woman was getting into a late-model Mustang. I put on my blinker and waited. A second later she pulled out, and I edged into the space and shut off the engine. I took the photograph I'd snapped all those years ago with my little red Swinger out of my pocket and put it on the passenger seat next to me as, on the radio, a very young John and Paul sang about places they remembered.

I put my head in my hands and started to cry.

ELEVEN

"Good news." Reed beamed as he stepped out of his car the next afternoon. "A couple of the leads we're following appear to be paying off."

I'd spent most of the morning spiffing up lawn furniture I'd found in the storage shed. Now I dragged Reed onto the patio. "Tell me," I said, ordering him to sit.

He balanced himself on a lounge chair and loosened his tie. "Okay, well, from the beginning the handwriting was a major source of interest. The uniformity of the lettering, and the assurance with which it's written, seem to suggest someone who's been profession-ally trained."

"You mean like a cartoonist?"

"More specifically"—Reed leaned forward eagerly, almost tipping over the chair—"an inker or letterer."

"A what or a *what*?"

"Publishers will hire three or four people on a comic strip," he said. "A writer to develop the story line. An illustrator—commonly known as a penciler—who draws the pictures. An inker to color the drawings, and a letterer, who prints out the writer's copy."

"And you think that's what Chaz does for a living?"

"It's possible. We're feeding writing samples from the major comic book houses into our system. We're also looking at rosters of names—freelancers who've worked as letterers or inkers during the past ten years. So far, no Chazes, but there are a couple of dozen close connects. Charleses and Charlies. Chasmaine, Chismare, Chesmont, that kind of thing. Matt's checking them out."

"That's it?" I couldn't help being disappointed. When he'd said "good news," I'd expected more than this—that Chaz may have, once upon a time, maybe, within the last decade, had a job lettering a comic strip.

But Corbin's spirits wouldn't be deflated. "It's fertile territory, Garner. Just give us some time."

"What else? Didn't you say there were a couple leads?"

Reed started to say something, then suddenly sprang to his feet. "Feel like taking a ride?"

"Sure," I said, following him to the car. "Where we going?"

He held the passenger door open for me. "Back to your other hometown."

Being on the open road with Reed Corbin was an almost spiritual experience. I tend to be critical in the passenger seat. To me, a good driver is someone who makes you forget about traffic lights and jaywalkers, or the guy in the car ahead doing twenty-five in a thirty-five-mile-an-hour zone. Good drivers, like good dancers and good lovers, invite you to sit back, and enjoy the ride.

I leaned against the neck rest, with the wind tousling my hair, for a long while. When I finally spoke, it was to say, "Turn on the radio."

Reed glanced sideways, with mock surprise. "You want music? I'm shocked. No twenty questions, Ms. Quinn? Surely there must be something else you want to grill me about."

"That's not my style," I said. "Besides, I know sooner or later you'll tell me everything you know. You can't help yourself."

"I'm just putty in your hands," he agreed.

The radio had been tuned to a classical station. Even Corbin's choice of music was safe. We sailed through Asbury Park on Vivaldi. I shut my eyes, imagining we were traveling at the lightspeed of violins. Unlike my sporty little classic, Reed's Volvo was quiet and impervious to bumps—a bank vault on wheels. The next thing I knew, a newscaster was reading the top stories of the hour in a soft, cultured, public radio sort of voice, and we were halfway through Monmouth Beach.

My stomach twisted in a knot.

Reed stretched one arm out until his fingers brushed the back of my neck. "It'll be all right, Garner. I'm not taking you back to the house." Without my having to prod, he went on. "We think we have a witness. Someone who may have seen him."

"Who?"

"A guy over at the local hardware store."

"Which one?" I went to lots of them. Like driving with a good driver, walking down narrow aisles filled with screws, nails, and paint cans also took me to an altered state of complete serenity.

"Over on River Road," Corbin said.

"That's Sid junior's." He made the left onto the bridge that would take us into Rumson, and I hunkered down in my seat.

"Our sketch artist is there now." Reed nodded. "Maybe we can finally put a face on this guy."

Again, my stomach burbled. I leaned over and turned off the radio. "Look," he said, "if this is too much, it's not necessary for us to be there. I just thought—"

"I'm fine."

The hardware store was located in a tiny riverfront town not far from where I lived. Reed pulled into the short-term parking lot behind the shop, slipping into a space next to a dark green van. "One of ours," he said.

We went in through the back entrance, walking past a loading dock stacked with lumber. The smell of sawdust had an immediately calming effect on me. I caught a glimpse of Sid junior in the back room, behind the counter where new keys were cut, huddling over a pad with the sketch artist. It

105

surprised me a little that she happened to be pretty, blond, and female.

"Garner." Sid scrambled to his feet when he noticed me. "I hope I didn't do wrong—" Sid was probably in his mid-forties, short and balding, with hunched shoulders and quick, worried eyes that seemed to be anticipating some coming trouble; but to his elderly mother, and his regular customers, he would always be "junior"—a mere chip off the giant block that the late Sid senior had been.

"Please God"—he pressed my hand—"I didn't screw up."

"You did fine, I'm sure." I stepped aside so Sid junior and Corbin could make their introductions.

The sketch artist had covered up her drawing. "I'm Sheila Fanning." She smiled. "It's a pleasure to meet you, Ms. Quinn."

"Garner," I said—I mean, she wasn't *that* much younger than me. I pointed to the pad. "Can I take a look?"

Sheila glanced at Corbin. "I usually wait until Reed gives the word," she explained. "That first impression is oh so important."

"Why don't I just get him then?"

"Oh, Garner." Sid junior took out a white handkerchief and mopped his face. "I told Mr. Corbin that I wasn't sure. I mean, it sort of looks like the guy who came in. I think. As far as I can remember."

"You did your best." I patted his arm. "That's all that matters."

"Yeah, but I really screwed up, talking to him in the first place," sighed Sid. "Not that

I thought it would do any harm. Who knew? This is a small town. You're our local celebrity. I never considered he might be out to do harm—"

I only half listened. Out of the corner of my eye, I was watching Reed and Fanning, their heads bent together, talking in hushed voices.

Reed came over to me and asked, "Ready?" He put his arm around my waist and guided me back to the table. Sheila lifted the cover off the pad.

I saw a man's face, sketched in smudgy charcoal. He had a broad forehead, and wide cheekbones under small but penetrating eyes. There was something vaguely Slavic in his bone structure. His nose flared at the nostrils, but his lips were thin, almost parsimonious, especially compared to the other features. He had long, straggly hair and a pointed chin. Fanning had shadowed the area around his beard line, as though indicating he'd needed a shave.

Thank God, I thought to myself. *This is no one I know.*

I looked up at Reed and shook my head. "Are you sure?" he asked, gently.

"I think maybe his eyebrows were thicker." Sid junior sighed. "His eyebrows and his neck."

"Tell me exactly what happened, Sid."

"Well, like I said to Mr. Corbin's people, the guy comes in maybe the second week in August. I noticed right away he wasn't from town. He had on all black, like some of the kids you see over in Red Bank wear."

I nodded encouragingly. "Did he come through the front door, or the back?"

"The back, I think."

"So you didn't see what he was driving?"

"No." Once again Sid junior sighed. "That I didn't, Garner."

"It's okay," Reed said. "Go on."

"Well, he went up and down the aisles and I followed, to help guide him toward his purchases," Sid said, "but also to keep an eye out, because I didn't know him, and you can never tell." His worried eyes darted from Reed Corbin to me. "And that's when I happened to see, he had a paperback kind of jammed in his pocket. *All Through the Night*, I think it was. I could see the top part, with the picture of the bloody knife and your name on it."

"Then what happened, Sid?" prompted Reed.

"I said something like, 'Great book,' and he says back, like, 'The best.' Sid wiped his brow with the handkerchief again. "And then I said, 'You know she's our local celebrity.' Which is what we always call you, right, Garner? You, and Bruce, and Jon Bon Jovi..."

I was losing my patience. "Did the man say anything about me?"

"He just said, 'Yeah, I bet you must see her all the time,' or no, maybe it was, 'If I stick around long enough, maybe I'll see her,' something like that." Sid junior frowned, attempting to remember. "And then I said— and here's where I could really kick myself— I said, 'Not for the next coupla weeks you won't.

She and her daughter went up to Maine on vacation,' I told him. 'If you'da come in yesterday you coulda seen her in here buying a floor mat for the car.'"

Chaz had known I was away. He could've staked out my property. Taken his time, gotten to know the lay of the land. I felt sick.

Reed handed Sid a business card, "We appreciate your help. Obviously, if you happen to see this guy again, you'll give us a call." It was not a question.

"I'm so sorry," the shopkeeper apologized again. "I wasn't thinking, shooting my mouth off to a stranger like that. If anything had happened to you and your daughter—"

"You couldn't have known," I said simply.

Sid junior shook his head. "It's getting to be such a crazy world."

"Sheila will make copies of the sketch, and we'll show them around to the other merchants in town," Reed said, "There's a good chance somebody else saw him."

Fanning folded the cover over her drawing and started gathering up her charcoal pencils. "By the way," I asked as an afterthought. "What did he buy?"

Sid junior pulled at his lower lip. "If I'm not mistaken, it was a small transaction," he said. "A package of throwaway plastic tarps and a roll of gaffer tape. I remember he paid cash."

Sheila Fanning drove off in a pale blue Volkswagen after having another private word with Reed. We headed back to Spring Lake without mentioning Chaz. I told Reed I had a headache and he handed me a tin of Advil. I washed the tablets down with a bottle of mineral water he kept in the back seat.

When we reached the gates on the edge of town, Reed spoke. "He didn't look the least bit familiar?"

"I told you."

"Yes," he said, then: "You're not holding out on me, are you?"

"No, I am not." I've been known to hold out information on occasion, but this wasn't one of them. I felt a stir of self-righteous indignation.

"I thought I saw something in your face," Reed said.

"Relief," I said. "You saw relief. Matt asked me to make a list of the people who might want to do me harm. Every time I thought it was complete, someone else came to mind. Eventually, I just gave up." We pulled through the gates. Reed put the car in park and let it idle. "I don't know why it matters, but I was just glad...that it wasn't one of the ones I knew."

Reed leaned over and took my hand. "Let me protect you, Garner," he said.

"No." I shook my head. "But you can kiss me if you want."

He pushed back his glasses. I saw the confusion in his face. "I don't want you to think that our personal relationship has anything to do..." he stammered. "I would never try to manipulate you that way—"

I grabbed his tie and pulled him toward me. His lips were still moving and his face was moist and smooth, as though he'd somehow managed to shave beneath the skin. I kissed him with purpose, and then, suddenly, he was twisting his body, trying to reach past the steering wheel, and his arms were grabbing me, pulling my shoulders up and toward him, and the gearshift was pressing into my thigh, and all that cool restraint seemed to have gone the way of the air-conditioning, out the vents and windows, leaving a steamy vapor in its wake.

It wasn't a very good kiss—too wet and earnest for my liking—but I told myself he'd relax and it would get better. He was a good man. Decent and caring.

I'd be safe with him.

TWELVE

"Garner," the voice said, "did I get you at a bad time?"

"Not at all." I tried to hide my surprise. Mercedes and I seldom spoke together on the phone. In fact, we hadn't talked since I stayed the night in her apartment. "Is everything all right?"

"That's what I called to ask," Mercedes said. "Mama told me you're moving back into the house this weekend."

"Sunday." I rolled onto my stomach. The comforter on the four-poster in Dudley's old room felt slippery cool against my bare legs. "Temple starts school on the eighth."

"Have I missed something?" A caustic undertone crept into her voice. "The last I heard, the stalker was still on the loose."

"The security firm is running down some leads."

"And so you've decided to pretend it's all okay and just move back? *Are you out of your mind?*"

"There's no reason to get upset," I replied.

"You got some crazed fan sending you letters, leaving boxes of shit at your door, Garner. If that doesn't upset you, I'd like to know what does."

"Everything's under control." I explained Corbin, Inc., was making progress, and described what had happened in the hardware store. "It's only a matter of time," I said, with a confidence I didn't actually feel, "before someone recognizes this Chaz guy from the sketch and he's picked up for questioning."

There was a pause on the line. "What if," Mercedes posed, "they catch the man from the hardware, and it turns out he's not your stalker?"

"That's ridic—" I began. "Of course, he is."

"A creep walks into a shop carrying a paperback book you wrote in his pocket." Mercedes sounded unconvinced. "Excuse me, but I think it's a huge leap to assume that, oh yes, *he* must be the one sending you those letters. Have you checked your royalties lately, girl? No offense, but there are a lot of insane people out there, reading your books."

"It's too much of a coincidence," I argued.

"Sid told him we were in Maine—"

"He didn't follow us up there, did he? How come, if he's so obsessed, he didn't get in his ride and go after you?" She dropped the strident approach. "Look, all I'm saying is maybe things aren't as under control as you think they are."

"There's a team of men guarding my property twenty-four, seven. It's a hell of a lot safer there than living in a doorman apartment in Manhattan." This was an underhanded move on my part. For such a strong woman, Mercedes Fields had really thin skin.

"I live in a highly secure building," she replied, all huffy, "in an excellent section of town."

"So do I." I swung my feet over the side of the bed and began pacing with the phone. "I can't spend my life hiding from this guy, Merce. I have to get back to work. And Temple's starting school—"

"Since when do you work at home, Garner Quinn?" she persisted. "And by the way, last time I looked, there were plenty of good schools around. Who says Temple has to go to one in New Jersey? She could come live with me for a while."

In my heart, I knew Mercedes meant well, but it was the worst thing she could have said. "Thanks for your concern," I replied coldly, "but I'm handling the situation in my own way."

"I hope you know what you're doing," she said. "If you don't care about your own safety, at least think about my mother, and that beautiful child of yours."

"Believe me, I do."

"All right then." Mercedes sighed. "But if the worst happens, and whoever this Chaz is makes a move, I expect *Front Cover* to get an exclusive on the story."

There was a click. Once again, one of the Fields women had managed to get the last word. I just couldn't tell if she had meant it seriously or not.

On the Sunday before Labor Day, Reed helped me move back into the house.

To my dismay, I'd found that by initiating the first kiss, I'd pried open floodgates that might've been better left shut. Like a lovesick teenager, Corbin seemed totally preoccupied with progressing swiftly along the bases. He could no longer talk without touching me, and after the first touch, he wanted more. "Andy's dropping Temple off any minute," I reminded him, pulling out of a clinch.

"Sure," he said, but zombielike, he moved in for another kiss.

"I don't feel comfortable here like this," I said.

He disengaged immediately. Reed Corbin, of all people, knew that no meant no. "Take your time with it then," he said.

I got up, tapping a key on the grand piano to break the silence. The house, which had been abandoned for the better part of a month, seemed sullen and unfriendly. In Spring Lake, I'd lived out of one suitcase, bringing in bags of food and other necessities only when the need arose. The rooms there were stripped down to basics, essentially nameless—anything I wanted them to be.

It suddenly struck me how much *stuff* was here. Furniture, carpets. Paintings and books. Did I even like any of them? Had I ever?

"Must be a little strange," Reed said, watching me, "being back."

"Yes."

"There's nothing to worry about, you know." He took a step in my direction, then thought better of it. "We've got you locked up tighter than a fortress."

I rewarded him with a wan smile and saw him melt.

I hadn't told Reed or Matt Raice what Mercedes had said about the guy in the hardware shop. It was almost as if speaking about it would do the same thing as the kiss—swing wide doors I'd regret having opened, and would then be unable to close. I wanted to believe that the skeevy-looking guy in the picture was Chaz. That Sheila Fanning and Sid junior had put a face on the devil. Because if I knew what he looked like, I could stand up to him; it was the blank awful facelessness that was intolerable.

"Could you leave a copy of the sketch when you go?" Already I was anxious for Corbin to leave. I needed to test the waters by myself. Get used to the place again. The great room seemed just too damn big, and too crowded.

Reed nodded. "I'll let you have some time with your family," he said.

Such a sensitive man. I wondered if I could ever love him.

Like a pair of jeans, the house felt better the more I walked around. Temple was thrilled to be going back to school. Sophomore year brought with it several hard-won privileges— her weekend curfew would now be an hour later, and she could go out in mixed company, although I stood hard and fast against one-on-one dating.

On Cilda's last night in Brooklyn, her son Deon had summoned up the nerve to tell her that his girlfriend was pregnant. At first Cilda was horrified. "Ow that boy goin' to support a child," she said, "and 'im not makin' t'ree hundred dollars a week?" But in a week's time, she was busy knitting. Blue booties. A blue and white blanket. A tiny blue sweater. Cilda said she knew it was a boy because when she'd suspended a threaded needle over the girlfriend's stomach, it swung back and forth in a straight line. There was, I knew from experience, no use in questioning this unscientific procedure.

I tried to downplay the whole Chaz thing, but Temple and Cilda weren't fooled. The lapping of the waves outside, which had always lulled my daughter to sleep, now seemed to stealthily muffle more sinister sounds. We spent those first few nights huddled together in my big bed, while, down the hall, Cilda slept with one eye open and a fireplace poker propped on her nightstand. Each morning the IAD man in charge went over the day's schedule with them. They understood that the IAD van would remain parked at the gate and that the three of us were supposed to carry our phones and beepers at all times. Instead of dialing 911, we only needed to call the guards, and help would be on the way.

By the end of the first week, we'd settled into an almost ordinary routine.

Reed came down every weekend. Often he'd show up late on Friday night and stay in the guest quarters with the other men until Sunday. I attempted to portray these visits as simply part of Corbin, Inc.'s security package, but Cilda and Temple weren't so easily fooled.

"I bet he doesn't pay this much attention to his other clients," my daughter teased. We were sitting in a movie theater while Reed waited in line at the concession stand. "Face it, Mom, he wants to *go out* with you." The one-on-one dating thing was never far from her mind.

"So what?" I sent out a trial balloon. "He's a nice guy."

"Really nice," said Temple. Even in the half-dark theater, I could read the postscript in her eyes. *But he's no Dane Blackmoor.*

"What a mob out there," Reed said, sliding into the seat next to me. "I was afraid I'd miss the beginning."

"Relax." My daughter reached for the popcorn. "The coming attractions haven't even started yet."

On weekday mornings I drove Temple to school, then headed over to my office. Knowing that Corbin's men were only a few hundred yards away was reassuring. The letters had stopped, and so far no one in the area other than Sid had reported seeing the face in the artist's sketch. Matt Raice felt Chaz's handwriting would eventually yield up the best clue to his identity. "Don't worry," he said whenever I called to check in. "Leave that to us."

After a while, I started to venture over the seawall and onto the beach, staying there for longer and longer periods of time. Although it was still warm in the sun, the breeze had a crisp aftertang of leaves and brushfires. Autumn was sneaking onto the Jersey shore, creeping inland a little more every day. In the woods, embolisms of color burst and bled through spaces between the tall, dark pines.

I began to think about working again. Maybe it was because I was still angry with Mercedes—subconsciously, I might've even been trying to ward off those doubts she'd planted in my mind—but for whatever reason, I found myself leafing through the Sea Bright arson file again. I was haunted by the image of those poor, lost souls—men who'd battled severe emotional problems, mental retardation, and alcoholism, and were desperately trying to better themselves—being set on fire while they lay sleeping simply because some of the locals didn't want a halfway house cluttering up their town. It would make a different kind of book. I'd never written anything so rife with social implications. I wondered if I was up to it.

A small voice in my head needled, *But isn't*

saving the world what you always wanted to do? I had to admit, a part of me wanted to take the risk, if only to prove to Mercedes that I was more than the diva of bloody white crime.

"Not to put any pressure on you," my agent, Max, would occasionally call up to say, "but I've still got two more kids to put through college. You ever going to write another book?"

"I might," I said.

Tentatively, I started taking notes. I spent the greater part of the mornings jotting ideas down in longhand; in the afternoons I sat at the Macintosh, fleshing these ideas out. For several weeks I went along this way, without fully committing myself to the project. The weather was beautiful, my daughter healthy and happy. I'd met a man who obviously cared about me, and my ex-husband was presently gallivanting on another continent. Life was good. And yet, no matter how many long walks on the beach I took, I couldn't seem to go on with business as usual.

I kept thinking about the man in the hardware store, picturing his broad face, his unkempt hair, and the hard line of his mouth, replaying the encounter with Sid. *Great book,* the shopkeeper had said. To which the stranger had replied, *The best.*

In itself, the comment signified nothing. As Mercedes had been so quick to point out, a lot of people read my books. Overzealous fans showed up in town all the time, asking questions, wanting to catch a glimpse of where I lived. It was no big deal. I was one of the local celebrities, part of the trio that included Springsteen and Bon Jovi.

The fact that no one else had reported seeing the guy bothered me, though. Chaz had been lurking nearby on the day I threw the sack of letters into the trash, yet not a single person had seen him. The sketch was circulated around the post office plaza—the Acme, the stationery store, the bakery, and the service station and pizzeria across the street. Corbin's man had come up with zip.

I figured there were two possibilities: one, either the guy in the picture had some kind of invisible-man act going on, or two, the guy in the picture wasn't Chaz. Both explanations made me extremely nervous.

It was in this state of growing panic that I happened to glance over at the book I'd tossed on my desk days before. The big bold letters on the cover seemed to scream at me.

THE FEAR FACTOR
by
Reed Corbin

*How Your PFQ (Personal Fear Quotient)
Can Save Your Life*

I picked it up and began to read.

It took me the rest of that day and partway into the next morning to finish, and by the time I did, Reed's book was riddled with underlined passages and scribbled margin notes.

The quality of the writing turned out to be a pleasant surprise, but it wasn't the style, it was the substance that held me spellbound. Batterers. Child molesters. Rapists and thrill killers. Assassins and terrorists. Corbin had catalogued them all. In the chapter about stalkers, he wrote:

Most of my clients can't conceive that the person sending them those threatening letters or making those disturbing calls may be someone they know. When I ask them to come up with a list of names—no matter how far-fetched or remote—they're at a loss. Then they remember someone at work, a quarrelsome neighbor, or a jealous ex. Invariably, though, just as our meeting is coming to a close, the victim's face will change. "This is really off the mark," she or he will say. "So-and-so just popped into my head and I can't figure why," my client will apologize. "It wouldn't make any sense."

And, dimes to doughnuts, you can be sure we've just found our stalker.

I read that paragraph over and over. Afterward, I made out the list Matthew Raice had asked for more than a month ago. I wrote it twice, ordering names, making additions and deletions. One popped into my head both times and stuck there—the name of my former assistant, Jack Tatum, a man I hadn't seen for years.

121

THIRTEEN

We kept our scrapbooks in an Irish pine cupboard in the great room. For my last birthday, Temple and Cilda had gone through the photo boxes into which I'd haphazardly been dumping photographs for years, and put them in bound leather books. It was a wonderful gift. I picked up the one marked *1990–91* and began leafing through it. It didn't take long to find a shot of Jack. Temple had snapped his picture as he was eating a submarine sandwich at his desk. Even with a mouthful of provolone, and his eyes beseeching in that pseudohelpless way, he was still a manly sort of guy—tall and bearded, slim, but muscular.

"I'm going into town for a bit." I stuck my head into the kitchen. Cilda, in front of the television set, watching Jerry Springer and knitting something blue, waved me off with a nod.

I slid Jack's picture into my pocketbook and walked to the car. Out of long habit I glanced into the back of the Volvo before I got in, startled for a moment by the likeness of the creepy man in the hardware shop staring back with his small, wide-set eyes. I'd left a copy of the artist's drawing on the seat and forgotten about it. It seemed appropriate that we all take this trip together—Jack, the long-haired stranger, and me. I threw my bag onto the passenger side and slid behind the wheel.

Corbin's IAD van didn't follow me through the gates. The deal was, I could do my errands without an entourage as long as I had my phone and beeper. I took my time, driving slowly through the back roads of Rumson. Nearly half of the trees had turned color, but some leaves hung on, doggedly green. After a wet summer, the fall had been unusually dry, with very little wind. The piles of brush along the curbs were modest for early October.

As I drove, I thought some more about Jack. Despite my insistence that I worked alone, he'd aggressively pestered me until I agreed to try him out as an assistant. A couple of years later he abruptly—but just as aggressively—walked out, after I told him there could be nothing personal between us. I hadn't heard from him since. Or so I thought.

Hold on, I warned myself. What about the handwriting? Jack's script was small and cramped. Chaz printed in bold, block letters. *But what if that was the point?* When I was out on the road, Jack would often sign my name on letters I'd dictated over the phone. I used to laugh that even I couldn't tell the difference between my own signature and his forgery. Had he simply changed his writing style to fool me?

I pulled into the last empty space in the parking lot behind the hardware store. It was so warm Sid had left the back door open for ventilation. The high, crisp scent of freshly cut lumber put a spring in my step. A thin man with a gray mustache was behind the counter. In the lower section Sid senior's elderly widow stood at the cash register, adding up items for a man in painter's overalls.

"Sid junior around?" I asked the mustached man.

"Over in pest control." He pointed to the aisle.

I found him stocking Have-a-Heart mousetraps. "Garner," he cried. "Just getting ready for the first frost. This weather can't last forever."

"You have a second, Sid?"

He glanced over at his mother, visibly relieved to find her occupied. "Sure, Garner, for you. Any news on that guy?"

"Not yet," I said. I took Jack's picture out of my bag. "There's someone else I want you to look at, Sid. I know he doesn't much resemble the person you described to the sketch artist, but I wanted to make double sure." I handed him the photograph. "Do you think there's any chance they might be the same guy?"

Sid junior squinted. Then he pulled a pair of plastic magnifying glasses from his pocket and took another look. "No," he said finally. "They're about the same age, but the one I saw had lighter hair and his face was bigger, I think. You know, wide and sort of flat." The shopkeeper shrugged apologetically. "Sorry."

"So you've never seen this guy?"

"Not that I can recall," he said. "Who is he?"

"Just someone who used to work for me."

This is totally ridiculous, I told myself. *Jack has no connection to the stranger Sid saw—no matter who he is. Jack has no connection to*

Chaz. "I'm getting a little paranoid, that's all," I rambled on. "Not thinking clearly, I guess."

"Maybe you should take a trip," Sid suggested. "Go to Florida. That's what I do when things get too much."

"Sidney!" his mother called from the register. "Sid junior—a customer needs some help here!"

I patted Sid's arm appreciatively. "Thanks for your help, Sid. Maybe I will."

Instead of heading to Florida, though, I walked out the front door and headed for the café across the street. I'd planned to show Jack's picture around to all the shops and businesses near the post office, but this bright idea no longer made any sense. Disheartened, I sat at the counter and ordered a chicken salad sandwich and a cup of coffee. It was still a few minutes before the lunch hour rush. The waitress was passing time doing a crossword puzzle.

"What's a seven-letter word for 'impasse'?" she asked me.

"Dead end," I replied, without thinking.

Sid had hired a local artist to paint an autumn scene on the hardware shop's windows. I walked by bright orange pumpkins ribbed in washable brown poster paint and a grinning scarecrow propped up against a cornstalk. On one side was a full, yellow moon and the sketched-in drawing of a witch riding her broomstick. Might be Sheila Fanning's work, I thought irreverently. Maybe, in addition to her crime sketches, she also did seasonal windows.

It wasn't until I rounded the corner that I remembered: I'd forgotten to lock the car. It was the second foolish thing I'd done today and it made me angry with myself. I glanced into the back of the car before getting in. It was empty.

Empty. The copy of Fanning's sketch was no longer there. My eyes traveled to the front. It had been placed neatly on the driver's seat, square to the wheel. Someone had made some quick but cleverly drawn changes to the face. The chin was no longer so pointed. The eyes became larger, more alive, and the tight, hard mouth had been widened, then twisted into a smile. A cartoon thought suspended above the man's head, a cloud trailing quizzical elipses toward his hair. Inside the balloon were the words—

WONDER HOW...?
WONDER WHEN...?

In the bottom right corner of the page, he had written, SOON, GARNER. And then he had signed his name, with kisses, XXXXXXXXXXXXXXXXXXXXXX CHAZ.

Within hours my great room looked like a satellite office of Corbin, Incoporated. Reed was in McLean, Virginia, at a meeting, but he'd made arrangements to take the shuttle into Newark. Matt Raice arrived first in a claret-colored Corvette, followed by two men in a dark Toyota.

"Mike will be acting as your personal body-guard," Raice said, nodding toward the older

126

one, a burly man in his fifties. "Jay is our forensic expert. He'll want to go over to the site. You didn't touch anything, you said?"

"Just the car door. One of the local cops gave me a ride home."

"From now on"—Raice followed me through the house—"you don't go anywhere without us. Is your daughter back from school yet?"

"Yes, but I'm trying to soft-pedal this."

"Give me a little time to organize things here," Matt Raice said, "and then I'll need three minutes with you, your daughter, and Mrs. Fields. A simple sit-down—no scare tactics, I promise." As I turned to leave he grabbed my arm. "The good news is, he's out in the open again."

"Don't leave anything out, Matt."

"The bad news is"—he gave me a rueful smile—"I think he just might've made his first real threat."

We sat on the sofa, three across.

"Before I begin," Matt Raice said in his most reassuring manner, "Do you have any questions you'd like to ask me—Temple? Mrs. Fields?"

"Yes," piped up Cilda. "Just 'ow many men will be staying to dinner?"

"Don't worry about us," Matt told her.

"People got to eat," she said flatly.

He went over the procedure for using the phones and beepers. "Until you hear otherwise, I want you to carry them with you everywhere—"

Temple raised her hand as if she were in class.

"My mother said I can't use mine to call my friends." She tossed her head. *My God, she was flirting with him!* "But I don't see what's so bad about a little recreational use, do you, Mr. Raice?"

"You can call me Matt," he looked amused. "But your mom's right, Temple. These babies are for emergencies only."

She sighed, disappointed that although Matt Raice might seem hip, he was evidently too old to remember what constituted an *emergency* to a teenager.

I heard the front door open, and the bodyguard called Mike speaking in a low voice to someone. A moment later Corbin strode into the room. His hair appeared windswept and flyaway, as if he'd driven here on the back of a truck, although his suit was as crisply pressed as usual.

"Hi, everyone." It was a general greeting but he looked only at me. "How's everybody doing?"

"Fine," I said.

"Any news?"

"Not yet," Matt told him, with a trace of impatience. "I just got here myself."

"Matt was going over the beeper procedure," I explained.

"Right." Reed loosened his tie, pulled a chair around, and sat down. "I think we also need to come up with a password. Our men will be rotating in shifts, and it could get confusing for you. But nobody goes anywhere with anyone unless he or she knows the secret code."

"We already have a password," Temple said, "It's Snowbear."

"Snowbear's fine." Reed scooted his chair closer. "You're all just going to have to be extra careful for a while, but there's nothing to worry about."

"Don't *you* worry," my daughter replied, looking him levelly in the eye. "My mother and I have been through this kind of thing before." She turned to me. "May I be excused?"

When I said yes, both she and Cilda got up to leave. "I count t'ree," the old woman said before disappearing into the kitchen, "unless the skinny one come back in the car."

"I guess you're all staying to dinner," I said.

Matt frowned. "They seem to be taking this situation a little too lightly if you ask me."

"Don't bet on it. It's been a crash course in living with fear around here." I sighed. "Cilda cooks. Temple talks to her friends. It's how they cope. But they're hanging on by their fingernails. We can't go on like this forever. I want to know what happens next."

Reed answered as though there were only two of us in the room. "Now we wait for Chaz to make his next move."

FOURTEEN

It was my idea to use myself as bait. From the beginning, Reed and Matt wanted no part of it. "I can't keep looking over my shoulder this way. It's put a major crink in my style," I told them. "That word he wrote on the bottom of the drawing—*soon*? Well, dammit to hell, that's all right with me. Only why should *he* get to determine where and when? Why can't I get a say?"

"Because that's not the way we work," Reed replied. "Our job is to get between you and this guy—not to throw you together and hope for the best." I realized he was speaking softly to control his anger, but it made him sound so goddam patronizing.

"Yeah, well, last time I heard, you weren't even handling this case, Reed," I said, coldly.

I turned to Raice. "Come on, Matt. We could pull it off. You know we could."

"This isn't one of your books, Garner," Matt replied. "It's real life."

"Real life is what I write."

"There are too many variables."

Despite Raice's hesitancy, I could tell he was intrigued. "Like what?"

"Well, for one, predators like Chaz don't think the way normal people do."

I pounced on that. "But you *know* how they think. Reed says nobody can get into a stalker's head like you. And anyway, you have the means to forecast violent behavior. Isn't that what Mr. PREDICT over there's always saying?"

Reed's expression was pained. "Forget it, Garner. If you want to kill yourself, you'll have to hire somebody else to help you do it."

I turned again to Matt. "He's the boss," he said simply.

Cilda appeared on the threshold. "You can use the upstairs bat'room to wash your 'ands," she announced. "Dinner's ready in 'alf an hour."

Reed stood. "Do we stay or do we go, Garner?" he asked.

"She already set the table." I shrugged. "The rest we can deal with later."

Matt came up behind Corbin, clapping an arm around his shoulder. "I told you this woman would be trouble, didn't I, pardnuh?"

Corbin's forensic expert found a lot of fingerprints in and on my old Volvo, but most of them turned out to be mine. The sketch itself yielded nothing. Apparently, Chaz had made his artistic corrections to the drawing while wearing latex gloves.

"So we're back to square one?"

"Not exactly. Now we have a better picture of what he looks like," Reed reminded me. "Jay Katz was able to find several hair follicles, dyed blond, and some black fiber. Not much help in finding him, but they might be important later on." Over the telephone, Reed's voice sounded flat and weary.

"Will you be coming down this weekend?" I asked.

"I'm up to my ears," he replied. "If you need anything, just ask Mike." Mike Fedora— "like the hat," he told Temple, as if she'd know what that meant—was the heavyset, older guy from the division called G&P, who'd been left in charge. Reed asked, "What're you going to do?"

"Oh, you know, put in my time," I replied, feeling sorry for myself. "If I'm good they let me out some mornings for a chaperoned walk."

"Try to be patient a little longer," Reed urged, halfheartedly. He already knew that patience wasn't one of my virtues.

On Monday morning I got a call from retired FBI special agent J. Emmett Hogan. "I was going through a drawer, and I found this postcard from Garner Quinn," he said. "Sue must've put it there by mistake, ha-ha." Hogan's wife didn't like me much.

"What's going on?"

"That's my line," my friend said. "It might be old news by now, but you mentioned you had a professional matter you wanted to discuss?"

"Unfortunately, that matter still hasn't been resolved," I admitted. "I'm getting letters from some guy. It appears as though he's also staked out my place."

"Can't you take him to court?"

"Probably," I said. "Once I find out who he is."

"This isn't anything to fool around with, Quinn," Hogan said sternly. "How come you didn't call me?"

"I tried, but your machine wasn't on at home." I didn't mention that I'd also called his number at the Bureau.

"You could've had me beeped."

"I know, but this stalking stuff isn't really your line, Hoge." I knew he wouldn't let up until he'd heard the whole story. "So I hired a protective security firm."

"Which one?"

"Corbin, Incorporated. Do you know them?"

I heard Hogan's sigh of relief. "Corbin and Raice," he said. "Yeah, they're top-notch. In fact, we're tied up together on this Warren Petty thing."

"Oh yeah? Thought you retired," I teased.

"Thought you did too. So how come we keep coming back?"

"Pure cussedness."

"Seriously though," he persisted. "I worry about you, out there by yourself in that house."

"I have Temple and Cilda."

Hogan said, "You know what I mean."

"Well, now I have Corbin too." I said this lightly, hoping to scoot it by Hogan's pin drop–sensitive radar.

"And you have me," he replied softly; then lapsing into his best James Taylor, he sang, *"You've got a friend—"*

"I know."

"Don't be a stranger," Hogan said. "Oh, and Quinn—keep your back covered and your head down."

I didn't tell him that it was good advice for what I had in mind.

Cooped up, with nothing to do, I passed the time dreaming up scenarios to trap Chaz. For the most part, they were lamebrain schemes which played out like the last act of a Lifetime movie of the week. *True crime writer Garner Quinn is in her office, working on her new book. The weather is warm enough to leave the front window open. It's going so well she loses track of time. The sun sets, and before she knows it, she's in the dark, typing by the glow of her Macintosh monitor.*

A muffled noise comes from the reception area. Then the office door creaks open. It's Chaz, with his plastic bags and gaffer tape. He's here to rape or strangle her, to shoot her in the head or slash her to pieces. But before he can make a move, Corbin's men rush out of the storage closet where they've been hiding. They handcuff him and haul his ass off to prison. The end. Finis. Bye-bye, you whacked-out Romeo, don't bother to write.

Of course, this wasn't just bad melodrama; the plan obviously wouldn't work. Chaz knew that the house was protected. I'd have to be on my own somewhere, out in the open, for him to make his move. Or else—I glanced out of my kitchen window—I'd have to get rid of them.

Them. The IAD team that had taken over my property and my life. The guys from PST—Protective Security Technologies—who wanted to put in a new alarm system and an electric fence. That G&P Fedora fellow whose mission in life was to follow me everywhere so he could Guard and Protect. I'd had it up to here with Reed Corbin's abbreviations and his polite army in their crisp khakis and ties.

I picked up the phone and punched in the number for Forked Brook. Reed was in Manhattan at a meeting, Tamara Ma informed me. Could she have him call me back? I said no, and asked to speak to Matt.

"What's up, Garner?" Raice's voice sounded harried.

"I've been thinking about...what I mentioned the other night." For some reason I had a sudden intimation of fear. I sat down at the table. "Temple's father just got back from Europe and he wants to see her next weekend, and Cilda is heading out to Brooklyn. So I'm on my own—"

"Give or take an armored division."

"That's my point," I said breathlessly. "What if I just dismissed them, you know, made a big show out of it, had a tantrum and told Corbin, Inc., to get out? I mean, it's not so far-fetched. I'm a prisoner in my own home, I can't go anywhere, it's driving me crazy—"

"For you, that's a short trip."

I ignored that. "But if we played our cards right, we could trick him. Sooner or later—and like he said, it's going to be sooner, Matt, I can feel it—he's going to come after me. And then the man you've left behind can pounce."

"Reed will never agree to it," Raice said.

"You can convince him. Tell him I'm nutty enough to go ahead without you." I paused. "I can't keep sitting around, doing nothing, Matthew. One way or another, I want this freak baited and bagged. It can't go on another week."

"I'll do my best," he said, without much hope in his voice.

"When's Reed getting back from his meeting?"

"I don't know. We don't keep tabs on each other every minute of the day, Garner, we just go about our business," Raice added, in a tone that was only half jesting. "And believe it or not, we do have other clients."

"I'd never guess from what you're charging me," I replied in the same semi-joking manner.

"All things considered, you're getting a cut rate," he shot back, "because the boss happens to be sweet on you."

"Talk to him," I repeated before hanging up.

The jittery feeling I'd been fighting gave way to an aching emptiness. Matt's light reproof— *We do have other clients* had hit home. I thought of Reed rushing into my house last Friday, hair flying, his upper lip beaded in sweat. This was a man many people counted on for their safety and protection, sometimes for their very lives; and yet, he'd flown a couple of hundred miles at a moment's notice to be with a woman who was hell-bent on throwing all his expertise and concern back into his face.

At dinner that night, Reed had seemed quiet and preoccupied. He'd accepted a ride back to New York with Matt, and politely pressed my hand goodbye. And for the first time in a long while, he hadn't come down to visit over the weekend. I'd assumed he was miffed, but now I wondered if it might be something more.

I stared at the clock. Only a few minutes after eleven. Reed's meeting might go on for hours.

Suddenly, I couldn't wait to talk to him. In a distracted state of mind, I went over to the coffeemaker and poured myself a cup.

Cilda stuck her head in the door. "Come look." She waved at me. "Mercedes is talkin' on the TV." I followed her into the family room, where the television was on full blast.

Mercedes Fields, vibrant in a mango silk suit, stood in front of an ornate iron gate. "In life"—she looked directly into the camera—"Warren Petty was known as an American success story. A risk taker who amassed a fortune by the age of twenty...whose real estate empire eventually spanned the globe...and whose art collection was the envy of most major museums.

"In death, however, Petty has become just the latest statistic in a growing American nightmare..." Mercedes paused dramatically. *"Terrorism."*

She continued to narrate as the live picture dissolved into a roll of pretaped video, saying that the FBI and other law enforcement agencies were trying to find out all they could about the group calling itself The Fourth Freedom, which had claimed responsibility for the downing of Petty's jet.

"See now," cried Cilda, "isn't that your friend Mr. Corbin standing next to that man wit' no 'air?"

It was. A second later Mercedes was back on screen. "If Warren Petty's death does indeed turn out to be a terrorist act, all of America joins in with his grieving widow when she asks the question"—Mercedes's

137

sculpted face softened plaintively—
"*why?*...Back to you, Brad."

"That dress she 'ad on," complained Cilda, "fit too tight haround 'er bottom."

"She looked wonderful. And she did a great job."

The old woman shook her head. "They going to get 'er 'opes up, them big TV men, and then some young girl will come along, hall white and pretty, and they'll give 'er a microphone and there'll be the end of hit."

"That won't happen," I said.

"Mark my words." Cilda made another dire prediction. "'Er will be down there in New York, forty-one years old wit'out an h'automobile or an 'usband, you'll see."

I didn't bother arguing. Instead, I called up a picture of Reed Corbin, walking among that group of serious, suited men. But my brain played a trick on me, and put Mercedes Fields into the scene instead.

"Get over yourself." Mercedes smiled into the imaginary camera of my mind, a vision in watery mango silk. "Not everything in this world is about Garner Quinn."

Reed called around four-thirty, prepared for a fight. "I spoke with Matt," he said. "To be honest, Garner, I think we're at a standoff here. You're either going to let me do my job or—"

"All right."

"What did you say?"

"I said okay. Do your job."

I heard a rush of air, as if he'd been holding

his breath and just let go. "Really?" His heart wanted to believe me, but his head was still screwed on straight. "Why the sudden change?"

"I've been acting like a brat," I said.

"Look." Reed was immediately conciliatory. "He came into your car. It's an awful feeling. Believe me, I understand. But if you can just sit tight for a little longer, we'll get a positive ID. I think we may have stumbled onto something with the comic book angle. Matt's checking out an underground strip called *Chasm* that's been around for a while. A lot of violent content, explicit sex. Fits our profile to a T."

"Great." I forced myself to continue. "Getting back to my brattiness, though—it's more than just me freaking out about this stalker, Reed. There's a thing I do when I get knee-deep into a relationship." I swallowed the knot in my throat. "I test people. Especially men...men I care about."

"In that case," Corbin said, "please feel free to test me as much and as often as you'd like."

By the next morning I was feeling antsy again. For years I'd flown solo, called all my own shots. Having a stalker and a high-end security company dictate where I could go and what I could do was simply unacceptable. I wanted my life back.

I'd promised Reed I would sit tight and wait, but as far as I was concerned, it wasn't an open-ended arrangement. If Corbin, Incorporated, didn't net my stalker soon, I planned to take matters into my own hands.

FIFTEEN

On that Thursday it rained for the first time in weeks—a lashing, blustery downpour that ripped leaves off the trees. High tide came at three in the afternoon, with the waves playing an awesome game of Can You Top This? over the hump of the seawall. At a quarter to five, the wind suddenly died and the rain faded into intermittent drizzle. Temple was on a class trip, an all-day outing to some Native American festival in south Jersey, and Cilda was watching *Oprah*. My cabin fever had peaked to almost hallucinatory levels: I imagined bars on all the windows and barricades at the doors. No question about it, I had to get out.

"I'm going to take a walk," I told Cilda. I put on my slicker and Reed's IAD cap and headed out to the beach.

My heavyset bodyguard—Mike Fedora, like the hat—followed at a discreet distance. For once, I didn't mind. In the thick fog that blanketed my private beach, it was easy to pretend I was alone.

The water had retreated, but the waves still beat the shoreline, taunting and recalcitrant. Tidal pools sparkled with an exotic array of shells, dismembered crabs, dead fish, and ocean effluvia. When I got tired of puddle jumping, I pulled myself up onto the jetty and began walking to the very end. I knew that although Mike Fedora would be cursing me under his breath, he wouldn't follow me out here. Not even the maddest of mad stalkers could lurk on these rocks. The only threat came from the cold, angry sea; the only danger, the slippery, wet surface.

I'd never climbed the jetty in a fog before. Salt spray kissed my face and hair. Mist curled out of the crevasses in the rocks. It was like walking in a dream. From far behind me I heard Fedora's voice calling, "Miss Quinn! Hey, you all right there?"

I yelled back, "Fine," but to my ears, the word sounded muffled, strangled, a mere wisp of cloud. Arms out to steady me, I pivoted, and turned toward shore.

"I completely lost sight of you out there for a minute," Fedora said, huffing and puffing as we walked back together on the moist, packed sand. The whites of his eyes seemed unnaturally large, and his big face shone with sea spray and perspiration. "If you don't mind me saying"—he wiped his cheek with the back of his hand—"seems like you sure enjoy pushing the edge of the envelope."

As I approached the house, I noticed the IAD van parked next to the garage. Cilda always brought a platter of food out to the men at dinnertime. The obfuscating fog all but erased them, but their laughter floated toward me, disembodied on the wind. I said goodnight to Mike Fedora at the back door.

The red light was blinking on the answering machine in the kitchen. I hit the play button and ducked into the refrigerator to get some water. "Hey, Mom?" Temple's voice said.

"Pick me up at the sports shed behind the school as soon as you can." There was a pause, and then she added, "Snowbear." I checked my watch. It was a few minutes before six.

That's funny, I thought. According to the permission slip I'd signed, the field trip wasn't supposed to be over until seven-thirty. Still carrying the unopened bottle of water, I went back to the machine and rewound the message. This time through I paid particular attention to the way Temple said "Snowbear," but even on the second listening, the word seemed free of any urgency or sinister meaning, peppered only with the sound of girlish laughter. At a pay phone, surrounded by friends, my daughter had once again slipped our code word in, as a secret gesture of love.

I pocketed the bottle of mineral water and started scouting around for my car keys. A shuffling noise coming from outside caught me up short. Then I saw Cilda at the door, an empty tray in her hand. "I have to go pick up Temple." I waved my keys.

"Mr. Fedora is over the guest quarters, using the bat'room," Cilda said.

I understood what she implied. "Then I'll take one of the other guys with me."

Corbin's men were still eating dinner when I reached the van. When they saw me, they rolled down the window. "Please, don't stop," I said. "I just need to zip over to the school to get my daughter."

"Mike'll be back in a second," said the one behind the wheel.

"She wasn't supposed to get in this early," I explained, already unlocking the driver's door of my car. "I don't want her waiting out in the dark. Tell Mr. Fedora I went on ahead."

"You're not supposed to—"

"I'll be at the shed behind the football field," I shouted over the drone of the Volvo's engine. "Fedora knows the way." I put it into gear and peeled away, spitting gravel in every direction.

The pea soup fog seemed to roll with me as I traveled inland. Visibility was almost nil. Snapping on my brights only worsened it, so I gave up, driving on instinct and my memory of the road. I told myself there was no need to worry. The teachers, and the school administration, had been informed about the special security measures we'd been forced to take. They wouldn't leave Temple alone in an empty parking lot. And at the first sign of trouble, she'd use her cellular phone to beep IAD.

My own beeper went off. I picked it up, and held it next to the dashboard light. It took me a second to decipher the code number; then I understood—Mike Fedora had completed his bowel movement and was paging me in a panic. *Poor guy,* I couldn't help thinking. He wasn't in the best of shape. I hoped the stress of this evening wouldn't kill him.

I tried punching in his number on my cellular, but bits of cloud were flying at me, covering the windshield like shredded cotton, and single-hand driving was out of the question. Up ahead, I could see the high school, its brick-and-mortar massiveness reassuringly unethereal. Only the clock tower had been eaten by the fog. I decided Fedora could sweat it out for another minute.

My first indication that something was wrong came as I made the next turn. The mercury vapor lights in the rear parking area floated like tiny alien mother ships, hovering above the mist, barely illuminating the lot. *Where are the buses? There should be buses.* Craning my neck, my nose nearly touching the dash, I coasted through the low-slung gauze. The football field had a topping of meringuey fog. I continued to edge along toward the dilapidated wooden shed where the coaches kept their sports equipment.

After school hours, this shed was a big meeting place. Much later, it became the place where the jocks and cheerleader types hung out, drinking beer and making out, spray-painting the battered exterior in huge bubble letters, with such thought-provoking sayings as "GO DAWGS" or "SHORE REGIONAL SUCKS." I prayed to God I'd see a couple of them there now—steroid-popping miscreants that they were—acting brash, trying to show off for my daughter. But I knew by the leaden feeling in my gut that I'd find what I found—a shuttered-up hut covered in graffiti and a shaggy mustache of fog.

I put the car in park, but left the keys in the engine. "Temple?" I slammed the door behind me. "Temple honey, I'm here!"

The wet ground made sucking sounds

under my feet. I tried another tack. "If you have my daughter," I shouted into the mist, "just let her go. This doesn't have anything to do with her." I kept walking toward the front of the shed. Its barn-style doors appeared to be fastened shut with a padlock.

"The keys are in my car," I continued to yell. "Let her drive away from here and then I'll go with you." Two filthy plate glass windows topped the doors, but they were set so high I had to pull myself up on the crossbar to peer in.

"Just the two of us." I held on to the bar and hung there, trying to see inside the shed. "That's what you want, isn't it?"

"Yes," said a voice behind me, "that's what I want."

He grabbed me by the back of the hair and yanked. "I thought we agreed you were going to grow this," he chuckled.

I crashed backward, smelling him before I saw him—a stink of sweat and male arousal that nearly made me retch. He rammed my face into the damp cotton of his T-shirt, then pushed me onto the ground, pinning down one shoulder, kneeling over me. I grabbed the bottled water out of my pocket and hurled it toward him. "What've you done with my daughter, you freak?" I screamed.

The bottle glanced off the side of his head, and for a split second he seemed disoriented. The next thing I knew, his fist was connecting with my jaw. A sound like a splitting log—*craa-ack!*—came crashing through my brain and I went sprawling. "You're even better than I imagined," Chaz said.

Flat on the ground, with his knees in my chest, I got my first real look at him—his wide forehead and Slavic cheekbones, his straggly bleached-blond hair, dark at the roots, the thin-lipped mouth. He was big, but pale and soft, with a doughy kind of musculature. Except for the chin, which was square, not pointed, Sheila Fanning's sketch had captured him perfectly; Chaz had been kind to himself in the corrections.

He tore off a length of gaffer tape. "I don't need your mouth just yet," he said, plastering it over my lips.

I forced myself to look him in the eyes, not wanting to give him the pleasure of seeing me cower. *He probably won't rape me here,* I thought, *so close to the road and the school. Maybe he has a car nearby.* With any luck he'd take me to wherever he'd taken Temple. He wound more tape around my wrists. As he lowered his head to bite the piece off, he burrowed his big face into my lap. I stared into the gauzy whiteness, blinking away tears of rage.

That's when the figure emerged from the fog. "Step away from her," Mike Fedora called with icy calm. I heard a slow click, the sound of a safety being removed. "I'll count to two and then I'll aim for the back of your head," Mike said. "One—"

Chaz scrambled off me. "Don't shoot," he cried. He put up his hands and the gaffer tape slid down on his skinny arm like a silver bracelet.

The IAD van came careening into the parking lot. "Got him, Mike," one of the

146

guys shouted. I watched Corbin's men drag Chaz to his feet and start to haul him away— just the way I pictured they would. And yet it was all so different than I'd imagined.

Fedora gently pulled the tape off my lips. "You okay, Miss Quinn?" His face was sweaty, the whites of his eyes preternaturally large, but this time nothing about Fedora's appearance made me want to laugh.

"Temple..."

"She's fine." He helped me into a sitting position. "I beeped her from the car, and she called on the cellular. The trip's running late. They won't be back till eight."

"But she called me," I protested. Fedora put his jacket over my shoulders. I heard the sound of sirens, and thought of my daughter, safe and secure, miles away, singing the beer barrel song on a bus.

"I'm sorry," I sobbed against Fedora's shoulder.

"Shush now, miss." He patted my head. "Everything's going to be all right."

SIXTEEN

Fedora insisted I get checked out by a doctor, and though I knew it would be a waste of time, I meekly submitted. The nearest hospital was only two miles away. To my relief, we found the waiting room empty. "They'll all come out," predicted the nurse at the desk, "soon as the fog lifts."

The emergency room doctor fingered my jaw, made me open and shut my mouth, and told me what I already knew—nothing was broken. He gave me some Tylenol for the pain. My face was swollen on one side and my shoulders felt as though I'd swum the English Channel. "Can we go home now?" I asked Fedora.

"Sure thing, Miss Quinn."

"Please call me Garner." I winced. "Or jerk or nitwit. Any old name you want. You just saved my life, Mike."

"Yeah, well, you saved my rear." Fedora held the door open. "If you weren't so tough, you might've ended up dead, and believe me, I wouldn't've wanted to be the one explaining that to Corbin."

Cilda met us at the door. "Oh, you going to take one of the ot'er gentlemen wit' you, is that right?" she asked crossly. "I'm not so old and feeble that I shouldn't 'ave seen that comin', Ga'ner Quinn." I threw my arms around her neck.

Temple was on the phone in the kitchen. She held out the receiver, saying, "Reed wants to talk to you," and somewhere during the pass-off, we ended up hugging. If Mike Fedora had been a little closer, I'd have hugged him too. It was just that kind of night.

"Hello?" I said, my arms still around my daughter.

"Everyone's assured me you're all right," Reed said, "but I won't be able to think straight until I hear it from you."

"Other than a case of impaired judgment—

148

which appears to be chronic," I said, "I'm perfectly fine."

"I really want to see you, but there's something I have to do first."

"That's okay." I ruffled Temple's hair. "We're all pretty beat around here."

"Put Mike on, would you?" I handed the phone to Fedora. Temple, Cilda, and I sat around the kitchen table holding hands as though we might at any moment break into some goofy campfire song, listening as the older man spoke to Reed, conversing in a string of nos and yeses.

After he hung up, Mike said, "You don't have to worry. They got that low-life crud in custody. Reed's gonna be there when they question him. He wants me to hang around tonight, if that's not a problem for you ladies. Not for any security reason except that this way you can leave everything to me, go get yourselves a good night's sleep."

"Sounds wonderful." I turned to Cilda and Temple. "I'll meet you upstairs, guys. I want to talk to Mr. Fedora for a minute."

"Don't be long." Temple kissed my swollen cheek.

"I won't," I promised.

"What's up?" Mike asked when they'd gone.

"I thought, with all the excitement, you might want to take another walk in the fog. Rock-climb the jetty, blow off some steam?"

"You sure are a piece of work"—he chuckled—"Garner." Then he added in a more serious tone, "At least we got the SOB, right?"

"Damn straight." I went over to a cabinet and took out a tin of cocoa and a small pan. "You like hot chocolate?" I asked.

"Sometimes," the old man said. "Especially days like this, moving into winter."

I heated up the milk and chocolate on the stove, then poured it into a pair of ceramic mugs and brought them over to the table. Mike Fedora and I sat there for a long while, warming our hands on the cups, not talking, just staring out the window at the evaporating mist and listening to the tide.

His name was Walter Dean Wozniak, a twenty-nine-year-old wanna-be comic book illustrator and sometime inker whose main claim to fame was a stint doing the print for the counterculture strip called *Chasm.* "That's obviously where the name came from," Reed told me over dinner the next night. "Not Chaz as in Charles, but Kaz as in *Chasm.*"

"What else?" I devoured every detail, looking for some kind of road sign that would make clear his path to me.

"He was born in Seattle. Mrs. Wozniak was fifty at the time. Apparently, she'd never been able to conceive, so Walter Dean came as quite a surprise. Mr. Wozniak committed suicide when Walter was seven. His mother managed to hold on to the house and keep food on the table." Reed pushed his plate of pasta aside. "But on the whole, I wouldn't call his a sunny childhood.

"Comic books provided an escape. As time went on, he added video games, heavy metal, and hallucinogenic drugs to the mix. The mother ended up having him arrested for stealing her Social Security checks and forging her name. Right after that he moved east. He was in Philadelphia for a while, then he headed over to New Jersey. Trenton, East Orange, Ridgefield Park."

"How did he support himself?"

"Working in head shops and comic book stores, mostly, among the *Spawn* and *Black Sabbath* set. Four years ago he managed to get an interview at DC Comics. They suggested he get some training, so he signed up for night courses at the Newark School of Fine and Industrial Arts."

Reed waited until the waitress cleared our plates before continuing. "He met a part-time teacher there, a guy named Brian Foote, who was doing illustrations for this strip called *Chasm*. Foote took a liking to him, and eventually threw some lettering work in Wozniak's direction.

"I spoke to Foote on the phone this morning," Reed said. "According to him, Wozniak started out pretty well. Didn't rag about the pay, and made all his deadlines. After a while, though, he began suggesting these off-the-wall story ideas for the strip. When the writers blew him off, he'd send them pages and pages of notes, outlining where he thought *Chasm* should be going. Brian Foote would check his mailbox at school and find it literally crammed with letters. Then he'd go home and find more of the same."

"Sounds familiar."

"The final straw came when Wozniak took to dressing all in black and showing up unexpectedly in places, like the main character of the comic strip, a demon warrior called Gorge. Foote said he'd walk into a room that he'd swear was empty and, out of nowhere, Wozniak would suddenly appear—"

Like at the shed last night, I thought.

Reed touched my hand. "You sure you want to hear the rest?" he asked.

The waitress stopped at our table. "Care for some coffee or dessert?"

"Two coffees," Corbin said, with that take-charge style I'd come to like.

"Tell me everything," I said, when she'd finished serving.

Reed stirred sugar into his cup, not looking at me. "With most comic strips, it's the old story of good versus evil. In *Chasm* the concept degenerates into evil versus more evil. One of the main story lines revolves around Gorge's violent union with a woman known as She."

"Please," I said, but I wasn't laughing. "Do people really read this stuff?"

"Read it. Or in Wozniak's case, live and die by it. The character of She is described as a red-haired sorceress whose *outward appearance is that of an angel, but whose soul encompasses the blackness of death.*"

"Oh, yeah," I said, facetiously. "That's me all right."

"Gorge must *become one* with her in order to possess all she knows."

"Which means, what?" I made him look me in the eye. "He rapes her?"

"Initially," Reed said. "He also cuts out her heart, then sets fire to her body."

"Jesus." I stared down into my empty cup.

"We're going to put him away, Garner." Again Corbin touched my hand. "For a long, long time."

The waitress came with our check, and we walked single file down the narrow center aisle of the trattoria to the cashier. "Was everything enjoyable?" the manager asked.

I forced a smile. "Yes, thank you. It was great."

Outside, the breeze coming off the river was cold. If I looked straight up, I could see the stars, like diamond studs on a perfectly ironed piece of dark cloth. Reed put his arm around me and we headed toward the car.

"What are you thinking?" he asked.

"I'm thinking," I said, snuggling into his shoulder, "Mike Fedora deserves a raise."

In the trunk of Wozniak's Plymouth, police had found a multipack of disposable plastic tarps, some nylon rope, a gallon of gasoline, and a hunting knife. There was also a stack of pornographic magazines, several hundred *Chasm* comic books, the complete works of Garner Quinn, and a dozen notebooks filled with page after page of Chaz's neatly inked printing and cartoon-style drawings—most of which showed my naked (and creatively zaftig) body being raped, mutilated, and burned.

"You draw these, Walt?" Matthew Raice had asked.

"Walt?" Wozniak snorted disdainfully. "Walt fucking Disney is decapitated in some walk-in freezer, butthead. I'm Walter Dean Wozniak. Ask Garner Quinn. She'll tell you who I am."

And Raice had looked him up and down. "Last time I spoke with the lady, Walt," he said, "she was calling you Loser."

Mike Fedora related this anecdote to me, adding something really interesting—among Walter Dean's personal possessions was a tape recorder and a cassette with Temple's voice. *Pick me up at the sports shed behind the school as soon as you can. Snowbear,* she said on it. In addition to this, a microcassette containing twenty-three old telephone messages from my office answering machine was discovered in the glove compartment of Wozniak's car.

When asked how the message cassette came to be in his possession, Walter Dean had sneered, "A little bird gave it to me. An American eagle, flew right through the red roof and left it, special delivery." At which point he'd laughed, then proceeded to bang his head on the metal table, until tears ran down his big, broad face.

SEVENTEEN

Mercedes wanted to interview me for *Front Cover.* She called from her office, very excited and upbeat. Segments on stalkers brought in a lot of viewers, she explained, and the fact that I was a famous author made the story even sexier. "No way," I told her. "I'm not about to make myself a target for every other nut in the world."

"You think you can keep this story under wraps?" she argued. "Every single network covered it last night. By the arraignment, the press will be all over you."

"I won't be at the arraignment," I said. "They took a statement and told me I wouldn't have to testify until the actual trial."

"Look, Garner," Mercedes persisted. "I respect your misgivings. Mama told me what Wozniak tried to do to you. But this would be a highly sensitive, extremely tasteful—not to mention, very *brief*—interview. You wouldn't have to discuss the attack itself. We could talk with you at home." She quickly amended, "Or anywhere you feel comfortable."

"I can't." There was a long pause on the line. When the silence became unbearable, I demanded, "You still there?"

"I was just thinking," Mercedes said, "how Garner Quinn would handle an uncooperative subject."

"She'd take no for an answer," I replied, but the bald lie made me feel guilty. "I'm sorry, Merce. If I was going to sit down with anyone, you know it would be you. But put yourself in my place. Think of Temple—"

"No, *you* think of Temple," Mercedes bristled. "Did you know that she's been calling me every night for weeks, desperate for someone to help make sense of this thing?"

"I—" I was stunned. "That's crazy. She knows she can always come to me."

"For what? A pep talk about how there's nothing to worry about, that she should just ignore the little gun-toting army camped out around the house? Do you really believe sweeping all the ugly stuff under the carpet makes it any easier for that child? What she needs is someone who'll listen, and be honest with her—"

"It's amazing how much you know about raising kids," I said, "considering you have none of your own."

"I'm sorry if I overstepped my bounds." Mercedes sounded hurt. "I was only trying to help Temple."

Shit, I thought, *why do we keep trampling each other's feelings?* I said, "I know you were. And I'm glad she had you to talk to, I really am. You're family, Mercedes—you're Auntie Merce. But as much as I'd like to do this interview for you, I just can't. I hope you can understand."

"Sure," she replied tartly. "You don't owe me any favors, Garner. I'm the one who owes you, remember? Say hello to my mother for me."

There was a click from the other end. I stood for a while staring at the phone. Cilda, who'd disappeared during our conversation, came back into the room. "I told her I couldn't do it," I said.

The old woman just shrugged. "A person 'ave to do what a person 'ave to do." But I could tell by the kindness in her voice that she was disappointed.

"How was your day?" I asked.

Temple tossed her backpack onto the kitchen counter. "Okay."

"Anything exciting happen at school?"

"Not really." She took a juice pack out of the refrigerator and kept on walking.

I followed her. "I thought we'd go out to eat tonight. Just the two of us. We could drive over to the Highlands, get a couple of lobsters. Talk."

She shook her head. "I've got that big team project due."

"Oh, right." I kept my voice upbeat. "Maybe tomorrow then."

"Sure." My daughter eyed me suspiciously. "Whenever."

Later, over an impromptu spaghetti dinner, I tried again. "This is nice," I said, beaming at my little family. "No vans in the driveway, no guards outside. Everything back to normal."

Cilda flaked Parmesan onto her pasta, making sharp little tsk-tsk sounds with the cheese grater as if to say, *When have t'ings ever been normal around 'ere?*

Temple said, "I miss the Fedora hat man."

Okay, I thought, *so she misses Mike.* That was a decent jumping-off point. "I do too, honey," I said. "In fact—" But I never got to segue into a more meaningful conversation, because just then the phone rang.

Temple cupped a hand over the receiver. "Can Jamie stay over? We really need to practice our presentation." She made her dark eyes go all puppy dog round and soft. "Pretty please? Her mom already said she'd drive her."

"It's a school night, Tem."

"We'll do our work and go right to bed. Scout's honor."

As if either of us had ever been a Scout. The second I gave the okay, she bounded happily out of the room. "You notice how that child talks to everyone but me?" I muttered.

"She's sixteen years old." Cilda shrugged. "And you're 'er mother."

"For what *that's* worth," I muttered.

The old woman stood up, dragging me over to the refrigerator by the scruff of my sweater, and throwing open the door. Inside was a lopsided cake. Across the top a childish hand had written the words "GOOD RID-DANCE!!!" in a piping of red food coloring. A gingerbread man with stringy hair was pinned behind black licorice bars. "T'ere," Cilda reprimanded me, "is what it's worth, Ga'ner Quinn."

I felt like an ingrate, sulking because my kid had confided her fears to someone else, when I had so much to be thankful for: Walter Wozniak was in custody; Temple and Cilda were safe; I had my old life back again—my old life, plus Reed.

Later that night, Temple and Jamie sneaked into the great room where I was reading the paper, dimmed the lights, and with hand trumpet fanfares, unveiled the surprise. "What's this?" I cried, suitably surprised and genuinely touched. "Oh my! Did you make this?"

"All by 'erself," said Cilda.

"Make a wish," Temple urged, setting the sloppy cake with its one candle down in front of me. I shut my eyes and blew.

Cilda cut four large pieces, and Temple plucked off the head of the gingerbread Walter, divvying up its limbs. "Well," she said with her mouth full, "that's the last of Chaz."

"Not quite." My stalker story had been picked up by all the New York papers, *USA Today,* the *Star-Ledger,* and the *Asbury Park Press.* I picked up the thick stack of newsprint and tucked it under my arm. "Come on, kids. We're going to have a little bonfire."

"Now?" Temple squealed delightedly. "In our pajamas?"

"Yep. In our pajamas." I grabbed a box of long matches from the hearth.

"Awesome!" cried Jamie.

"Crazy people," grumbled Cilda. "You catch your deaths out t'ere in the cold. I'm going to bed."

The sweatshirts we threw over our flannel PJs proved to be unnecessary. Despite Cilda's prediction, the night was windless and humid, with a thin cover of pinkish clouds. What stars were visible appeared to be trillions of miles away. We walked briskly to the sea-wall, our slippers slapping the flagstone, the sound of our breath amplified by this vacuum of silence. Even the ocean was hushed and still.

We combed the beach for driftwood. I

walked behind, listening to Temple regale her friend with the inside dope on Walter Wozniak. "God, an obsessed stalker." Jamie's voice sifted through the quiet air. "How intense is that? Your mother must be, like, so brave."

"It's being in the public eye, that's all," I heard Temple say with a world-weary sophistication that made me want to laugh and cry at the same time.

When we'd gathered enough wood, the girls crumpled up the newspaper and added it to the pyre. Each of us took a long match, and one after the other, we struck them against the side of the box. The tiny flames caught, licking at the newsprint until it shriveled, then disintegrated into black ash.

Wavery heat buckled from the fire. I peeled off my sweatshirt, stamped my feet, and howled up at the sky. Temple did the same. Then she grabbed my hand, and I grabbed Jamie's, and we spun around the fire, shrieking and laughing at the top of our lungs, going faster and faster, until we became so dizzy we fell down on the sand. "Ms. Quinn," Jamie hiccuped breathlessly, "you are totally cool."

Later, as we were putting the plates into the dishwasher, Temple said, "I bet I know what you wished for when you blew out that candle."

"And what's that?"

"You wished they'd put Wozniak away for a hundred years, right?" She looked at me earnestly.

"How'd you know?" I hugged her close. Actually, my wish was to always feel as close to my daughter as I did tonight, but I didn't want to jinx it by telling her.

EIGHTEEN

A few days later Walter Dean Wozniak was arraigned at the superior court in Freehold. Wozniak, wearing a black jacket, a *Chasm* T-shirt, black jeans, and black sneakers, doodled on a pad as his court-appointed public attorney argued, somewhat dispiritedly, that since her client had never been arrested for any violent crime, he should remain free on his own recognizance.

The prosecutor then read a few passages from Wozniak's notebooks—detailed descriptions of what he planned to do to me. "Walter Dean Wozniak continues to exhibit a perverted obsession with Garner Quinn. He admits that his sole object is to rape and murder this woman—why, he's been sitting here drawing pictures of her throughout this entire proceeding." The district attorney gestured toward Wozniak's pad, and for the first time, Walter smiled.

"Ms. Quinn lives in fear of her life, Your Honor, and the life of her daughter. Allowing Walter Wozniak back on the street would put them both in grave danger."

The judge set bail at $500,000. Assuming that Wozniak passed a psychiatric evaluation establishing he was fit to stand trial, jury selection would begin during the last week of November. Reed Corbin and Matthew Raice were happy with the ruling. Walter had left an outstanding balance at the motel where he'd been staying; the only thing he owned was his car and his comic book collection. He wouldn't be getting out of jail anytime soon.

"Did he really just sit there drawing me?" I asked them at the Chinese restaurant near the courthouse where we met after the hearing.

"You"—Matt shrugged—"or She. The guy isn't exactly clued into reality."

"The main thing," Reed said, shooting a reassuring smile in my direction, "is that Garner can go back to living normally."

"Yeah, right. Baking brownies, perfecting her golf swing, puttering around in the garden." Matt elbowed me. "He doesn't know you very well, does he?" There was a sudden awkward silence, during which time I considered that Raice might be right.

The hostess, a small, exquisitely lovely girl with a heavy Chinese accent, had been eyeing us through the clear waters of a fish tank as we ate our main course. Now she came over to our table, carrying a tray of fruit and ice cream. "Dessert," she said, setting it down in the center of the table. "Special for you."

"Thank you." Matt managed to catch her averted glance. "It's beautiful, just beautiful." I remembered what Reed had said about his partner having a girl in every port.

Corbin may not have figured me yet, Matt honey, I thought to myself, *but he sure has you pegged.*

"To Walt Wozniak." Matt raised his glass in toast. "May he rot in jail."

"Hear, hear," Reed and I both said.

The next morning, to spite Matthew Raice, I baked a tray of brownies. They came out burned on the bottom with a syrupy middle, but still, I considered them a small victory. Since Wozniak's arrest, even mundane things—opening the mail, going out for a walk, hopping in the car for a ride—had become exhilarating experiences.

Every day was a new adventure. I took care of my correspondence in a timely manner. I was personable to salesclerks, bank tellers, and the parents of my daughter's friends. I didn't even complain when Cilda sent me back to the grocery store for one small item she'd left off her list.

Occasionally, I dreamt about driving through fog, or that Temple was lost and I couldn't find her. Or I'd be sitting at the computer and a vivid flashback of that night would grip me. But I'd had post-traumatic stress attacks before, and I knew how to handle them.

I'd picture Wozniak sitting on the bunk in his small cell. Then I'd mentally slam the barred door, and lock down those metal prison walls, and I'd take the key and walk out to the farthest point of the jetty, and toss it as far as I could into the ocean. At that point, my breathing usually slowed and my pulse returned to normal.

I wasn't about to let Walter Dean Wozniak invade my life, or thoughts, ever again.

"The McCarthys are only *this* far from making an offer," Peggy Boyle squealed on the phone. "Their parents absolutely adored the house. I told them they'd better hurry, though. There's been a *lot* of activity. With all this *interest,* I've no doubt we'll be hanging the Sold sign out before Thanksgiving."

Thanksgiving? I found the notion oddly disturbing. I pictured the McCarthys eating turkey in Dudley's dining room. Did they have children? I wondered. Or would it be a quiet holiday—just the two of them, sitting at opposite ends of the table, as the in-laws debated wallpaper patterns for the powder room?

After I hung up, my ambivalence started to subside. The more I thought about it, the happier I felt. It would be good not to have to think about the old place anymore. I looked forward to the day I could drive by and see, not my father's home, but someone else's.

Reed still came down to see me when he could, but more and more frequently he was out of town. He'd call from some movie set where he was visiting a client, or a hush-hush meeting at the FBI or NTSB.

"I'm worried about the poor bastard," Matt Raice confessed during our weekly update call.

"This pace is going to kill him," I agreed.

"Not just the pace." For once, Matt sounded completely serious. "We've always made it a practice to watch each other's backs. But with Reed's book, and the Petty case—not to mention all the other plates we've got spinning..." He sighed. "We've got too much going, on too many fronts. I keep telling Reed we have to scale down, but it seems to go in one ear and out the other. Maybe you can talk some sense into him."

The implication made me uncomfortable. "I can't tell Corbin how to handle his life," I told him.

Still, the next time Reed and I were together, I commented on how preoccupied he seemed. "Sorry," he said. "It has nothing to do with you. It's just the cases I've been working on lately." He pushed his glasses down and rubbed the bridge of his nose. "Plus this damn book party."

Corbin's publisher planned to launch *The Fear Factor* at a lavish, celebrity-studded party at Tiffany's. In the words of his editor— what better place for the security expert to the stars to make his literary debut than a showplace for priceless treasures, which also happened to be as safe as Fort Knox?

I said, "It'll be fine."

"It would mean a lot"—he took my hand, almost shyly—"to have you there."

"I wouldn't miss it," I said. In truth, I had to admit I liked Reed Corbin more the way he was now—distant, a little moody, his brow creased, his eyes weary. I found him way more attractive than the Reed Corbin of earnest hands and wet kisses who'd only weeks ago been so urgently courting me.

When he slid behind the wheel of his Volvo for the long drive back to New York, I leaned into the driver's window. "The party sounds like it might go on pretty late," I said.

"You could always leave," Reed said, jumping to the conclusion that I wanted out.

"Actually, I thought I might spend the night in town." It was ridiculous the way my heart was hammering, as though I were a kid, not an experienced woman of almost forty.

Reed's eyes widened. He took a breath. "Sounds smart," he agreed. "You could get a hotel, or...you could stay with me."

"That might be good," I said, noncommittally. And then I kissed him and ran into the house without waving goodbye.

NINETEEN

Whether by design or coincidence, Reed's book launch had been scheduled for the day before Halloween. Mischief Night never got too out of hand in the affluent communities of the Jersey shore, but although most towns had an eight o'clock curfew, there would be a lot of soaped-up windows and toilet paper–hung trees by morning. The pranksters always stopped short of the remote end of the peninsula where we lived, though. By autumn, the woods were too dark and lonely for the average thrill-seeking kid.

Temple had been invited to a costume

party at her friend Jamie's house. For weeks, she'd agonized over what she should be—a flapper, an accident victim, a bag lady. It all depended, she explained, on whether she wanted to be pretty or funny. As a rule, funny made for a better costume, but pretty was the way to go if you expected someone to ask you to dance.

I considered her lucky; I had no choice but to put in an appearance at the bash this evening as plain old Garner Quinn.

My daughter poked her head into my bedroom. After experimenting with make-up that was supposed to resemble an open wound, she'd discarded the accident victim idea. Instead she and Cilda had whipped up an Arabian princess outfit from a pair of sheer curtains, with astonishing results. Her face seductively half covered by a transparent scarf, her midriff bare, a paste ruby gleaming from her navel—there could be no doubt that someone would ask this young woman to dance tonight.

"You're wearing *that*?" Over the veil Temple's dark eyes were critical.

I glanced down at my black suit and white piqué vest with tiny pearl buttons. "What's the matter with it?"

"It's pretty stodgy," said the girl with the ruby in her bellybutton. Then her face lit up and she dashed out of the room, returning a moment later with a dress in a dry cleaner's plastic bag.

"I can't wear that."

"Why not?"

"For one thing, it's too small," I said. "For another, your father bought it for you to wear the night he got engaged to Candace, that's why."

"So?"

"I think there's some kind of law against second-engagement party dresses being worn by first wives," I explained through gritted teeth.

"Let me know if you need help with the zipper," Temple said as she closed the door.

The dress fit like a dream. Differently than it fit Temple, but still—like a dream. I spent a few seconds trying to talk myself out of it: the hemline was too short, the neckline too daring, the midnight-blue velvet too soft, too midnight blue. Finally I gave up. There was a certain sweet justice, I told myself, in going off to a romantic tryst wearing a dress picked out and paid for by my ex-husband.

"Isn't it funny?" Temple giggled, making me turn round and round. "Both our dress-up parties are ending in overnights."

I came to a sudden stop. Had there been a slight teasing in her voice when she'd said "overnight"? With the veil on her face, it was impossible to tell. But of course, she was just excited about Halloween, and the prospect of staying at her pal Jamie's—thrilled with the sky's-the-limit potential that any Saturday can hold when you're sixteen.

"And by noon tomorrow we'll both be back," I reminded her. "In time to take Cilda out for brunch." I held out both hands.

"Yick," she said. "Your palms are sweaty."

"Temple!" Cilda called from downstairs. "Jamie's mot'er's 'ere to chauffer-drivver you to the party—"

"Have a great time, kiddo." I kissed her forehead.

"You too, Mom," she sang, and then she was gone in a swoosh of gossamer and a flash of cut-glass gems.

I was rummaging through my closet, trying to decide which wrap to wear, when a summer blazer slid off its hanger and fell on the floor. As I was putting it back, I noticed something in the front flap pocket—a small snapshot of a dark man with a dangerous profile and a gaze that, even when averted, could scorch a young girl's soul.

Shutting my eyes, I let the feeling overtake me again, and for a brief moment, his scent (ironed shirts and the dry astringency of plaster, simmered over heat) filled the closet. My palms tingled with the remembered pressure of fingers as they went about the slow, soft extrication of my hands from those lapels.

"Are you telling me I'm never going to see you again?" I'd asked. To which Blackmoor had replied, "That's something I have to figure out." He'd send me a sign, he said.

Are you done figuring? I wondered. I looked up from the picture. Studied the reflection I saw in the closet mirror—a white-shouldered woman in a slip of a dress, her face shining and radiant, looking as though she were on the cusp of something—*what?*

This is your last chance, Dane, I whispered. *The clock's ticking. If I'm supposed to forget about you and go on with my life, so be it. But if there's any chance for us—dammit, now would be a good time to send that sign.* I brought the picture over to the lamp on my dresser, the better to see it. But Blackmoor's eyes steadfastly avoided me, so after a while I put the picture down, and shut off the light.

TWENTY

Reed suggested that I meet him at his apartment on East Sixtieth Street so we could go to the party together, but when I got to the Lincoln Tunnel only a single inbound lane was open, leaving traffic backed up for miles. "Don't worry," he said when I called him from the car. "I'll see you there. If you come before cocktails, we can still grab a few minutes together before all the hoopla starts."

I detected a note of distraction in his voice. "Is everything okay?"

There was a long blitz of static; then Reed came on the line again, in midsentence, "...with them, and I ended up staying up half the night going over...which isn't exactly wh—"

"Reed," I interrupted, "I'm losing you." The line went dead. I decided to just turn off the phone and concentrate on getting through the tunnel.

By the time I parked the car, it was nearly

eight. I grabbed my shawl, my purse, and the good-luck present I'd brought for Corbin, and made a mad dash toward Fifth Avenue. The cocktail hour started in less than half an hour. I'd wanted to give Reed my gift before the other guests arrived, but at this point it was probably too late. Now I'd be stuck carrying this big-as-a-bread-basket box around all night.

As I passed Trump Tower, a couple of Asian businessmen emerged with several very tall, thin women in sequined Mardi Gras masks. They made me think of Temple in her Arabian costume; I wondered how her party was, if she was having fun.

Tiffany's windows were like open jewelry boxes, richly textured tableaux of subdued sparkle and light. Two liveried doormen stood in front of the art deco facade, and velvet ropes hung from stanchions, marking a path for the people who would soon be pulling up to the curb in their taxis and limousines.

"I'm early," I said to one of the doormen, "but Reed Corbin's expecting me." He opened the door, without asking my name.

In the first quick second of stepping inside, time froze. My mother, a celebrated beauty in her time, had died alone and destitute in a halfway house for alcoholic women. At her funeral, a teary blonde in a molting mink coat had grabbed my hand. "Don't cry, sweetie. We'll see her again, on the first floor of Tiffany's, someday," she sniffed.

"Pardon?"

"Why, that's what your mother always said

171

heaven would be," the woman said. "Like the first floor of Tiffany's, all polished to a shine, and golden." If my mother was hovering on some astral plane over these glittering counters, I'd never seen her, but in some odd way I always felt closer to her here.

"Ms. Quinn," Tamara Ma greeted me. She was wearing a black dress with a slit up the back, her long hair caught up with an antique silver clip. "You look lovely."

"So do you," I said, commenting, "what a beautiful comb."

Tamara smiled. "Don't you love it? Matt gave it to me for my birthday."

A reception table had been set up inside the front entrance. Poster-sized reproductions of the front and back cover of *The Fear Factor,* celebrity endorsements, and early reviews were prominently displayed at either end. Two women in evening wear sat behind two large guest books. Behind them, near the escalators, a meeting between Corbin's people and members of the Tiffany staff seemed to be breaking up.

"Reed's already upstairs. If you'll wait a moment," Tamara went on, "I'll have someone take you to him."

Matt Raice appeared out of nowhere. "Don't bother, Tam," he said. "I'll escort the lady myself." He leaned over and gave me a kiss. His cheeks were cold, as if he'd just come in from outside. "You look scrumptious," he whispered.

But not half as scrumptious as he. Raice had probably owned a tuxedo all his life, and it showed in the wearing. In honor of the occasion, he'd even shaved off the fashion-page five o'clock shadow. His skin gleamed like his starched white shirtfront.

"How's it going, Matthew?" I asked as we walked toward the elevator banks.

"Like one big fucking security nightmare, to put it bluntly," he muttered good-naturedly. "The good news is, Madonna bowed out at the last minute. The bad news is, that still leaves six big names on the Hollywood A-list—not to mention Hizzoner the mayor, Mr. and Mrs. Kissinger, Gloria Steinem, and Donald Trump."

"Have you spoken to Reed?"

"Have you?" Matt held the elevator door for me.

"Not really."

"He's nervous, a bit preoccupied. But I've known him long enough not to be fooled. The more scattered and unfocused he seems, the sharper he'll end up being, once the rubber meets the road."

The elevator stopped with a well-bred little ding. "Third floor. Fine crystal," Raice said. "Check your belongings, everybody out."

I stepped off the car into a shimmering wonderland. When I'd first heard that Reed's publishers were throwing him a party in the crystal department of Tiffany's, I'd thought, *How droll*, but now I saw it was a stroke of genius. *The Fear Factor*'s stark, foreboding cover loomed—over and behind a transparent backdrop of Baccarat, through a filigreed maze of Waterford, around sculptures of blown glass.

The spires, globules, and stems, made a powerful statement about the intrusion of violence on our one-of-a-kind, fragile lives.

"We've got a pressroom in back with a satellite linkup," Matt explained. "All the big newsmagazine shows are here. Primarily"—he rolled his eyes—"because they were expecting Madonna. But also because violence, as you well know, happens to be one of those hot-button topics. We're allowing them to shoot B-roll during cocktails, but they have to clear out once the dog and pony show starts. The celebs'll probably go to the pressroom for interviews while Reed's signing books."

I caught a glimpse of skirted tables through the display case, like a corps de ballet in some enchanted crystal forest. Uniformed waiters were bringing in platters ladened with fruit and cheese, and lacy plates of finger sandwiches and petit fours. A tower of champagne glasses had been arranged on the main banquet table, flanked on either end by two large deco figures—a man and a woman—sculpted in ice.

IAD men circulated around the room, doing their pre-event security check. On the dais, Reed Corbin was scribbling a note to himself on the Lucite podium, oblivious to all the activity. Behind him was a projection screen and a banquette stacked with at least six hundred copies of *The Fear Factor*.

Matt's walkie-talkie made a chirruping sound. "Early arrivals," he said. "Lucky me, I'm running interference downstairs. Well, have fun." He gave me a farewell peck on the cheek.

I set my shawl and my gift down at an empty table and started toward the dais. Halfway across the room, Reed looked up. "Garner." He seemed relieved. "I was beginning to worry that something might've happened."

"Oh, I know how to take care of myself." I smiled. "I read the book."

"You look—" He stooped over to kiss me, but I broke away quickly.

"Thank you."

"So what do you think of all this?" Reed straightened up, stuffed his notes into his pocket, and swung off the platform. "A bit much, isn't it?"

"I rather like it."

Mike Fedora came over to us in a shiny black suit a size too small for his bulk. "Hey, Garner. How are things down the Jersey shore?"

"Quiet and clear," I said.

"That's good." He gave me a big smile. "We got a seat saved for you, right next to the podium."

"Any calls, Mike?" asked Corbin.

"Nothing yet, boss," he replied.

Reed frowned. I noticed dark circles under his eyes. He'd slicked his thin blond hair back, and it made him appear older than his forty-odd years. "Keep me posted," he told Fedora; then he turned to me. "Come on, let's take a walk."

"What's going on?"

He shook his head. "I'll tell you about it later."

We strolled around the back of the dais, where there was another aisle of crystal sculpture. For several minutes, we stood in front of a display case, eyes straight ahead, not speaking. Reflected in the glass, our bodies looked half erased and floating—Reed in his tuxedo, and me in my velvet dress. I got a small, voyeuristic thrill from seeing the way his hand looked, touching my waist.

"Which one do you like?" he asked.

"Oh," I said, "I don't know anything about glass."

"But you must have a favorite."

"That one." I pointed to a heavy, cristalline slab in which a three-dimensional etching of a castle was suspended. Like us, the image seemed to float inside the glass.

"It's yours then."

"Reed—"

"Don't argue with me," he said. "I want you to have it."

"Tonight isn't the night for *you* to give presents." I walked him around the dais, toward the table where I'd left the package. "Open it up now," I told him. "Before it gets too crazy in here."

"You know, I'm a sucker for surprises." Corbin was clearly delighted. "Probably stems from my deprived childhood, yada, yada." He shook the box. "Feels heavy." He balanced it in one hand, playing with the ribbon.

"Just open the thing."

Reed unwrapped the first figure, his face lighting up like a kid's. "Batman." He whistled softly. "I've never seen one like it."

The minute I'd spotted the bookends in the window of a collectible shop in Red Bank, I knew I had to buy them, but halfway through the purchase, I'd noticed a rack of *Chasm* comic books, and it had taken all my willpower not to drop everything and run. "The other bookend shows him wearing a smoking jacket and tie," I said.

"Ah, yes. Batman's alter ego, millionaire Bruce Wayne." He set the two ends together, admiring them. "Thank you, Garner. I'm going to treasure these forever."

"It's just a few minutes to showtime," I said, helping Corbin put the figures back into their tissue paper sheaths. "An hour from now they'll be calling 'Author!'"

Together we found a hiding spot for the bookends, under the banquette's long white tablecloth. Reed touched my arm. "Are our plans for this evening still on?"

"As far as I'm concerned."

He took a key out of his pocket. "Here. Just in case you decide to cut out early." He drew me close. "I'm really glad you're staying tonight. Not just because..." He was hugging me so tight he seemed to be holding on for dear life. "God, it's been a hell of a month. I feel like I've spent the past few weeks just going round and round in circles—"

"Oh, there you are," someone cried. Corbin and I moved guiltily apart. A woman of about fifty, in a bouclé knit suit and lots of Chanel jewelry, clattered toward us on high heels.

"Hello, Madeleine." Reed turned to me. "This is Madeleine Garth, the publicist who's working on the book. Madeleine, I'd like you to meet my friend Garner Quinn."

The woman's face lit up and said tilt. "Ms. Quinn, what an honor," she said, producing a business card like magic and pressing it into my palm. "I handle a lot of writers. Maybe someday the two of us could sit down together and chat." Without skipping a beat, she turned to Reed. "Of course you heard Madonna canceled. But she sent a video congratulations, which we'll play—what do you think, before the President's letter or after?"

"Um, I should let you—"

I tugged Reed's sleeve before she could go on. "Good luck. I'll see you later. Nice meeting you, Madeleine."

"Nice meeting *you*." The second I turned I heard her sigh to Corbin, "*Ay chihuahua—* that one! What I couldn't do for *her* career!"

I shot a backward glance at Reed and our eyes met in a smile.

TWENTY-ONE

Several television crews had stationed themselves around the room, and a well-dressed battalion of on-camera talent marked out turf, digging trenches around the most promising locations.

"Hello, Garner." I spun around at the sound

of a familiar voice. Microphone in one hand, Mercedes Fields was somehow managing to shimmy the waistband of her form-fitting, kiwi shantung skirt around with the other.

"Mercedes!" I couldn't hide my surprise. "This is great—"

"Yes." She gave me a wry smile. "Imagine finding me here."

"I was just on my way to the rest room—"

"I'd join you," Mercedes said, "but I'm on the job."

"Your mother didn't tell me..."

"She didn't know. I don't speak with her as often as you do."

Mercedes called to her cameraman, "Manny—make sure you get a shot of the book cover next to that Steuben piece with the skyline."

"Well," I said, "I'd better leave you to your work. Maybe I'll see you later."

"Garner." Mercedes stopped me. "We're doing interviews in the pressroom after cocktails. Stop by and say something nice about Corbin's book," she invited, adding with biting sarcasm, "That is, if you don't feel it would invade your privacy or compromise your principles."

"I just might do that," I said.

"Oh, and by the way," Mercedes added, "fabulous dress." She said this as if she knew that it couldn't possibly belong to me.

"I'm glad you approve," I replied, coolly.

I hung out in the ladies' room for twenty minutes or so, just wasting time. When I emerged,

179

the room had filled up considerably. Celebrities glided between the glacial aisles of crystal like sleek ocean liners, nodding to any worthy ship they passed. Politicians and prominent businessmen worked the tables, pressing flesh. It was one of those high-profile affairs I usually avoided. Standing alone, with my hands dangling at my sides, in uncomfortably high heels, I remembered why. I snagged a glass of champagne from a nice-looking waiter in a white jacket, and headed for a quiet corner where I could watch the scene without being in it.

A crowd of well-wishers had circled Reed. I saw his eyes dart furtively over one man's shoulders, looking for me perhaps. Mike Fedora came over and touched him on the shoulder, whispering something into his ear.

"Look," said a voice behind me, "there's Isabella Rossellini! God, for a woman that age, she's fucking beautiful."

I wanted to see what she looked like—this cretin who'd make a dig about a person's age, and in the next breath, use the F word within hearing of complete strangers. When I turned, I found myself gasping. "*Annie?*"

The girl blinked with rapid-fire lizard eyes that seemed to look me up, down, and sideways. "*Garner?* Is that really you? Oh my gosh, this is sooo cool." She gave me a huge hug. "I would've never recognized you. You cut your hair, and my God"—she squinched up her small, angular face—"you've lost weight, haven't you?" For Anya Houghton, a walking eating disorder, this was the ultimate compliment.

"Maybe a little," I lied.

"A little?" She wiggled a bony finger. "Garner, you're like *this*! I swear, you're absolutely, drop-dead, unfuckingbelievably gorgeous," she said in a reverential hush. It made me wonder how bad I must've looked to her, a couple of years ago, when we first met, in the reconverted Bucks County mill that Dane Blackmoor once used as his studio.

"What are you doing here?" I asked—although her presence tonight, among this A-list elite, made a certain kind of sense; Annie had always managed to inveigle her way into the most interesting situations.

She tossed her ash-blond hair. "Oh, it's a long story—"

"I'll bet."

"Well, you know I've been working for Dane, right? Over in Paris?"

I didn't, but Annie went on anyway, her little eyes on fire. "Oh, Garner, it's soooo wonderful. You've got to come. The city is completely like..." Words failed her. "Well, God, it's—*Paris*. And I know all these cool places. We could have the best time together. Promise you will—"

I told her I'd see. I didn't want to spoil her evening by mentioning that her boss Blackmoor had moved all those miles away specifically to avoid me, and that maybe she should check with him before sending out a blanket invitation. Instead I said, "So who else went over there?"

"Well, Richard Lewan came for a while, but he quit," she said, talking of the apprentice sculptor who had worked for Dane. "Oh, and Roberto just left to live happily ever after in Amsterdam with some new guy."

"What about you? Still dating that soap opera actor?"

"God, no," she groaned. "After the second face-lift I said to myself, *Annie, what the hell are you doing with a man who's fixed every sagging part but his prick?*"

I looked around, praying that no one near us had heard. "You haven't changed a bit, Annie."

"*Au contraire.*" Her little lizard face realigned itself demurely. "The whole experience with Mr. All My Fucking Children turned me completely off men older than fifty."

"Which still leaves quite a segment of the Parisian population."

Annie beamed. "Actually..." she said, lowering her voice to the perfect level for juicy dish.

All at once, Annie Houghton's smile vanished and her bright eyes darkened. I followed her gaze toward one of the white-jacketed waiters. At first I thought her sudden distress came from the fact that he was carrying a tray of frosted cakes—a terrifying sight for someone like Annie—but eventually I realized Annie was staring at the man himself. "What's the matter?" I asked.

The waiter passed by, and some of the life came back into her face. "He looked like somebody— Forget it." Annie's thin shoulders shuddered. "I'm creeping myself out, that's all."

"Well, if he bothers you later," I joked,

"there are a couple dozen security men here who'll be more than glad to take care of him."

She smiled, and touched my hand, the one holding the champagne flute. "It's so good to see you, Garner," she said.

"Same here, Annie," I replied, thinking to myself, *Could this be it? Could this be the sign?* Granted, it was a little weak, but surely it meant something, running into—of all people—Dane's assistant, tonight. I tried to order my thoughts. There were a million and one things I wanted to ask.

At the front of the room, someone started tapping the podium mike. "Ladies and gentlemen," said an elegant man, who I assumed was Reed's publisher. "If you would take your seats—"

"Come on." I nudged Annie.

"You go ahead," she said, a little regretfully. "It's an SRO audience and I didn't come with a ticket, if you know what I mean."

"Look, Reed Corbin is a good friend of mine," I told her, "and to be honest, it would make me a wreck to have to sit up there with a smile plastered on my face, knowing how nervous he is. I'm much better off back here, where I can pace."

"You really like this guy, huh?" And her cunning little face posed the unasked question—a question about Dane Blackmoor, for which I had no answer. At least, at the moment.

The lights were dimming. "Go on," I said. "They're saving a seat right next to the podium for me."

"Are you sure?"

"Yes." I gave her a quick hug, and then said again, "Go."

I watched her scurry happily away. The publisher had already begun his introduction, calling Corbin "an advocate, an innovator, and a hero." Up on the dais, Reed looked pale and visibly nervous, not very heroic at all. I realized that Annie was right; Blackmoor or not, I really did like this guy.

"For many here tonight," the man was saying, "Reed Corbin is the person you called upon to help get you through your darkest moments. How gratifying it is, then, to be able to celebrate the publication of his wonderful new book, in this, his finest hour. Ladies and gentlemen, please join with me in welcoming the author of *The Fear Factor,* Mr. Reed Corbin."

The applause was enthusiastic. Reed shook hands with his publisher, who stepped off the dais, taking a seat in the front row next to Annie Houghton. When I craned my neck, I could see Mike Fedora's wide back next to Annie's skinny one.

"Good evening." Reed adjusted his glasses and cleared his throat. "You'll have to excuse me, I seem to be experiencing the fear factor..."

The audience laughed, and Reed moved closer to the microphone, suddenly confident and relaxed. "I know many of you have already read the book. A few of you were nice enough to say some kind words about it—words which I immediately, and quite shamelessly, put in big print on the back cover." More laughter. "Those of you who are, or have been, clients know my theories about the predictability of violence. So tonight, instead of talking about what I wrote, I'd like to tell you who I wrote the book for. Someone whose name doesn't appear in the opening acknowledgments."

My heart jumped to my throat, then dropped to my shoes. I thought, *If he says Garner Quinn, I'll die.* But to my relief, Reed Corbin went on, "I wrote this book for a ten-year-old boy. I don't know his name, but I can tell you about him. He's living at this very moment in a house, or an apartment, or a trailer somewhere in the United States, and he's living in fear. Fear of doors that open and slam in the night. Of raised voices and thrown chairs. Of threats, and slaps, and those moments of hushed, terrified silence that he knows—from long experience in his short life—means that things are about to escalate to another level."

Corbin leaned forward on the podium. "If I close my eyes, I can see him. I can listen to him, listening—for the next signal, the next sign. In his head, that little boy is predicting the level of violence to come...sifting and correlating evidence in much the same way my firm's PREDICT system does."

He cleared his throat again. "Friends, this is where it all starts. Every killer, stalker, assassin, and psychopath I've met or studied knows that fearsome place—the little boy, and those steps in the unspoken dance of cruelty.

"I myself lived in that place, but thanks to

some very special people I ran into along the way, I was able to take the hard lessons I'd learned and make something good out of them. I was one of the lucky ones." Reed smiled shyly. "And that's why I wrote this book. For that ten-year-old boy and the folks around him. To let them know they can use their fear—not as a justification for cruelty in the future, but as a way to survive *right now.*

"Because, although the world we live in is an increasingly dangerous place, when it comes to violence, we all have an inner voice." And here his grew raspy with emotion. "And we also have a choice."

This time the applause was thunderous. Corbin waited it out, looking grateful but a little embarrassed. After a moment he held up a hand. "I have a stack of books up here to sign, but before I'm allowed to do it, they tell me there are a few messages from some folks who couldn't be here."

The lights dimmed further. On the projection screen, Madonna sent kisses and positive thoughts to her "knight in shining armor," Reed Corbin. *Otherwise known as the man I'm going to sleep with tonight.* I smiled back at her.

Tom Cruise and Nicole Kidman sent their videotaped best wishes, as did two senators and the director of the FBI. During this last testimonial, I headed toward the champagne, mouthing silent Excuse me's to the other standees I passed.

Once the tape was over, the lights brightened again. Reed moved to the end of the banquette where there was a long box. Yankee hitter

Don Mattingly had sent him a baseball bat, with a note to the effect that, when Corbin was calling it, he was always "safe." The audience laughed appreciatively.

A look of boyish surprise passed over Corbin's face. He picked up another box and shook it. It was a flat wooden case with a flip-up top. I remember thinking it was probably the President's commendation and that Madeleine Garth had wisely decided to save it for last.

I was sipping champagne when the explosion occurred. The initial blast sent a shock wave of heat and sound—first this incredible bang, then the awful, overlapping, high-pitched aftermath of terrified screams and shattering crystal. One second, Reed was standing on the stage opening the lid of a box; I took a sip of champagne, and suddenly Reed and half the stage were gone, buried under a pile of smoking rubble.

People began running toward the back of the room, knocking over tables that hadn't been uprooted by the blast, beating their way toward the escalators. I rushed forward, fighting against the panicking tide. The bomb had taken a big chunk out of the dais, blowing the podium right off the stage. Shards of glass and broken crystal were everywhere.

I started calling Reed's name. One of Corbin's IAD men caught me by the shoulder. "Don't go up there," he told me. "There's nothing you can do." I shrugged him off, and seeing my resolve, he began wading through the wreckage with me. We passed two men half carrying a woman. Her face was black with soot, she had a huge gash on her forehead, and she was making a low keening wail.

A well-known tennis player spotted us. "You security?" He grabbed the IAD man's arm, panting breathlessly. "There's a couple really hurt up front. One of them is stuck under the podium. If you give me a hand, I think we can pull him out."

I followed along behind them, and then stopped.

Annie Houghton was lying facedown and motionless with a jagged shard of glass in her back. Mike Fedora slumped between the stage and the first row of seats, as though in that final moment he'd been trying to shield the girl and still get to Corbin. The pedestal of the podium rested on top of his chest.

"It looks like he's still alive," cried the tennis player. By now several IAD men had made their way to the spot. Three of them carefully began removing the debris, preparing to lift the huge Lucite stem off Fedora. Another one, a young guy whose face I recognized, shouted, "I'm going up!"

In a state of shock I began moving after him. Smoke hung in the air, and glass covered the floor like gravel. The bomb had singed a hole right through the projection screen, and propelled the banquette back at least ten feet, smashing it into one of the crystal display cases. Corbin's young man stepped cautiously, clearing a path as he went. He stooped to upend a jagged piece of something, part of the banquette maybe, or the back of a display, and I heard him say, "Oh God, no," then, "Oh, Jesus."

It suddenly occurred to me that this was the guy who'd been manning the gatehouse at Forked Brook on the morning of my visit there. His name was some tool—Hammer? No, *Mallet*—and in that same moment, I saw Reed's arm protruding from the pile of twisted metal, glass, and wood. His hand had been blown off. Bits of ceramic shard and nails made bloody stab wounds through his jacket.

A few feet away, one part of the crystal castle I'd admired less than an hour ago lay split down the middle by shrapnel. I walked over to the shattered sculpture and picked it up. *Goddam you, Blackmoor,* my dazed brain screamed. *I was waiting for a sign. But not this...not this...*

I started to cry. Mallet heard me. "Stay back," he commanded. I could tell he was working hard to compose himself.

"Please, I know him. I...I'm—" But I couldn't find the words to tell the young man who or what I was.

From behind me came the sound of a commotion. Glancing over my shoulder, I saw a mad rush of cameramen scrambling toward the dais. The *Front Cover* guy appeared to be in the lead. It seemed that the press had beaten out Matt Raice's backup team, as well as the bomb squad, who were only now advancing through the wreckage in their helmets and Kevlar suits.

The cameramen spread out, jockeying for

position. I dropped to my knees in front of Corbin's body. My eyes were tearing, my dress soaked in champagne and splattered blood, but unlike Reed—exposed and defenseless—I was still in one piece.

Suddenly, someone pushed past the cameras, elbowing through, shooing them back. Mercedes Fields had taken charge and she was angry. "Leave her alone!" Mercedes ordered, shielding me with her body. "Turn the cameras off! You hear me? I said, get back!"

PART TWO

PART TWO

We had to evacuate the building while the bomb squad determined whether or not there were more explosives on other floors—an eventuality I hadn't even considered. By the time I got outside, the entire section of Fifth Avenue between Fifty-sixth and Central Park had been blocked off, clearing the way for an armada of emergency vehicles, police cars, and fire trucks. The seriously injured were being loaded into ambulances; others were treated for cuts and symptoms of shock.

Corbin's men worked with the police, trying to calm people as they emerged from Tiffany's and organize them into groups. I went up to one and asked if he had heard any news about Mike Fedora.

"From what I understand, it's pretty bad."

"What about the young woman sitting next to him?"

He shook his head. "She never stood a chance."

A special area had been roped off for VIPs. Visibly shaken, and somewhat annoyed, the tattered celebrities huddled together while Tamara Ma did a quick head count. I walked by, opting for the anonymity of the nameless crowd.

Additional camera crews from all the local news stations had already begun to arrive. It occurred to me that I should call home and tell Cilda and Temple I was all right, but I couldn't find my purse. I'd probably left it on the dais. Near Reed.

A man in a tuxedo carrying a clipboard and wearing a Corbin, Inc., ID touched my shoulder. "Are you Garner Quinn?"

"Yes."

"Were you hurt in any way, ma'am?"

"No," I said. "I was in the back."

"We've arranged secure transportation for certain high-profile clients still on site, Ms. Quinn. Should you feel it necessary to leave, one of our people will take you wherever you want to go," he said. "But Mr. Raice said—if you're feeling well enough—he'd appreciate it if you stay a little longer and give your statement here."

"That's fine."

"I'll come back for you as soon as the bomb squad gives the okay. In the meantime, is there anything you need?"

"Could somebody make a call to Jersey for me, let my family know...?"

"That's being taken care of," he said. "I have the number right here." His eyes traveled up from his clipboard for the first time. "Are you sure you're okay, ma'am? You're shivering."

"I lost my shawl." It was such a stupid thing, given the situation, but it made me want to weep.

"I'll send somebody over with a blanket," he promised. I watched him walk away—one of the many kind, efficient security men who hadn't been able to save Reed Corbin's life.

The pressroom had been turned into emergency headquarters for Matt Raice's team, the

NYPD Intelligence Unit, the bomb squad, and the FBI. A pot of hot coffee and some leftover cake provided meager comfort to those invited guests still waiting to answer questions. The hired help—servers and waiters, members of the Tiffany staff—had been corralled into an area on another floor for interviews.

Except for a passing glimpse of an ashen-faced Matthew Raice, I hadn't seen anyone I knew. I sat down in a corner, and closed my eyes.

"You still breathing?" Mercedes stood over me, hands on her hips.

Normally, I would've come back with some wiseass remark, but the sight of Mercedes Fields sparked such an overflow of gratitude that instead I launched into an embarrassingly emotional—and rather incoherent—speech, thanking her for what she'd done by shielding me from the cameras.

Mercedes shrugged. "It's no big deal, Garner," she said. "I wouldn't ambush anyone at a moment like that."

"It was a big deal to me. I won't forget it, Merce," I insisted; and then I did something really stupid. "That interview you asked for? Whatever you want. You just let me know, and it's done."

Her face contracted like a muscle. "You're really something, Garner." The words seethed from her. "You can't stand to be indebted to me for one second, can you? What, does it disturb the unspoken equilibrium? The balance of kindness can only run one way—from the rich white girl in the big house, down to the rest of us? Well, let me clue you in." Her eyes flashed. "I'm not Kathianne, getting misty over some used dining room set. *And I'm not my mama either.*"

"Mercedes—" I reached out to stop her from walking away, but succeeded only in knocking over the Styrofoam container of coffee on the table next to me.

Mercedes stood there for a moment, watching me blot up the spill with a handful of napkins. I must have looked pathetic, in my dirty velvet dress, with the coarse woolen rescue blanket falling off my shoulders, because she took the wad of soggy paper from my hand. "Your teeth are chattering, girl," she said. "It's about time one of these idiots wrote up your statement and let you out of here."

She turned on her heel and strode purposefully away. In a matter of minutes, I knew, she'd be browbeating some detective. Mercedes would do that—not for me, but because it was in her nature to stand up for what was right. Anything more than that, I couldn't expect. The distance between us was simply too great.

I'd always assumed that the rift had its roots in an odd kind of sibling rivalry, a competition for Cilda's affection. Now I realized that explanation didn't cover it. *Open your eyes, Garner,* I could hear Mercedes chide. *Not everything in this world has to do with you.*

But sitting here, wrapped in a scratchy wool blanket, with Reed Corbin lying dead in the next room, it seemed altogether intolerable to believe as Mercedes Fields did—that the rift between us was predetermined; that it had been in place long before our births; that no matter how many clumsy attempts I made to bridge it, the vast gap between black and white would remain set and unbreachable.

If it was that kind of heartless, hopeless, arbitrary world I was sitting in—then, dammit, I didn't want anything to do with the world at all.

"Garner." I ran into Matt Raice in the hall, on my way to be interviewed. His tie was off and there were stains on his white shirtfront and sooty tracks down the sides of his face. "Keep me company for a minute." He beckoned me toward a quiet corner.

"What's the good news, Matthew?" I asked softly. "Tell me that there *is* some good news."

Raice shook his head, and I put my arms around him. The minute I did, his body started to heave with sobs. "I still can't understand how it happened. Christ, we went over every inch of this place. Oh God, it's all my fault. My own fucking fault..."

"Stop it," I said. "You know that's not true."

"I've had a bad feeling for weeks," he said, wiping his eyes with the back of his hand. "What am I going to do now, Garner? He was like a brother to me."

"I know." I touched his sleeve.

"I let Reed down." Matt clenched and unclenched his fists. "If I'd been on top of the

Petty case, this never would've happened. But I got too emotionally involved... God-dammit, PREDICT is the most sophisticated violence indicator in the world. We've got a file on every terrorist and assassin known to man, and yet these bastards walk in right under our noses—"

"You think it's the same group? The Fourth Freedom?"

Raice leaned up against the wall. "Looks like it," he said, "from the similarities in the bombs." I myself had wondered if there might be a connection, but I'd warned myself not to jump to conclusions. The flip side of the security business was danger. There were probably hundreds of unsavory characters with motives for wanting Reed Corbin dead—including any Walter Wozniak–style crazy hell-bent on publicly proving that violence can't always be predicted.

I broached another subject. "What about Mike Fedora?"

"They don't think he's going to make it," he said. "The girl sitting next to him was killed instantly."

Raice rubbed his mouth, choking back another surge of emotion. "Jesus. You know, when the call came over the radio, saying an unidentified woman up near the podium had been killed in the blast, I thought for sure it was you—"

"It could've been." I turned to him. "I knew her, Matt."

He faced me, slowly. "The one who died?" I nodded. "My God, Garner." He didn't seem to know what to say; then his expression changed. "She hasn't even been identified yet..."

"Her name was Anya Houghton. Annie," I said. "She was an office assistant for Dane Blackmoor."

"The sculptor?"

I'd left the blanket in the other room, and was starting to feel trembly again. "I met her at his studio a couple of years ago while I was researching a book. When Blackmoor moved to Paris, Annie went with him." I shrugged. "We hadn't spoken since. Until tonight."

Raice looked confused. "Did she say what she was doing here?"

"No. I only ran into her a few minutes before—" I glanced down at the floor. "Before the speeches began. She said something about not being able to sit with the invited guests, and so I told her to take my seat. At first she was reluctant, but I insisted..." I bit down hard on my lower lip to stop my teeth from chattering. "That's me—always willing to do a favor for a friend."

Matt put an arm around me. "Fuck this guilt," he said bitterly. "Fuck all of it. The worst thing is, I keep wanting to call Reed. Ask him what I should do next."

"Listen, Matt. This might have nothing to do with anything." I broke free and began to pace, trying to keep warm. "But Annie Houghton reacted pretty strangely to one of the waiters here tonight."

"What do you mean?"

"The guy just passed by carrying a tray, and Annie completely lost track of what she was saying. All the color drained out of her face. She was shook. When I asked her what was wrong, she shrugged it off. Said he looked like somebody—"

"Who?"

"She didn't explain. I probably wouldn't have given it a second thought, but under the circumstances, I thought you might want to run a check on the guy."

"Absolutely. Do you remember what he looked like?"

"Dark hair, dark complexion. In his late twenties, maybe thirty. About five eight or nine, one-fifty." I tried to picture the man, but his face remained hazy. Did he have a mustache? "To tell the truth," I admitted, "I was looking more at Annie, but I'm pretty sure I'd be able to pick him out if I saw him again."

"That's great," Matt said. "They've got the staff downstairs now. Let me see what I can find out."

A detective stuck his head into the corridor. "Ms. Quinn?"

Raice pressed my hand. "Stick around if you can. We may need you to make an ID later." I said I would, and went inside.

Special Agent Bob Barrow looked like a tough guy, but he handled me with kid gloves. "I understand that Reed Corbin invited you to attend the party this evening as his date," he said.

200

"I came as his guest." I made the subtle distinction.

"How did you know Mr. Corbin?"

I explained that I was a client of the firm and that, through our professional association, we'd become friends. Barrow acknowledged this with a knowing smile. He asked me if during the course of our *friendship,* Reed had given any indication that he felt his life was in danger.

"No," I said. "But I understood that his work brought him into contact with people who at any time could become violent."

The agent nodded. "What about tonight? Did you notice anything different about his behavior?"

"He was a little nervous—which was understandable. I also got the impression that he was worried about a case."

"Which one?"

"He didn't say specifically, but I assumed it had to do with Warren Petty."

Barrow made a note. "Anything else? Anything you noticed tonight that might be considered unusual?"

When I told him about Anya Houghton, Barrow's routine politeness sharpened to a fine point. "Could you spell that name for me?" he said, scribbling furiously. Next came a barrage of questions. Where was she from? Did I have any idea why her name wasn't on the guest list? Had she mentioned where she'd been staying in New York?

I suddenly realized how little I knew about

the young woman. "All I can say for sure," I told him, "is that for the past few years now she's worked for the sculptor Dane Blackmoor at his studio in Paris."

"And she never explained how she happened to have come all the way from France, just to crash a book party?"

Something in his voice put me on alert. "Are you suggesting—"

"I'm not suggesting anything, Ms. Quinn. I'm just trying to get this straight. Someone who lives and works in Paris shows up at a New York party, unexpectedly and alone—"

"Look," I said. "Anya Houghton turned up in all sorts of places. She was drawn to influential people—" I stopped, feeling as though I'd just made matters worse.

"And she worked as a sculptor's assistant?" Barrow raised an eyebrow.

"More like a gal Friday. In Blackmoor's office—"

Barrow exhaled with a whistle. "Judging from the labels on her clothes, the man must pay his office staff pretty well."

It was true; the plain beige pantsuit Annie had been wearing had probably set someone back at least a thousand bucks. "Annie dated older men with lots of money," I explained. "They spent a lot of it on her."

"Do you know any of their names?"

"One was an actor on a soap opera." I squirmed in the leather armchair. "Look, I'm telling you, it's pointless to concentrate on Annie. Besides, if she'd known a bomb was set to go off, why would she have taken a seat right up front?"

Barrow made another note, and I went on, "Something odd did happen while I was talking with her, though." I told him about Houghton's reaction to the waiter, and gave him the same general description of the man that I'd given Matt.

The agent didn't seem to process this information the way I'd expected him to. "She told you this waiter was someone she knew?" He frowned.

"No," I repeated. "Annie said he looked like someone..."

"Ah. *He looked like someone,*" Barrow echoed, writing some more. "And you never saw the man after that?"

I shook my head. "A minute later, the lights dimmed."

The agent leaned back in his chair. "And you invited Ms. Houghton to take your seat." As insensitive as it was of him to remind me, I looked him straight in the eye and said, "Yes."

Barrow made a few more notes; then he asked if I knew the name of Annie's next of kin. I told him no. He said he realized how trying (his word) this evening had been for me, and should anything else come to mind "pursuant to this inquiry," would I please give him a call?

I took his card. Before I could say my goodbye, Barrow's cellular rang; he signaled me to wait. His face remained impassive throughout the brief conversation.

"Does the name Alex Haver ring a bell?" he asked after hanging up.

"No. Who is he?"

"It appears he's the waiter who upset your friend," said Special Agent Barrow. "In fact, you two may have been the last people to see him. According to what I just heard, he's been missing in action since the bomb went off."

One of Corbin, Inc.'s security men was waiting out in the hall with my purse and wrap. A moment later Matthew Raice appeared. The shadow of beard stubble had reasserted itself on his face, but instead of making him look stylishly hip the way it usually did, he seemed older, frayed to the bones. "You hear about the waiter?" he asked in a low voice.

"Yes. What does it mean?"

"At the very least, we've got an unaccounted person on our hands," he replied grimly; then he straightened the shawl around my shoulders. "There's nothing more you can do here, Garner. Where are you staying tonight?"

It was a good question. I thought of Reed's key, tucked into the bottom of my evening bag, but I couldn't face walking into a strange, empty apartment alone. Besides, for all I knew, a team of detectives were over there now, searching the place.

I said, "I want to go home."

"I'll have someone take you."

"No, the drive will relax me," I said. "I'm wired for sound." Matt insisted that one of his men accompany me to the parking lot. We hugged, both promising to keep in touch.

On the way out, I passed Mercedes, cinching the waist of her trench coat while a nice-looking man in a gray suit stood holding her purse and her tote.

She flagged me down. "You're not heading back to Jersey now?"

"Yes, I am."

"That's ridiculous. It's after twelve. Here." She rummaged through her bag while the man was still holding it. "Take my key. You can get a fresh start in the morning."

I looked at Mercedes and the gray-suited man, who waited in a hushed but patient silence while the fate of his evening was decided. His stiff arms looped with Bottega Veneta and Vuitton, he resembled one of those metal stands you see in shops displaying expensive leather.

"Thanks anyway," I told Mercedes, feeling suddenly vengeful. "But you know how I can't stand to be indebted to you."

TWENTY-THREE

Like the careful man he was, Reed Corbin had left a letter detailing his final wishes. He wanted his organs to be donated and his body cremated; unfortunately, the manner in which he died made the first impossible and the second nearly unnecessary.

A few days after Corbin's death a memorial service was held at the Episcopal church in Tarrytown. Temple and Cilda both offered to take the drive with me, but I insisted I wanted to go alone. I didn't want to hurt their feelings with the truth—I needed a shoulder to lean on, but not a mother's or child's. I needed a friend's. One that was shoulder-level with my own.

Mercedes might've fit that bill, but I wasn't about to set myself up by asking.

By the time I got to Tarrytown, the streets around the church were already lined with cars. I managed to squeeze into a space two blocks away, locked the Volvo, and started walking. The wind scattered leaves along the sidewalks. November had arrived, and my blood felt watery thin, unready to face it.

At the front entrance, a funeral parlor hearse decked with a bower of autumn flowers formed a somber backdrop for camera crews as they recorded the faces of arriving mourners. I yanked down the brim of my hat and moved quickly past them.

Once I was inside, my knees buckled at sight of the funeral urn standing amid a spray of golden chrysanthemums. I played the awful game—picturing the Reed Corbin I knew, six feet of lean, rangy muscle, turned to cinder and ash. It was more than I was prepared to handle, so I forced my eyes away.

The pews were loosely packed. I noted the straight backs of Corbin's security squad peppered throughout the congregation. Others patrolled the narthex or stood beside the doors on either side of the altar rails. I took a seat in one of the back rows, blessed myself, and bowed my head. I wanted to pray for

Reed, but instead I found my attention drifting. *Who are all these people?* I wondered. Apart from his parents, who were dead, the only family Reed had ever mentioned was a brother—the irresponsible druggie, Mark, who lived in Amsterdam.

Discreetly, I craned my neck, trying to peer over the heads of tall men and hatted women. Matthew Raice sat in the first pew, close to the aisle, between a well-dressed gentleman with a shock of white hair and a very thin woman, both in their sixties, who I assumed were his mother and father. Dr. Raice had been Reed's mentor. I could tell by the defeated slump of the old man's head that he was devastated by this loss. Tamara Ma had positioned herself directly behind Matt; I saw her lean forward to whisper some words of comfort.

As my gaze wandered, I caught a glimpse of several famous faces, stoic behind tinted dark glasses. The majority of those who'd come to say goodbye to Reed Corbin appeared to be ordinary people. Many were women, my own age or younger, sitting alone or banding together in groups of four or five. These were the battered wives and girlfriends, the ones who had been terrorized by former lovers, or stalked by lunatics they'd never even met. It was almost possible to pick them out. A faint whiff of fear still clung to them like the vestige of some strong perfume.

From the belfry, the hour chimed.

"I will lift up mine eyes unto the hills," said the priest in a grand voice, *"from whence*

cometh my help." All around me heads bowed, but I kept mine stubbornly high, my eyes fixed on the small vase, in its place of honor.

"*The Lord himself is thy keeper; the Lord is thy defense upon thy right hand; So that the sun shall not burn thee by day, neither the moon by night.*" The priest read the words of the Psalm, and then invited the congregation to pray. Again I passed, angry with God for having failed to keep Reed Corbin as safe and protected as he had kept so many others, including me.

After the service, someone touched my sleeve. "Mr. Raice asked if he might have a word with you," a raw-faced IAD man said.

I glanced toward the front pew and saw Matt, still seated next to his parents, waiting patiently as the queue of mourners filed past the urn containing Reed's ashes. Once the crowd thinned, the guard and I made our way forward.

We passed Tamara Ma, who stopped to shake my hand. She appeared paler than usual, and her eyes were tinged with red. "How's everybody holding up?" I asked.

"Matt's a mess," she whispered. "Between trying to get to the bottom of this and keeping the firm going, he's got a lot on his shoulders. But I told him we'll do fine. Reed might've founded the firm, but it's always been a two-man operation. Matthew brings in most of our biggest clients, anyway."

It felt like a betrayal, listening to her talk about the corporate restructuring of Reed Corbin's dream while he lay in a heap of ashes only a few feet away. I offered her my condolences, and hurried away.

"Garner." Matt Raice rose as soon as he saw me. I kissed his cheek; his skin tasted of salt tears. "I'd like you to meet my father, Dr. Gerald Raice, and my mother, Mary." He stepped into the aisle, making the introductions. "Mom, Dad, this is Garner Quinn."

"Mattie told us you were a client." Mrs. Raice pressed my hand, her immense diamond ring cutting into my palm.

I turned to her husband. "Reed spoke so highly of you, Dr. Raice."

The white-haired man momentarily brightened. "He was like a son—" He stopped, his voice choked with emotion.

Two men in dark suits approached the altar. One carefully picked up the urn, the other lifted the spray of flowers. We stayed silent as they passed, and then Matt said, "Mother, maybe you should take Dad out to the car. I'll be with you in minute. I have something I need to discuss with Garner."

We shook hands again and I watched the couple walk slowly up the aisle, the old man leaning against his whippet-thin wife for support. "He's never going to get over this," Matt said, reading my thoughts.

"What about you?"

He lifted his shoulders in a halfhearted shrug and sat down on a pew. I sank down next to him. It had been days since I'd gotten any sleep. The hard wood felt like a mattress. "The good news is," Matt said, "they've upgraded Mike's condition from critical to serious. He has no memory of the blast, but at least he's conscious."

"That's great." I paused. "What's the bad news?"

"It turns out your friend Annie was staying at the Plaza."

I tensed. "What's bad about that?"

"The FBI found terrorist literature in her room."

"That's ridiculous," I cried. "What is that, anyway—'terrorist literature'? Some Harlequin romance set in Arabia?"

Raice said, "Religious and political pamphlets. Very extreme."

"I knew this girl, Matthew," I argued. "Annie was a party animal, not a political animal."

"Hey." He held up his hands. "Don't shoot the messenger, okay?"

"This is that FBI agent Barrow's idea." I tried to speak in a hush, but the empty church just threw my angry words back at me. "I told him it made no sense. If Houghton knew about the bombing, there's no way she would've walked up to that stage and taken a seat in the first row."

"What if she didn't know?"

"Come again?"

Raice leaned forward in the pew. "You admitted Annie had gotten herself involved with some wrong guys. What if one of them used her to unwittingly plant the bomb?"

"But if she'd been *duped,* then why was she carrying around political handouts from the Middle East?" I countered. "You can't have it both ways. It doesn't make sense."

"I see what you mean." Matt sighed, then checked his watch. "Look, we're heading over to Forked Brook for an informal ceremony. Anybody who knew Reed is invited to say a few words. Afterward, we'll scatter his ashes on the grounds. Why don't you come with me and my folks? I can always drive you back later."

"I can't." I stood.

"Garner—"

"I'm not good at these things, Matt," I said. *As if anybody was.*

We walked out of the church together. "I wish you'd change your mind," Matt said as we stepped into the cold November morning.

Most of the cars had already pulled away. A driver was standing by the open door of a black limousine. In the back seat I could see the pale silhouettes of Dr. Raice and his wife.

"Give him a good send-off," I whispered hoarsely, pressing Matt's hand. "Tell him that Garner says goodbye."

TWENTY-FOUR

I came home and slept for twenty-two hours straight. When I awoke, I felt weak and chilled to the bone. Cilda padded into my room just as she'd done when I was a child. "You're burning up," she said, touching her palm to my head.

She and Temple began playing nursemaid, bringing trays of tomato soup sprinkled with crumbled crackers, and cups of tea to wash down Cilda's bitter island remedies. They'd seen me this way once before—feverish and fastened to my bed—after Dane Blackmoor stole away like a thief in the night, with my heart tucked under his arm. Temple must've also made that connection.

"Do you believe that everybody has one person they're really meant for?" she asked, out of the blue, one late afternoon. Something in her face told me that this wasn't a question I should just blow off.

"Well gee, honey," I said. "The world is a big place. People come in and out of each other's lives all the time. Sometimes whether they end up together or not is just a matter of, um, timing—or fate."

She frowned. "Auntie Merce says everyone has a soul mate." The red flag went up; if this was something my daughter had already discussed with Mercedes, I definitely wanted in.

I drew my knees up, leaned back against the headboard, and patted the bed. Temple snuggled up beside me. "What do *you* think, Tem?" I asked.

"I think there are the group-date kind of guys, guys you might go out with for pizza, or if they asked you to slow-dance, it would be okay—like you and Reed Corbin." She spoke slowly, reasoning out her ideas. "Then there's the kind whose picture you'd want to keep next to you when you fall asleep."

I followed her eyes toward the small black-and-white Polaroid of Blackmoor on the bed-stand. "Oh, Tem, that's just an old..." I stammered. "It fell out of one of my pockets, and I happened to put it there—" I would've gone on that way, hemming and hawing, had I not remembered one of the cardinal rules of mother-daughter heart-to-heart talks: *It's never really about you; it's about them.*

Immediately, I backtracked. "You aren't by any chance keeping somebody's picture by your pillow, are you?"

Her smile managed to be both innocent and mysterious at the same time. "His name is David Wescott and he's a senior," my daughter told me. "And even though he thinks it's like verging on child abuse that you won't let me date for another year, he's cool with it, because he really likes me."

"How do you know that?"

"Because I *asked* and he told me, Mother," Temple scoffed. Was it really that simple? I wondered. At sixteen, my daughter certainly seemed to have it all figured out. She picked up Dane's picture and studied it under the light. "That girl Annie who got killed was a friend of his, wasn't she?"

"She worked for him, yes."

"Dane must be feeling as rotten as you. Why don't you go see him?"

"I can't just pick up and go to Paris, Temple."

"Why not?"

"There are a million reasons," I said. "Your grandfather's house is on the verge of being sold. I have the Wozniak thing—not to mention the fact that Max is bugging me for another book."

"Max is always bugging you for another book," Temple said with a jaded sigh. "And the stalker trial doesn't start for weeks. The guy's in jail, Mom, he's not going to bother us. It's a perfect time, if you ask me."

"Yeah, well," I teased, shifting the focus, "somebody has to be here to keep an eye on you and your pal David."

"What about Cilda? And Daddy and Candace, and Auntie Merce..."

I took the photograph from her and put it facedown on the bed table. "It's a lot more complicated than that, kiddo. There are a lot of issues—"

"Yeah, yeah." Temple swung her feet off the bed impatiently. "Dane told me."

I caught her arm. "Dane said something to you? When?"

"The day he left. I could tell he didn't want to go. I told him you loved him." My daughter looked me straight in the eye. "He said he knew, but that you'd always let too much other stuff get in the way to ever follow your heart." Temple shrugged her shoulders. "I guess he was right, huh?"

Early Sunday morning I called my friend Hogan. His voice sounded rusty, as if he hadn't used it in a while. "It's me. Are you alone?"

"Yeah." He yawned. "Sue and the kids went to Mass."

I'd figured. Hogan's wife, a devout Catholic, divided her time between daily church services and confession, mostly praying, I suspected, for the strength to go on in a marriage that had been rocky for years. Sue had once accused Hogan of being in love with me. I'd laughed when he told me that. Hogan had sheepishly chalked it up to a case of insane jealousy, but from that point on, we carried on our professional relationship in a sneaky, clandestine manner, like guilty lovers. "Look, I hate to ask," I said, "but is there some way we could get together? I need to talk."

Hogan coughed up phlegm for a solid minute. Then I heard him spit. "I've got a meeting in New York in the p.m. tomorrow. If I make it to your place by breakfast, I'm yours till noon."

I kicked the covers off and swung my legs out of bed. "Thanks, Hoge," I told him. "You're the best."

I'd known Hogan for years. When we first met he was a criminal profiler in the FBI's Behavioral Science Investigative Support Unit in Quantico. I was an already successful, but still wet-behind-the-ears, writer of true crime. We careened into each other with the force of two freight cars speeding toward the same point from opposite directions; yet somehow we managed to survive the crash, and go on to catch a brutal killer named Howard Beech.

Along the way, we discovered we liked each other. Immensely.

But in all that time, I'd never been introduced to Hogan's wife or his children, nor had he visited my home, or met my daughter. So seeing him standing in my doorway, with a box of Dunkin' Donuts tucked under his arm, on this bright, crisp morning, seemed strange to say the least.

"Jesus, Quinn, could you live any farther out in the sticks?"

I grinned. "Let me take your coat."

"I better keep it," he said, "for a quick getaway. You still haven't told me why you lured me out here."

"I ask," I corrected, leading him through the great room and into the kitchen. "I don't lure."

He gave me a look and said, "Whatever."

I took the doughnuts from him and tossed them on the counter. "Those things'll kill you. Cilda made muffins."

"I'll pass. When I'm with you, I need all the sugar and preservatives I can get." Hogan sat down at the table and stretched out his legs. A hint of a crisp, pin-striped dress shirt and an expensive silk tie peeked out from his trench coat.

I poured us both mugs of coffee. "How's Sue?"

"I told her the meeting was bumped up." He shrugged. "She probably didn't believe me."

"You *were* lying," I reminded, passing him a plate.

"You're going to lecture me about telling the truth?" My retired special agent friend laughed.

I took a muffin for myself. Hogan brought the doughnuts back to the table and opened up the box. Bright pink, white cream, and glistening chocolate—they looked like fat little women, decked out in frilly dresses. He picked out a glistening glazed number, saying, "Come to Papa," and afterward—Hogan's highest tribute—he sang, *Oh, baby...I like it like that!*

For fifteen minutes or so, we sat shooting the bull and sipping coffee. He asked about Temple, and I told him she was at school. He spoke of his own kids, the eldest of whom was already in college. We commiserated about the swift passage of time, and, as he always did, Hogan made me feel old.

He insisted on rinsing the plates and mugs and stacking them, with machinelike precision, in the dishwasher, saying Sue had programmed him to the task. Then he turned to me and said, "Okay, Quinn. Why don't you show me your ocean?"

I grabbed a jacket and we headed for the beach, climbing over the seawall and walking with our shoes on, the way year-round shore people did. The sky was blue and the waves rolled onto the sand with a little shudder, as though they were trying to shrug off the infringing cold. "This is beautiful," Hogan said.

"You should come up sometime in the summer," I said, "with the family."

He shot me a quizzical look, then reached out and ruffled my hair. "For a person so smart, you really are clueless, Quinn."

Not having a ready answer, I stared straight ahead and kept walking. After a few minutes, I was having difficulty keeping up with him. I called out, "I need a favor, Hogan."

"I know." He stopped short and we nearly collided.

"What happened to Reed Corbin..." I began tentatively. "Have they brought you in on it?"

"I've been consulting on the Petty thing," Hogan admitted. "I'm assuming it will be announced at this meeting that the two cases are connected."

"The girl who was killed, Annie Houghton, was a friend of mine."

"That I also know."

"Matt Raice says the FBI believes she had something to do with the bombing." I hoisted myself up onto the lower lip of the jetty.

Hogan took out a handkerchief, placing it flat on the rock, before he sat. "The missing waiter's name wasn't Alex Haver." In the open air, his voice sounded defeated and weary. "From the descriptions we have, in all probability he's a Jordanian named Abdul Amer. Very little is known about him other than that he was a student for at least a year in Paris. He managed to get into this country illegally from Canada. It appears he has some connection with a Muslim radical already convicted of terrorist activities."

"A member of The Fourth Freedom?"

"No." Hogan shook his head, with something like disgust. "This Freedom cell must be an offshoot. Before Petty's jet blew up, we'd never even heard of them."

"How can you be sure they're the same group that killed Corbin?"

"I'm not going to go through the forensics, Garner." He stood, shaking off his handkerchief and putting it in his coat pocket. "I shouldn't even be talking to you. All I'm going to say is that Abdul Amer wasn't working alone. He needed someone else, innocently or not, to plant that box there. Anya Houghton fits the profile of the kind of woman these assassins use—young, attractive, a risk taker, someone who can easily blend into an upscale crowd."

"I was watching her face when she spotted this guy Amer," I argued. "He scared the shit out of her, Hogan. And you're telling me they were partners?"

"I'm not telling you anything. I'm not even here, remember? I'm at a meeting in New York. Just ask my wife." We fell into step together again, heading back toward the wall.

"It doesn't feel right to me," I grumbled.

"Forget it, Quinn," Hogan advised. "You can't solve this one. Your friend Corbin's death wasn't a typical murder, it was a warning from a bunch of Middle Eastern terrorists who wanted to send a message that no matter how rich, or smart, or careful you might be—nobody's safe." He grabbed the back of my neck, swivelling my face until I looked at him. "Watch my lips, Garner. This is way, way over your head."

Hogan turned down Cilda's invitation to lunch, warding off her wrath through song— a rendition of "Dancing in the Dark," which ended with him spinning and dipping the old woman across the kitchen tiles. "Ooo-ee, Mr. O'gan," she panted, shooing him away. "Take your bad doughnuts and your wild dancing and go 'ome!"

I walked him out to his rental car. "Your friend is dead, Garner," he said. "Sooner or later the FBI will close in on Amer and the chips'll fall where they may." Of course, he knew as well as anyone that patience had never been my strong suit.

"Keep your head down, Quinn," he said as he started up the engine.

"Watch your back, Hogan," I mouthed, tapping on the front windshield and blowing him a kiss.

TWENTY-FIVE

Peggy Boyle called the next morning as I was heading out the door. "Oh, Mrs. Quinn." She sounded exasperated. "I hope this isn't a bad time."

"Actually," I told her, "I'm on my way to New York." After a little arm-twisting Matt Raice had agreed to meet me at Reed's apartment.

"Well, I'll be brief," Peg said, undaunted. There was a small dramatic pause on the line before she announced, "The McCarthys' marriage is over."

At first, I drew a blank, and then it came to me. "The couple interested in the house? I thought you said they were signing a contract today."

"Not anymore," sighed Peg. "Now they're getting a divorce."

What kind of a world are we living in, I wanted to scream, *where crazy men can stalk their favorite crime writer, and terrorists set bombs in jewelry stores, smashing wonderful people into bits like pieces of broken crystal, and couples shop for multimillion-dollar shorefront mansions on their way to divorce court?*

Out loud I said, "You're kidding."

Peggy Boyle quickly showed what a true Diamond Salesperson of the Year was made of. "I told them it was their loss." I wasn't sure whether she referred to the relationship or the house. She went on, building momentum, "I've already visualized that Sold sign out in front by Thanksgiving—now all I have to do is make it happen. Visualization is the first step toward actualization, Mrs. Quinn."

I visualized hanging up the phone. It must've worked because a second later, Peg Boyle told me she had a closing to attend, wished me a pleasant ride into the city, and said goodbye.

I'd purposely left an hour to spare before my appointment with Matthew Raice. It was just enough time to stop by St. Luke's Hospital to say hello to an old friend. When I walked into the room, I thought the patient was sleeping, but a second later his eyes flickered open.

"Hello, Mike Fedora, like the hat."

"Thank God," he rasped in a weak voice. "I thought it was that lady with the magazine cart coming by again. I think she has a crush on me."

"Can you blame her?" I gave his bandaged and battered body the once-over. "Just look at you."

Fedora smiled, and patted the bed. "C'mere. How are things down the Jersey shore?"

"Not so good," I said.

Under the skullcap of gauze, Mike's eyes filled with tears. "Hell of a thing to happen," he said.

"Is any of it coming back to you?"

"Not much. I remember the publisher talking. A girl sat down in the seat next to me." The old man's eyes turned wistful. "For a second I thought it was you. Then Reed stood up—" Fedora grimaced in pain.

After a moment, I prompted him again. "What about earlier? Reed had been expecting a phone call, hadn't he? You came over to him before the program started and whispered something in his ear."

"I did?" He looked confused. "Reed wanted me to look out for his special guests. Madonna...she didn't come..." His voice trailed off. "Thank God that girl wasn't you, Garner. Hell of a thing, though."

"I brought you candy." I put a small shopping bag on his bedside table. "And there's homemade cookies from Cilda, and Temple made a card."

"Thanks." He found my hand. "You know, Reed really had his cap set on you. I knew that boy for a lotta years. There was always some woman chasing after him, but no—he had his work and he had his standards. Then you came along, he says to me, 'Hey, Mike, I think this is the one.'"

For the first time since Corbin was killed, I started to cry. I curled up on that hospital bed, with Mike Fedora's big, bandaged hand patting my hair, and carried on as if my heart would break, for a man I never even loved.

Reed's doorman recognized my name immediately. He said Mr. Raice was waiting, and that I should go right up. I took the elevator to the fourth floor. Number 405 was at the end of the hall. Before I had a chance to ring, Matt opened the door.

The change in his appearance shocked me. Since the funeral service, he'd dropped at least ten pounds. Inside his shirt collar his neck looked like a wrung chicken's, and his unshaven cheeks sank into a concave hollow. "I could kill you," he said, "for talking me into this."

"I won't ask how you're doing." I walked past him and into the living room. Reed's apartment was much as I'd pictured it—sparsely furnished, but elegant in an understated sort of way. Other than a few, dramatic Oriental pieces, most of the decor had that arty-but-functional MoMA style. I sat down on a flat, backless leather sofa with fifties-era peg chair legs. Matt Raice lowered himself into the matching chair, gingerly, as if every part of his body hurt. "Refresh my memory," he said. "Why the hell are we here?"

I took Corbin's key out of my pocket and tossed it. "I wanted to return this."

"Next time, Garner"—a faint smile played over his lips—"do me a favor and use Fed Ex."

"I know I'm a pain," I admitted. "I just had to see the place."

Matt's eyebrows shot up. "You mean this is your first time?"

"I was supposed to meet him here the night of the book party," I said lightly, "only things didn't work out." I stood up. "Is it all right if I look around?"

"Be my guest." Raice put his feet up on the leather ottoman, watching me. "But if you're searching for some Garner Quinn true crime clues, forget it. Like I said on the phone, the feds already went through here with a fine-tooth comb. Then a team of our guys took a pass. There was nothing unusual. No dark premonitions in Reed's computer journal, no hastily scrawled messages, nothing."

"What about the note he was scribbling on the podium before the speeches started? Did you find it?"

"I'm afraid there's no delicate way to put this, Garner. When we finally found him under all that wreckage—" Raice stopped. "Let's just say, if there had been a note in Reed's pocket, it's cinder and ashes now, like the rest of him."

For a long moment we stayed silent; then I crossed to the bamboo bookcases. Reed's shelves were stocked with scholarly texts— sociological tracts dealing with the issues of domestic violence; government reports on crime and terrorism; psychological case studies; treatises on a variety of sociopathic disorders; manuals outlining state-of-the-art security technologies; computer workbooks; a few self-help and personal-growth best sellers.

"Pretty dry reading," I commented.

"That's our boy." Matt smiled sadly. "All work and no play. Forever putting other people's lives ahead of his own. And for what?" It was a chilling echo of Dane's last words to Temple, something about the stuff I let get in the way that prevented me from following my heart.

Matt's eyes darted furtively toward his watch. "I know you have to get back," I said. "Could I just take a peek at the bedroom before we go?"

He got up with exaggerated difficulty. "I wouldn't do this if the boss wasn't so fond of you."

"You're the boss now," I reminded him.

Matt shook his head, his expression serious. "Once a second banana, always a second banana. Everybody knows that, Garner." He snapped on the hall light and I caught a glimpse of a bronze-tiled bathroom. "I'm just the poor fuck who got left holding the bag."

He opened the door at the end of the hall and hit the switch. Reed's bedroom was luxuriously carpeted, with expensive recessed lighting. An antique Chinese chest of drawers stood on one wall, a desk and a chair on the other. The futon was on a raised platform at the center of the room. "You really think you're going to uncover some piece of information that all of us big, bad professionals have overlooked?" Matt Raice's eyes followed me as I walked from spot to spot.

"Not really."

"Then what's this about?"

"I keep thinking about something Reed said when I called him from the car before the party that night. The connection was lousy, but I remember him saying he'd been up all night, that he'd been going over, I don't know, a file maybe, or some papers—"

"The manifesto." Matt nodded. "We already confiscated it."

"What manifesto?"

"The Fourth Freedom's ranting and—take it from me—nearly indecipherable statement of intent, telling how they planned to systematically undermine the U.S.'s sense of domestic security." Raice sounded disgusted. "It was mailed anonymously to the FBI after Petty's jet crash. They released it to us the day before the book party. That must've been what Reed was referring to when you called. I was up that same night, poring over it myself."

"Oh." I couldn't help being disappointed. "I suppose the next thing you're going to tell me is that the feds found a copy in Annie Houghton's hotel room."

"Sorry, Garner." Matt's eyes were sympathetic, but already I was looking past them, at a coatrack just beyond the door. A single hat dangled from its wooden arms—a baseball cap with the letters IAD embroidered on the brim. I took the hat and sat down with it, on the step ledge of the platform.

"All of Reed's horses and all of his men..." I put the cap up to my face. He hadn't even left a scent behind. But then, he was such a clean man. "I need a glass of water," I said.

Matt walked me down the hall, through the living room, and into the small kitchen. As I was running the faucet his beeper went off.

"Go ahead." I gave him a weak smile.

"I'll be in the living room, if you feel like you're going to faint." He managed a grin. "If you're going to barf, you're on your own."

"You're a pal."

Reed's glasses were arranged according to height and function. I filled up a tumbler with tap water and drank it. Still a little wobbly, I sat on one of the padded breakfast stools. A copy of *The Fear Factor* was on the counter, facedown, under the wall-mounted phone. I ran my palm across the back cover, caressing it all the way from Blackmoor's typeset praise to Reed's unsmiling picture. Oddly enough, I could feel small indentations in the smooth, glossy surface.

I scrambled off the stool, my eyes roaming around the immaculate kitchen. In a drawer I found several sharpened No. 2 pencils, but nothing to write on. I searched through the storage shelf, which had been well stocked with plastic garbage bags, rolls of aluminum foil, Saran wrap, and wax paper. I ripped a piece off the latter and went back to Reed's book.

While my left hand held the thin, waxy paper flat against the jacket, my right swept the side of the pencil point up and down, in much the same way as an artist would shade a drawing. Amid the sea of gray graphite, a name and a number appeared: Adrian Nadeau, 01 42 71 14 33. Underneath them, was one more word. *Paris.*

Okay, Blackmoor, I hear you, I muttered to myself. *I give up. You win.*

Raice was folding up his cellular when I came into the living room. "I've got to get back to the office, Garner," he said.

"Take a look at this." I waved the wax paper in front of his nose.

"What—?"

"I rubbed it off the back of the book he had on the counter. Reed must've been leaning on it when he wrote this name down."

"Adrian Nadeau." Matt frowned. "Paris."

"Does it mean anything to you?"

"No," he said. "But I'd have to check with Tamara to be sure. Over the years, we've built up a pretty extensive list of international contacts."

I went over to the sofa and took a pad from my purse, writing out the name and number and handing it to Matt. "Check it out," I said.

"Will do." Raice tucked it into his jacket. I stood near the bookshelves while he went through the apartment, shutting off lights

228

and closing doors. When he returned, he said, "Look, Garner. I want you to promise you'll stay out of this. If—and we're talking a big if—there's a connection between that name and the Fourth Freedom group, things have to be handled very carefully, you understand?"

"I understand."

I stood in the hall, watching him lock Reed's front door. "This isn't an ordinary murder investigation," Matt went on, echoing Hogan's words. "It could have international implications."

"I realize that," I said, as we walked toward the elevator.

"Then how come I get the feeling I'm wasting my breath?" He hit the button and an elevator car opened immediately.

"I have to go to Paris."

"Fuck me." Raice leaned heavily against the mirrored wall of the elevator, and closed his eyes for the length of the descent.

The elevator opened and we stepped into the marble foyer. "I swear I won't do anything to interfere with the investigation. This trip is strictly personal." Which was mostly the truth, I thought, if I was granted a little leeway on the "strictly" part.

"You can't go," Raice said suddenly. "The Wozniak trial starts in a couple weeks. You're set to testify."

"I'll be back in plenty of time for that," I assured him. Reed's doorman held open the door. Once we emerged onto the busy sidewalk, I grabbed Matt's arm. "I need closure on this thing with Annie. Dane Blackmoor might have some answers."

"So call him up on the phone, Garner. They do have phones in France."

"It's not so simple," I said. "There's more to it than just Annie."

"You have a history with this guy, don't you?" Matt searched my face.

"Yeah. That's the bad news." I reached over and patted his scruffy cheek. "The good news is, you'll have me out of your hair for a while."

TWENTY-SIX

From the start, I knew it would be a gamble. Three was either going to be the charm, or the third strikeout.

I'd been to the City of Light twice before. Once on a midsemester break from college, when I discovered that the R word in *April in Paris* wasn't romance, but rain. The second time was on my honeymoon. I rest my case.

In theory, I was supposed to have slept on the plane, but nervousness kept poking me in the ribs and nudging me awake. I'd done all the mental math—the pluses and minuses of the eight-hour flight divided by the six-hour time difference—to no avail. My body sent out warning signals that its store of adrenaline and anxiety was just about used up. And yet, flying into Orly on such a clear November morning, I could almost believe that this time I'd get it right.

A yellow Citroën taxi was waiting at the curb when I emerged from the airport. The driver, who'd given me only a sullen nod when I told him where I was going, cooed and sent great, smacking kisses through the air to the huge black poodle sitting on the front passenger seat as he drove. It was still very early when we reached the outskirts of Paris. A few cafés and wine bars had already opened; other proprietors were washing down the sidewalks in front of their businesses.

Using a rather skewed logic, I'd opted to stay in the same hotel where I'd spent part of my honeymoon. Located on a lovely street on the Ile St-Louis—one of two small islands floating in the Seine at the very center of Paris—it was gracious in an old-world sense. I figured that it would give me a lift each morning just to wake up in one of the sunlit rooms, and count my blessings that I wasn't there with Andy.

Postcard to my agent:

Dear Max,
By now Stacy will have told you the news. Please don't be angry— I need some more time before I can commit to another book. It's like spring here, only not raining. I'll bring back a peace offering—
Garner

Mr. Max Shroner
Shroner Literary
Associates
708 Third Avenue
New York, NY 10017

231

My room was small, but nicely furnished. Through one of its long windows I had a charming view down the rue St-Louis-en-l'ile; through another, I could see the flying buttresses flexing from the east facade of Notre-Dame, like the spiny wings of some great prehistoric bird.

A few minutes after I arrived, the proprietress came to my door with a breakfast tray of warm croissants, fresh butter, marmalade, and hot coffee—which tasted especially wonderful in the soup bowl–sized cup. "I don't do this many times," the woman told me. "Only because you are Irish, *oui*?" I smiled and said *oui*, afraid that if I told her I was fourth-generation American she might take the food away.

After breakfast I fought the almost irresistible urge to sleep by taking a shower and washing my hair. I waited until ten-thirty to place a call to Blackmoor's studio.

"*Bonjour*," said a cheerful voice.

"*Je voudrais parler à Monsieur Blackmoor, s'il vous plaît*," I said, carefully reciting the line I'd practiced.

The woman responded in a flurry of fast French. "I'm sorry." I gave up without a fight. "Do you speak English?"

"*Oui*," she replied. "Monsieur Blackmoor is away from the 'ouse this morning. Who shall I say is calling?"

"My name is Garner Quinn—"

The woman cut me off. "Yes. Yes, I see. The American writer. When I begin this job, the girl who trains me says that perhaps one day Garner Quinn telephones, and no matter what the circumstances, she must be put right through."

I could almost hear Annie giving her those instructions. It made me want to laugh and cry at the same time. I said, "If I could just leave a message—"

"*Mais non,*" the secretary said. "Dane is all day in Montparnasse. I am going there later too. You would like to meet me, perhaps, at, um, three o'clock this afternoon? I will take you to him myself."

Suddenly I wasn't so sure. "You'd better check with Mr. Blackmoor first."

"I cannot, um, communicate with Dane right now," the young woman said. "It will be good, I think. Not to worry." She told me the address was 1 Place Denfert-Rochereau.

"Walk past the barricades," she said. "Tell them you are looking for Nicole. I'll be waiting inside." It was only after I'd hung up that I realized I probably should've asked Nicole what she looked like; then I reminded myself that if she worked for Blackmoor, odds were she'd be young, attractive, and dressed in black.

I knew if I stayed in my room I'd fall asleep. It was a short walk to the Pont St-Louis, the bridge that connects Ile St-Louis with the oldest part of Paris, the Ile de la Cité. The streets around Notre-Dame were packed with tourists and locals, making the most of the warm, sunny weather. For a moment I considered joining their ranks, but in my present sleep-deprived state, tackling the huge cathedral would've been tantamount to climbing Everest. I decided to leave it for another day.

By the time I reached the forbidding walls of the Préfecture de Police, I was beginning to feel hungry again. I flagged down a woman, asking her in halting French if she knew of a café in the area. She waved me off and hustled away. I had no choice but to keep on walking. The police headquarters stretched ahead endlessly, dreary and gray. I could no longer get my bearings on the pocket street map I was carrying.

A balding man in a light overcoat passed by. *"Monsieur—"* I held out my map, but he just shook his head.

Then I glanced up and saw a vision—a tall spire soaring against the blue sky. After the flat, dull facade of the police building, the effect was almost magical.

"Qu'est-ce que c'est?" I stopped another woman.

"Sainte-Chapelle." She shrugged.

Tucked away shyly on the far side of the island, Sainte-Chapelle seemed like the lacy virgin bride of the powerful Notre-Dame, as if the cathedrals were betrothed to each other in some otherworldly, eternal sense. I walked through the front portals. A spill of colored light sifted through the stained-glass kaleidoscope of the massive rose window. There were a lot of people moving up and down the aisles. I followed along until I found an empty prayer railing. Under this arching, star-studded vault, I knelt down and lit a candle for Reed Corbin and Anya Houghton.

Postcard to my family:

Hi guys,
Well, now I can see why
Blackmoor feels at home
here— the average
Parisian is as arrogant as
he is. Seriously, though, the
city is a big kid's toybox.
Next trip, you're both com-
ing!

                Love, Me

MISS TEMPLE MATERA &
MRS. CILDA FIELDS
1 PENINSULA POINT ROAD
TWO RIVERS, NJ 07701
U.S.A.

It took me longer than I'd like to admit to get dressed. After a few tries, I settled on a deep red Edwardian-cut jacket, a white shirt, a long brown skirt, and brown leather boots. Then I knotted a man's silk tie around my neck and put on a brown cloche hat. On the pink-and-green-plaid coast of the Jersey shore, a person might end up getting hung as a witch for wearing such a get-up, but I was in Paris, and I'd waited a long time for this moment; I wanted to make an impression.

I took a taxi to Montparnasse. The driver, a Middle Easterner, whose French was only negligibly better than his English, seemed polite and friendly, but when I pointed out that the best route wasn't through the Arc de Triomphe, he took both hands off the wheel and smacked his head, as if my destination had only then become clear to him. "Ahh, Montparnasse...!" he cried.

"*Oui,* Montparnasse," I said, mentally subtracting a few centimes from his gratuity.

It wasn't until he turned onto the boulevard Raspail—a street I recognized from my pocket map—that I relaxed enough to appreciate the surroundings. We passed a huge cemetery. Unlike the rolling green burial grounds of the United States, this one was divided into rigid sections. Several elaborate tombs soared above the more common plots. My driver turned his head, puckered up his lips, and pointed. It took me a moment to understand—we were passing the famous cubist sculpture *The Kiss,* which showed a primitive couple in a passionate embrace.

"Okay, *ça y est!*" said the driver when we finally reached 1 Denfert-Rochereau, *"Les catacombes."*

The catacombs? I thought. There must be some mistake. But once I saw the film trailer, and the paparazzi and curious onlookers pressing against the barricades, I knew that I'd come to the right place. I gave the enterprising driver a bigger tip than he deserved, and elbowed my way into the crowd. A muscular young man in a dark suit stood out in front. He had ears pierced in so many places they appeared to be made of silver, like bionic mechanisms grafted to his head. *"Est-ce que Nicole est là?"* I asked.

"Are you Garner Quinn?" he replied in English.

"Yes."

"Come this way." He led me through the front entrance. "Watch your step," he advised.

He should have said steps, because there were about a hundred of them, winding downward. With each twist and turn, the passage grew darker and colder—a clammy kind of cold that seeped through clothing and got under skin. Eventually, the steps bottomed out into the mouth of a tunnel.

"I have to go back," my muscular guide said. His earlobes glinted in the half-light, like a cluster of stars. "Nicole and the others are a quarter of a mile ahead." He gestured toward a sign. It said: *Arrête! C'est ici l'Empire de la Mort.* Even with my rudimentary French, I could translate the warning—*Stop! This is the Empire of the Dead.*

"Wait," I called to the young man. "What's going on here, anyway?"

"I thought you knew." He turned, shrugging his massive shoulders. "It's a television shoot. Blackmoor's doing a commercial."

For a second I just stood there, listening as the man's footsteps grew fainter, then disappeared. Blackmoor was making a commercial. In the clammy dark, I almost laughed. For what? Mountain Dew? Cheez Doodles? Pepé Le Pew's Mortuary?

I pulled down the narrow brim of my hat, took a last look at the grim welcome, and walked into the Empire of Death.

TWENTY-SEVEN

The bones in these catacombs didn't belong to particular bodies.

There were no full skeletons, no picked-clean corpses in repose. Remains had been categoried by type, then stacked and piled. Jawbones mutely jabbered against jawbones. Femurs lined up like the peg legs of pirates. The flat disks of vertebrae became poker chips in a fixed game of cosmic poker. Skulls, blank-eyed and yellow, formed crumbling pyramids.

Death here was starkly impersonal. Leg bones of saints coupled with sinners'. The extraordinary and the barely ordinary looked exactly alike.

To put it mildly, it made you think twice about your own mortality.

After about a hundred yards the tunnel divided. I stayed to the right, following the soft, reverential whisper of a Gregorian chant. Up ahead, the catacomb widened. Arcs of artificial light cut eerie haloes out of the darkness. A film camera mounted on a pedestal dipped and swiveled through a spidery web of cables and electrical wiring. About a dozen people stood, as still as cardboard cutouts, blocking my view of the rest of the scene.

One of them, a female, turned around and waved. "Garner?" She mouthed my name. When I nodded, she beckoned me closer.

Nicole *was* young and dressed in black, but with her heavily browed eyes, aquiline nose, and thin lips, she couldn't really be considered pretty. Still, there was an assurance in her movements, and in the unfussy way her hair had been pulled back into one long braid, as if to say, *Look at me, I know exactly who I am.*

She whispered into my ear: "Dane doesn't know you are here." Her skin gave off a warm scent of wine and garlic in the cold, musty air.

"Maybe I should—"

Nicole put a finger to her lips, pushing me forward, into a small space between the shoulders of the other observers.

This catacomb had been decorated in a nightmarish mosaic. Some warped, creative hand had fashioned shapes out of the remains— a heart made of skulls, a star-burst cluster of ribs, a crazy tibia-spoked wagon wheel. The Gregorian chant seemed to waft out of the walls of the tunnel itself. And in the midst of all this— surrounded by cameras and lights and a scalloped backdrop of human hipbones—was Dane Blackmoor.

Dressed in black, his face turned away from me, he was in the act of creating one of his plaster cast sculptures. A model sat on a chair in front of him. The long white dressing gown she wore fell in folds around her comely body. But at this point, her face remained a provocative mystery. Other than two straw-sized holes under her nostrils, the model's entire head was encased in hardening plaster.

Blackmoor crouched like a cat, never taking his hands off her—smoothing, shaping, caressing her jawline with the heel of his palm. Behind him, a clothesline fluttered with long, wet, white bandages. Every once in a while he reached up and took one, swiftly working it with his fingers until it formed another layer of the plaster mask.

"That's the director," Nicole whispered, pointing toward a short man with long blond hair. "He is very avant-garde, you know? Very stylish and smart with the editing."

"What's the commercial for?" I whispered back.

"Some financial company. Creation out of the ruins. Birth, death." The girl shrugged. "It's all very conceptual."

No kidding, I started to say, but just then Blackmoor turned and the first clear sight of him knocked the wind out of me. The harsh television lights softened his face some, making him appear younger, and more conventionally handsome, than he actually was. Over the years, the old wounds—the broken nose, the wandering scar on his chin—had faded. I used to fancy, though, I could catch a glimpse of these past hurts, at odd times and in certain lights, looking into his eyes.

Nicole nudged me. "Watch this."

If I'd been inclined, I could have told her that I'd seen Blackmoor work before. It was no surprise to me when he picked up the mat knife, and with a rock-steady grip, proceeded to slice a seam down both sides of the model's head until the hardened cast fell into two perfect pieces in his hand.

Quite unexpectedly, it was the sight of the model's face that made me gasp.

Under the coating of protective jelly, her

skin was a network of wrinkles, parchment pale, and loosely slung over the skull. The woman had to be close to eighty years old. Next to her, Blackmoor stood holding the plaster cast—the woman's face as it once had been, lineless and sweet. The juxtaposition was startling.

"Cut!" cried the director in heavily accented English, then: "Fantastic!" There was a smattering of respectful applause from the peanut gallery. Blackmoor took no notice; he sat on his heels beside the model, conversing with the old woman softly as one of his assistants toweled off her face.

"Yesterday," Nicole explained, "Dane did the same sort of trick, only inside the face mask of a very old woman was a young girl of thirteen."

"Sorry I missed it," I said.

"Yes, well..." She gave another *je ne sais quoi* shrug. "I don't know what it means. It's very conceptual, you see."

One of Dane's assistants helped the old woman off the platform. Blackmoor turned. His eyes fixed first on Nicole; then his gaze stopped, retracing toward me. He paled as if he'd just seen a ghost. For one fleeting second, the ice man actually seemed to lose his composure.

A sudden thought popped into my head: *He thinks I'm Gabrielle.* The idea that my mother—whom Blackmoor may or may not have had a passionate love affair with as a young man of twenty—should still haunt him made me angry.

He started to move in my direction, but the director intercepted him. "Perhaps if we could just do one or two close-ups—"

"No more." Blackmoor shook him off like a flea and kept walking. All around, people started edging away, as if his steady gaze might pose some kind of health problem, the way radiation from an X ray or prolonged proximity to a microwave oven does.

"Dane—" Nicole began.

Blackmoor ignored her. There was very little space between us now. He reached out and removed my hat. "You cut your hair," he said.

The lump in my throat made it impossible for me to speak. Blackmoor handed me back the limp, brown cloche and turned to Nicole. "Call for the car. Tell him to meet us on the other side."

"Good show, Dane." An assistant tossed a coat to the sculptor. Blackmoor carelessly threw it on. "Let's get out of here," he said.

The walk out of the catacombs seemed to last forever. It took me two steps to match each one of Blackmoor's strides; within the first few minutes my breath was labored and shallow. "That was really something," I said, trotting along beside him. "Very conceptual—"

He gave me a withering look. "It's advertising, Garner. The packaging is all." A self-deprecating smile wreathed his lips. "A perfect medium for me, actually."

A little while later, in a gesture of unexpected kindness, Dane slowed to a stop. "Take a moment," he suggested wryly. "Soak in the scenery."

I collapsed against the wall of the tunnel. The time difference that had overtaken me hours ago came back to trample my body again. I felt light-headed, sick to my stomach.

Blackmoor nodded to a disintegrating heap of skulls and broken bones. "You think that's God's idea of modern art?"

"The whole place gives me the creeps," I said.

"Before the Revolution, certain members of the French nobility used to throw drunken parties down here." Blackmoor slouched against the wall next to me. His coat smelled steam-pressed, very clean and dry. "Of course, during World War Two the tunnels became the headquarters for the Resistance—which was really, really small as parties go, although ask any old Frenchman and he'll swear that he attended."

He stood up straight. "Ready to go?"

"I came because of Annie," I told him flatly.

"I realize that," he said.

"They think—"

Dane put his hand up and shook his head, as though the skulls might still have ears. But they were long past remembering how to hear, past even remembering how to remember. "We'll talk about it later," he said.

It was nearly four-thirty when we stepped out onto the street, blinking in the weak autumn light. "The walk was worth it," Blackmoor said, glancing up and down the sidewalk. "At least it appears we shook the photographers."

The multiply-pierced muscleman was waiting in front of a silver Jaguar. "Here you go, Dane," he said, holding out the keys.

Blackmoor walked around to the passenger side and held open the door for me. When I got in, he crossed in front of the car, and the sight of him through the tinted windshield, walking briskly in his long dark coat, was vaguely surreal. *What have I done?* I thought to myself. *How in the world have I ended up here?* At that moment, I wanted to trigger all the door locks, put my jacket over my head, and go to sleep.

"How long have you been in Paris?" he asked as he slid behind the driver's seat.

"I arrived this morning."

He put the car into gear and pulled out into traffic. "Where are you staying?"

I told him the name of my quaint pension on the Ile St-Louis. He nodded in approval, then said, "We can have your things moved over to the Marais later."

"The Marais?"

Blackmoor kept his eyes on the road. "I've rented one of the old *hôtels* there. There's plenty of space. You'll be much more comfortable."

"That won't be necessary." I took my hat off and shook out my hair. "I'm not planning on being in Paris very long."

We drove for a while in silence. "I'm really tired," I said finally. "Maybe you'd better just take me back—"

"You should fight it for as long as you can." Blackmoor cast a sidelong glance at me, and in my jet-lagged state, I completely lost the thread of the conversation. *What should I fight? Wasn't I already doing that? Struggling in vain against myself?*

"We'll have something to eat," Dane was saying, "and then we'll talk about Annie."

There seemed no use in arguing, so I just sat there, fighting the good fight, silently, with my hat in my lap.

TWENTY-EIGHT

The word marais, Blackmoor explained, meant swamp. It originally referred to the marshy wetlands of the Seine. By the fourteenth century, its unspoiled beauty and proximity to the Louvre had turned the Marais into the preferred residence of the royal court. Members of the wealthy classes moved in, building sumptuous mansions here, which the French called *hôtels*.

After the Revolution, these grand houses were overrun by the common people and fell into decay. A section of the quarter eventually became a ghetto for Polish and Russian Jews fleeing religious persecution. The once splendid architecture continued to deteriorate until 1962, when Charles De Gaulle pronounced the Marais a historical monument. Almost immediately developers began to restore the *hôtels*, and trendy boutiques and cafés started to pop up along the narrow medieval streets.

Blackmoor's narrative, combined with the

forward motion of the low-slung car and the hum of the engine, put me into a near-trance-like state. We passed one of the most famous squares in the world, the place des Vosges, dormered and arcaded with gingerbread cutout symmetry. I leaned back, listening to Dane talk of the knights who'd jousted across these manicured lawns.

"See that place over there?" He pointed through the windshield at an imposing stone structure built in a U, like some Renaissance castle.

"What is it," I asked listlessly, "another museum?"

Blackmoor laughed. "I'm afraid I'm the only relic in it."

"Don't tell me that's where you live."

"Makes for a large studio space." He shrugged.

I sat up. "Well, aren't we going in?"

"Not yet." He stepped on the gas. "First we're going to get something to eat."

He took me to a Middle Eastern restaurant on the rue des Rosiers. The aroma of roasted lamb assaulted me as soon as we walked into the place. I suddenly realized how hungry I was.

The waiter, who knew Dane, sat us in a quiet corner of the small dining room. Blackmoor asked if I had any preferences; I told him whatever he suggested would be fine with me. He spoke to the waiter in French, and the man gave me a big smile.

The moment we were alone I said, "I need to talk to you about Annie."

"By all means, then, talk."

"I was there when it happened, Dane. When the bomb went off." Although no one was seated at the tables next to us, I kept my voice low.

Blackmoor didn't look surprised. "I saw your name in the *Times*. I also had a call from an FBI agent named Barrow. He said you'd identified her as one of my employees." The waiter came back with a bottle of red wine and poured a glass for each of us.

"It was awful," I whispered, miserably. "I couldn't even tell them where she was from."

Dane reached across the table and lightly touched the back of my hand. "It's all right. Her parents live in San Francisco. I flew out there for the funeral."

The idea that only days ago, Blackmoor and I had been on the same continent *and he hadn't even bothered to call* seemed a grievous outrage. It took all my restraint not to pick up my glass of wine and throw it right into his clean-shaven face.

"I hadn't planned to go, actually," he went on, almost to himself. "Annie worked in my studio for almost four years, but I scarcely knew her."

He shrugged off his introspective funk. "Still, she was the last of the old crew, the only one left. Have you noticed how unhealthy it is"—Blackmoor's mouth twisted up into a wicked smile—"for a person to stick around me for any length of time?"

The waiter came back with our food. Dane pronounced the falafel "the best in all of

Paris" and cautioned me about the Moroccan salad, which he said was very spicy. Everything tasted delicious, but I was more interested in our conversation than the niceties of the meal.

"Why did she go to that book party?"

Blackmoor put down his knife and fork. "What cause are you championing now, Garnish?" he said, reverting to the nickname he'd given me as a child—Garnish, *a little something good enough to eat.*

"Have they made you an honorary agent of the FBI? Or maybe you've joined Interpol? Is this interrogation grist for another book? Because if it is, I'll pass this time." Dane savagely ripped off a piece of flatbread. "You can quote me on that."

"I'm not writing a book," I snarled in a low voice; then I grabbed his hand. "I haven't written anything in a long while. Stop looking at me that way—"

"What way?"

"*That* way," I sputtered. "The way you look."

I let go of him, and like wary prizefighters, we both went back into our corners. "The only reason I'm here," I said, falling back into an easy lie, "is because a bomb killed two people I knew and liked, and now it appears that one of those people is going to be blamed for it."

"Ludicrous!" Blackmoor spat out the word. "Annie Houghton would've had a hard time finding the Middle East on a map. How's a girl like that going to get mixed up with revolutionaries?"

"They found some kind of manifesto in her hotel room from the same group who set off a bomb in Warren Petty's jet. The Fourth Freedom."

"The Fourth Freedom." Dane laughed bitterly. "What the hell is that? Sounds more like a branch of the DAR than a terrorist organization."

I took a long sip of wine. "You never answered my question," I said. "About how Annie ended up at that party."

"I'll tell you exactly what I told Barrow," he said. "I have no idea."

"And that was the truth?"

Blackmoor locked eyes with me. "I don't lie, Garner."

I flinched first. "Did she tell anyone else at the studio that she was going to New York?"

"Not that I know of. But I wouldn't say that was out of character." Dane took a sip of wine. "When she put her mind to it Annie could be remarkably focused and sharp, but then someone she met in a bar would invite her to Monte Carlo, and off she would go. If she planned to be gone for more than a week, she'd call. Sometimes she asked me to wire money."

"What about her boyfriends?"

"They were legion."

"Does the name Abdul Amer sound familiar to you?"

"No, but there are thousands of Middle Easterners in Paris. Jews, Muslims, Jordanians, Palestinians, Israelis, Iraqis, Iranians."

"How about Alex Haver?"

"If you're planning to go down a list, you

may as well save your breath. You can ask my apprentice, Stephanie Rubin, when we get to the studio. The two of them socialized together."

Again, I lowered my voice. "You don't think it's possible, Dane? That maybe Annie got in over her head with the wrong man?"

"They were all the wrong men," Blackmoor said. "But not that kind of wrong."

TWENTY-NINE

By the time we left the restaurant, it was dark. Back on the road, I posed the $64,000 question. "Can you think of any connection that Annie might've had with Reed Corbin?"

This is a test, a voice in my head whispered, *only a test.*

"Not directly." Dane kept his eyes on the road, "except for the fact that his firm did some security work for me." But of course, I already knew that. I'd read those words of praise on the back of *The Fear Factor.*

We'd reached the Renaissance mansion Blackmoor called home. At night, with its facade splashed with floodlights, it looked even more impressive than before. The entrance drive was flanked by a pair of stone gatehouses. Dane took a security pass from the glove compartment, rolled down the window, and inserted the card into a metal slot. The heavy iron doors swung open, and we drove inside.

The courtyard was immense. Two classical statues, artfully lit, loomed over formal French gardens. The interior walls were ornate, with carved pediments and lacy accents around the windows.

Blackmoor turned off the ignition, but made no sign that he wanted to leave the car. "A little over a year ago," he said in a low voice, "someone broke into the house."

"This house?" I was amazed. "It's a fortress."

"Now." Dane leaned back in his seat. "I found out the hard way that the old security system was pretty much a joke."

"Did you get hit bad?"

"It could've been worse. Fortunately, no one was here. I had a show opening in Rome that required a full staff. It was obviously a professional heist. As it turned out, the burglar had good taste. He walked out with a Fernand Léger painting...an Egon Schiele erotic drawing...three dozen pieces of faience porcelain...a small but stunning Rembrandt...and the Vermilion Coronation Egg, one of a handful of privately owned Fabergé eggs in the entire world—truly a work of art, all gold lattice and diamond frost flowers, with a miniature replica of the tsar's palace inside." He added with sly amusement, "None of my sculptures were taken."

"Was anything ever recovered?"

"No. I'd been told that these people often come back, so I did some checking around and ended up hiring Corbin."

"Then it's possible," I reasoned, "that Annie met him when he was here."

"No." He shook his head. "I only met Reed once, at the home of one of his clients in London."

I was dying for details, but I kept to the matter at hand. "I guess you must've dealt with Matt Raice, then."

"Initially," Blackmoor said. "The man who actually handled the installation was a fellow by the name of Alan Neary."

"Did he come into contact with Annie?"

"Maybe once or twice." Blackmoor's shoulders were too wide for the sleek little Jag. He was clearly uncomfortable, but he seemed to be putting off going inside. "What about you, Garnish?" He flattened me with one of those half nelsons of the eyes. "Was your relationship with Reed Corbin professional or personal?"

Bingo, I thought. So that's why we've been sitting out here in the car. I'd waited a long, long time to see Blackmoor squirm. "It started out as business," I said, drawing out the moment, allowing the words to register.

Then I took a deep breath and I told him about Walter Dean Wozniak. I went through the whole sick, twisted story. The letters, the threats, that awful night in the fog. Dane didn't say a word, but the edgy, dark part of him—the dangerous part that smashed cameras and landed photographers in the hospital, the rage that seethed out of his pores while he was sculpting—filled the cramped interior of the Jaguar like a slowly inflating air bag.

"So where's this guy now?" he asked finally.

"In jail, being held on a half-million-dollar

bail, until the trial," I said. "Which is one of the reasons why I have to get back home."

"Yes," Blackmoor said gravely. "And of course, you probably already miss Temple." It shocked me that he should know that before I realized it myself. But then, it never took long for the ache to set in when I was far away from my daughter.

Dane abruptly got out of the car, walking around to open my door. Now that the sun had gone down, it was colder. As we made our way across the courtyard, I found myself starting to shiver. Blackmoor took off his coat and put it around my shoulders. "How is she?" he asked. "Temple?"

"Oh, she's amazing. Beautiful, smart, wise beyond her years." I laughed. "Did I mention we're related?"

"And Mrs. Fields?"

"Cilda's Cilda."

Blackmoor stood in front of the massive door, his eyes cast downward. "I hope they don't hate me too much," he said.

The interior of the *hôtel* had been recently renovated. I'd expected—oh, I don't know— Versailles, or at the least, dripping Belle Epoque excess, but during Dane's tenancy as lord of the manor, the rooms had been stripped to barest essentials. In the reception hall, floor-to-ceiling mirrors reflected gold-leaf paneling, marble mantels, crystal chandeliers, and nothing much else. An immense mural showing the Queen of Sheba being carried on a golden litter spanned the walls of the ballroom.

"The oldest section was built in the 1600s," Blackmoor said, "by a gambler who later lost his entire fortune in one night."

He led me down a long hall with gold-coffered ceilings. Several of his plaster cast sculptures stood like silent sentries, guarding the way. "Living quarters for me, and for a few members of the staff, are in the east wing."

"Is that where Annie stayed?"

"Yes," he said. "I can show you if you'd like, but unfortunately there isn't much to see. French Interpol already went through her personal items and removed them. What was left I had sent back to California." We'd come to an arched passageway. "Through here is the studio."

I started toward it, but Dane caught my arm. "Before..." Again, his composure momentarily flagged. "I have this...commitment I can't get out of, at the Pompidou."

"That's all right," I said. "When do you have to leave?"

"In about an hour."

He was trying to tell me that he had some tarted-up French babe waiting in the next room. "No problem," I said. "I can talk to your apprentice some other time."

"The thing is," Blackmoor went on, "I was hoping that you'd come with me."

"Tonight?" I hated myself for sounding so giddy. "Oh, I can't. I didn't bring a dress—"

"That's not an issue." He was back to his old arrogant self. "I'm sure you could find something here." Many of Blackmoor's sculptures were fiberglass figures, fully dressed right down to their underwear. I bristled at being packaged like another one of this man's creations.

"I've been up for thirty-six hours," I told him. "I'm about to collapse." In truth, the spicy meal had given me a jolt of renewed energy.

"The program isn't long. We'll leave as soon as it's over." Dane must've sensed me weakening, because he cupped his hand under my chin and turned my face up to his. "Please. Having you there would make the evening almost bearable."

You will not melt, I told myself. *You will not melt.* "I don't want to be out too late," I sighed, melting.

"I promise to be a perfect gentleman, and return you directly to your hotel," he replied. It was such a bald lie, that gentleman part. Blackmoor might've traveled the world, accumulated a fortune, and mingled with the elite, but he still retained the rough edges of a young man who'd started out with nothing and succeeded only by the sheer force of his wits and will.

Just then a young woman came clattering into the hall. "Dane!" she cried. "We've been frantic. They've been calling from the Center—"

"Yes, yes," he said. "Garner, this is my colleague, Stephanie Rubin." *The girl who'd socialized with Annie.* Pleasingly plump, with long dark hair, olive skin, and a generous mouth, Rubin was Houghton's physical opposite, yet something in the way her eyes sharply appraised me made me see how they might've been friends.

"I'll be escorting Ms. Quinn to the concert tonight," Dane told her. "She'll need a dress to wear. Can you find something?"

Rubin didn't look overly happy, but she said, "Sure, Dane."

"I'll be back soon," Blackmoor said; then he strode down the corridor, through the ranks of his plaster cast honor guard.

THIRTY

Blackmoor's studio was an immense, airy room fronted by a row of French windows. Rubin explained that during the mansion's glory days, this open space had served as the grand salon. A work-in-progress sculpture stood in the center of the room. "So you're Dane's apprentice." I spoke as loud as I could, trying to be heard over the *rat-tat-tat* of Rubin's clogs on the parquet floor.

"Apprentice, assistant." The young woman shrugged. "I came to Paris a few years ago to study sculpting. Dane saw my work, and offered me a job. It's been a great experience, but I don't see a future in it."

"How come?"

"To be honest, Dane's techniques don't do it anymore. People aren't clamoring after his art. It's *him* they want—the Blackmoor package, the mystique. Not that Dane doesn't deserve it," Stephanie qualified. "He's a master at reinventing himself—the films, the commercials, this thing tonight."

We walked into another sumptuously pan-eled room. "What is it exactly, a showing of his work?"

"Didn't he tell you? He's designed the scenery for an avant-garde opera. It's a very big deal. One of the hottest young French cou-turiers designed the costumes. The tickets have been sold out for months. You're lucky to be going with Dane." For the first time, she smiled. "Otherwise you'd be standing out front like the rest of us."

"I was a friend of Annie's." The words tumbled out suddenly.

Stephanie's face brightened. "I thought your name sounded familiar. You're the writer."

"That's me."

"Well, then you understand what a special person she was. I've been a mess ever since it happened. I just can't believe she's not coming back." Rubin stopped in front of a recessed entranceway, fitted seamlessly into the paneling. When she opened the door, lights came on inside a storage room stacked with racks of clothing.

"This is wild," I said.

"Our stylist Martine goes to Clignancourt every weekend, scouring the market for finds." Rubin walked over to a rack of gowns. "One of these should fit you."

"Dane told me you and Annie were close." I sat down on a stool, watching her go through the dresses.

"Yeah. After Roberto left, we were the only Americans," Stephanie said. "At the end of the day, if nothing else was happening, we'd head over to Le Pick-clops or one of the gay bars—which are, by the way, aplenty here, and really a lot of fun if you don't mind being one of the only girls."

"What about men?" I asked. "Did you know any of Annie's boyfriends?"

Rubin laughed. "Keeping up with Houghton's romantic life would've been a full-time occupation, and I already have a job. I did meet a few of them—" She stopped, holding up a slinky green satin sheath for my approval. "No?"

"No," I said, nixing it flat. "Did Annie ever show any interest in the man from the security firm?"

"Alan Neary?" Stephanie shrugged. "I thought he was kind of cute, but Annie said he looked like Gomer Pyle."

"Is the name Abdul Amer familiar to you?"

She shook her head. "Uh-uh. I would've remembered that one."

"How about Alex Haver?"

"Nope. Like I said, Annie ate 'em up and spit 'em out pretty fast." Rubin smiled. "I did get the feeling she had her scopes set on someone over the summer, though. She disappeared for a couple of weeks in July and came back all dewy-eyed and sexually satisfied. But whoever he was sort of just faded from the picture, I guess, until—"

"Until what?" I prompted.

"She didn't say, but I think that's who she went to meet in New York."

My skin went all tingly, the way it always did when a new piece of information was about to fall into place. "Annie told you where she was going?"

"No. But I knew she had something exciting going on. Before she left she threw her arms around my neck and said"—Rubin smiled sadly—'Wish me luck, Steph.'"

I was digesting this, when the girl let out a sudden cry. "Voilà!" She held up a hand-crocheted dress in the most amazing shade of violet gray. "It's perfect." It was long, very narrow, with a scooped neck and no sleeves.

"I don't have the right underwear," I protested.

"Garner, darling." Rubin's eyes twinkled wickedly. "Under a dress like this, you don't wear a blessed thing."

THIRTY-ONE

Sitting beside me in the back of the chauffeur-driven limousine, Dane Blackmoor was unusually quiet. Stephanie Rubin had found a pair of gray satin shoes with high, wedged heels and straps that buttoned. She'd also put a lot more makeup than I was used to on my face, and spritzed my hair with something shiny. Then she'd handed me a drawstring purse and a hooded cloak and said, "Dane's going to absolutely die."

But when Dane entered in his tuxedo he just fell silent. "If you'd like, you could use the phone to call home before we leave," he said, after a long, awkward moment.

259

I'd taken off my watch, but with the time difference, I figured it would be only early afternoon back in Jersey. Blackmoor told me how to dial out, and then he and Stephanie left the room. I reached Cilda right away.

"Everyt'ing's fine," she told me; she was watching Erica Kane on the television, and Temple was in school. I explained that I wouldn't be able to call back tonight, but I'd speak with them both on Saturday.

I dialed out again, catching Matt Raice just as he was about to leave for lunch. "What's the good news?" I asked.

"Well, they're releasing Mike Fedora from the hospital today."

"That's wonderful."

"And your old pal Walt has just been deemed competent to stand trial."

"Even better." I shrugged off the chill that came from hearing Wozniak's name. "Did you find anything on Adrian Nadeau?"

"He runs a gallery on the Left Bank," Matt told me. "We're looking into it now. I want you to stay away until I get some answers."

"I will."

"What else you doing over there in gay Paree?"

"Touristy stuff," I said, glancing down at my opera clothes. "The catacombs, the Pompidou Center, that sort of thing." Raice told me to send him a postcard and I promised I would.

"Do you know a gallery owner on the Left Bank named Adrian Nadeau?" I asked Dane in the car.

He scowled. "You don't want to have anything to do with him."

"How come?"

"He has a bad reputation. The artwork he sells is of questionable provenance." Seeing the look on my face, he put it more plainly: "It doesn't come to him through legitimate channels, Garner."

"Oh." I leaned back against the leather seat, feeling suddenly—and I feared, irrevocably—sapped of energy. I closed my eyes for a minute. The next thing I knew, Blackmoor was speaking again.

"It's the hair," he said softly, in the darkness. "You're not that school girl anymore."

"I know." I stared straight at him. "It took years, but I finally grew up."

There appeared to be a phantasmagoric light show going on in front of the Pompidou Center. Television news trucks nosed against the street barricades. In the sloping plaza outside the main entrance, a Felliniesque circus of fire-eaters, jugglers, and street performers were keeping the crowd amused, while, in the mouth of a spitting fountain, a pair of immense red lips lasciviously turned.

Just beyond, the Center itself crouched like a fat-bottomed woman lying dead on her belly, with her inner organs turned inside out. Blue, yellow, and green arteries flowed through the steel skeleton. A red escalator stepped up the glass spinal cord. This was Paris's mecca of modern art—a piece of architecture that one critic had likened to an oil refinery.

Blackmoor's chauffeur inched up slowly, then stopped. When I saw the cameras, and just how many people the rickety wooden horses were keeping out, I started to hyperventilate. Dane reached over and took my hand. "Just keep hold of me," he said, "and everything will be fine"—this from the man whose disappearing act rivaled Harry Houdini's.

A man wearing a security pass opened the car door. "Monsieur Blackmoor," he said, then, "Madame." Dane stepped out first and I scooted out behind him. There was a surge from the crowd, photographers calling, "Dane! Dane!" Blackmoor just put his head down, gripped me tighter, and headed toward the door.

I glanced up. A huge digital clock was showing a countdown of seconds. "That's the time left in the millennium," Blackmoor said into my ear. Between the jet lag and the frantic scene, I really felt we were on a fast track to some apocalyptic end. With my cloak flapping behind me, I clung fast to his hand.

In the lobby, televised images played above our heads, while on the ground, reporters shoved their microphones into Blackmoor's face. "My goodness." I spoke loudly, wanting to be heard over the commotion. "They really love you here."

"Yes. Me and Jerry Lewis." He broke into a scornful smile and a dozen flash bulbs went off.

As we approached the bottom of the snaking

red escalator I saw a familiar face in the crowd. For a second, I thought I'd really lost my grip. It wasn't until Mercedes Fields waved that I realized I wasn't imagining things.

"Dane." I tugged his arm. "The woman over there. That's Cilda's daughter..."

He stopped and said something in French to the security guard. The man went over to the barricade and motioned for Mercedes to come through. She walked toward us, a vision in bronze-ruffled taffeta. "Hello, Garner," she said.

"Wow," I said. "We must be on the same wavelength."

"Just a plane ride behind." Mercedes smiled.

"Dane, this is Mercedes Fields." I let go of his hand so they could properly greet each other. "Mercedes, this is Dane Blackmoor."

"Wonderful to meet you, Mr. Blackmoor." I swear, she actually batted her eyes.

"Call me Dane, please. I'm an old friend of your mother's."

Ha, I thought. *And he said he didn't lie.*

"I know you have to go inside," Mercedes said, adding—rather brazenly, at least to my mind, "but could you spare a moment to say a word to your American fans?"

Whoa, boy, I snickered to myself, *is she ever barking up the wrong tree.* To my surprise, Dane was completely amenable. He followed Mercedes to the barricade, where he allowed himself to be interviewed for a full three minutes. Once the camera was off, I sauntered over to them.

"I was just telling Mercedes," Blackmoor said, "that she's more than welcome to stay at the studio while she's here."

"It's sort of a blanket invitation," I said, facetiously.

Mercedes met my gaze. "I'm only in town over the weekend, and I've already imposed on you enough," she said. "Thanks so much for the interview, Dane." She pressed his hand and then flashed me a dazzling smile. "Enjoy the show, Garner."

As we were walking away, Blackmoor leaned over and whispered in my ear, "Your friend Mercedes seems like a real dynamo."

I didn't bother telling him that he was only half right.

We followed the security guard into the Grand Salle. It was a fashionably late and very conspicuous entrance, accompanied by a smattering of applause, which I hardly heard. My attention was focused straight ahead, on the stage.

The set, bathed in watery light, looked like a gigantic Tinkertoy covered in moth wings. Three platforms of varying heights and sizes were connected by suspension bridges that seemed to levitate, midair, with no visible means of support. From out of the cross-supports of each platform, a writhing plaster cast figure fought to get free.

"It's about ghosts," Dane said.

I nodded, not trusting myself to speak. I told myself it was a visual trick—a Rorschach test that would evoke different things to different people. To me, however, it was as though Blackmoor had designed a looking glass image of my father's house. Mercifully, when the lights went down and the opera started, the impression faded.

The music worked hard at being experimental—ear-assaulting dissonance broken every so often by atonal arias which seemed to go on forever. After a while, I gave up trying to figure out who was who and what they were singing about, and gave in to the electric discomfort of being wedged into a tight theater seat, breathing the heavy scent of a thousand perfumes, while Blackmoor's body butterfly-kissed my shoulder in the dark.

I didn't fall asleep, but I went into an altered state. The music had all the vicissitude of a test pattern; the more I tried not to pay attention to it, the more mesmerizing it became.

A split second before it happened, Blackmoor tensed, as though he were trying to signal a warning, but I was in a time-change warp, and the sudden explosion caught me unawares. Up on stage, the performers writhed and twisted, in a choreographed dance of death. Laser pellets of light bounced off them like bullets. With their last breaths they emitted horrible, screeching sounds.

I started to shake uncontrollably. "Come on." Blackmoor all but lifted me to my feet, and carried me up the aisle.

"I'm sorry," I croaked as we emerged from the auditorium.

"It's my fault. I forgot—" he said. "I should've made the connection."

He asked me how I felt. I told him I wanted to find a ladies' room. When I came out, I discovered he'd already sent for the car. "You can't leave," I told him. "I don't want to ruin your night."

Blackmoor pushed a strand of perspiration-soaked hair from my face, and said, "You *are* my night, Garner. This is it, right here."

THIRTY-TWO

Postcard to a friend:

Dear Mike, like the hat— Here I am, envelope-pushing and enjoying the view. Matt told me you finally got away from the magazine lady. When I return, we'll have you down to the Jersey shore for some real R&R. *All the best, Garner Quinn*	MR. MAX SHRONER SHRONER LITERARY ASSOCIATES 708 THIRD AVENUE NEW YORK, NY 10017

There was a knock at the door—my Irish-loving proprietress bearing breakfast. I wondered how to say *merci* with a brogue.

Putting a lilt in my voice, I opened the door. *"Bonjour—"*

"Bonjour," Dane replied, annoyingly amused. "Sleep well?"

I'd conked out in the back of the limousine riding back to the hotel last night—collapsed against Blackmoor's chest in an unattractive, slack-jawed, down-for-the-count stupor. This morning, I woke up in bed wearing the crocheted gown and a man's tuxedo jacket. I had no recollection beyond that. And now my hair was wet, I had a robe on, and there were hokey postcards of the Eiffel Tower on my writing table. At a time like this, I had no choice but to be honest. "I'm really embarrassed," I said.

"Don't apologize." Blackmoor put the paper bag he was carrying down on the cards. "That composer's music is enough to sink anyone into a coma."

The smell of warm croissants and coffee emanating from the bag almost made me swoon. "Are these for me?" I asked.

"Eat up," he invited. "Then put on some sensible clothes. I'm taking you out."

"No more human bones or explosions," I warned.

"I promise," Blackmoor said, adding mysteriously, "Everything else but."

We took the metro, heading toward the northern outskirts of the city. It was another beautiful day, the sort of weather where you could feel comfortable in a light jacket without fear of freezing or sweating. I was surprised to see how many people rode the subway on a Saturday. Macramé totes hung limply from the arms of the older women; the young ones—frail birds with tough little faces—

hung limply on the arms of their tattooed boyfriends. I saw a girl about Temple's age and was nearly bowled over by a flood of homesickness. What was I doing here?

You're trying to clear Annie's name, I reminded myself. Then why was I standing in a crowded metro car, being tossed and jostled against a man who, only two years ago, had purposely walked out of my life. *And why was he looking at me that way?*

"Clignancourt," Blackmoor said. "This is our stop."

We followed in the steps of the other disembarking passengers. "It's about a fifteen-minute walk." Dane steered me through the crowd.

The neighborhood was squalid, and smelled of sweat and urine. Wooden stalls lined both sides of the street, displaying an array of battered hubcaps, rusted kitchen appliances, and *Hello, Kitty* paraphernalia. "Don't worry, it gets better," he said.

A man in a filthy butcher's apron waggled a bunch of wilted roses in our faces. *"Pour la belle mademoiselle!"* he called.

Blackmoor pulled me closer. Sunlight had soaked into his leather jacket, so that it radiated a soft, lazy heat. "Welcome to the Marché aux Puces," he said. "That poor bastard's family has probably been peddling dead flowers here for the past two hundred years."

As we walked farther, I began to notice an upward shift in the quality of the merchandise. Empire baubles and ornaments appeared among the bric-a-brac. "All told, there's about fifteen acres of this," Dane explained. "About here it starts to break down into specialized markets. My stylist comes just about every weekend, looking for props and costumes I can use for my sculptures. I believe the gown you wore last night came from the Marché Vernaison, beyond that building there."

"Speaking of the dress," I said, picturing the way it had looked, slept in and wrinkled, "I'll return it as soon as it's been cleaned."

"I'd like it very much if you kept it. It was clearly made for you"—a compliment maybe, but he said it brusquely.

We wandered through the maze of stalls. One area was entirely devoted to old furniture. Not antiques necessarily—secondhand sofas and chairs, some still spruce and showy, others that made you want to cross yourself and walk quickly by.

"Dead people's stuff," Dane commented, with a dry smile.

I stopped short in front of a beat-up leather club chair. "Dudley had two of these in his library. The realtor who's selling the house bought them from me."

Blackmoor's face darkened at the mention of my father; there had always been bad blood between the two of them. "The Spring Lake house is up for sale?"

Why do people always act so damn surprised when I tell them? "Up until a couple of days ago, it was virtually sold," I said, moving away to inspect a brass lamp, "but the couple who wanted it decided to get a divorce instead."

Blackmoor had a funny look on his face. "What?" I asked him.

"Nothing. Somehow I always pictured you there."

"Too many ghosts." I dismissed this lightly.

"So paint the place," he said. "Put in some new windows, air things out."

"I did. It helped, but..." I couldn't put it into words. "That house never seemed like a home to me. There was always something missing."

Dane shrugged. "Who am I to argue? I live in a *hôtel* built by a luckless gambler, on the grounds of a goddam swamp, in a foreign country whose national pastime is hating Americans."

I reached up and boxed his chin. "But they *love* you."

Then Blackmoor did an unexpectedly goofy thing—a Jerry Lewis impression (*"Hey, Professor!"*) that was actually very funny. "Okay," I amended, "you and Jerry."

"Don't forget about Woody." He slumped into a Woody Allen posture, rubbing the bridge of his nose, and adopting a New York accent that was breathless and defensive. "I—I—I mean, it wouldn't be right to overlook him, would it?"

"Enough," I laughed. "I get your point. The French have very warped taste."

He caught me around the waist, pulled me toward him to kiss me, and I thought, *Oh God, I hear bells! I'm floating!* But after we kissed for a while in the middle of the market, I realized that it wasn't my imagination. The minute Blackmoor lifted me off my feet, a dozen little clocks in the market stall had started chiming twelve o'clock. One of the flea market peddlers in the neighboring stall called out, *"L'amour...toujours l'amour..."*

We broke apart. I could feel a little indentation on my cheek from where the collar of Dane's leather jacket had pressed. "Come on," he said. His loosely slung arm around my shoulder felt almost as good as the kiss. "I have some business to take care of in that building over there."

The sprawling warehouse was packed with stalls. Dane headed toward a shop in the far corner. *"Bonjour,* Monsieur Blackmoor," the merchant greeted him, but his small, shrewd eyes were on me. I wondered if I had lipstick smeared on my face.

"Has that Le Corbusier chair come in yet, Paul?" Dane asked.

"Ah, monsieur, it's even more fantastic than they described—'ere, let me show you." The shopkeeper waved us around the counter, unlocking the door to a private room. The chair in question was red, with slender metal legs, and a sleek geometric design. I saw Dane's eyes light up. The two men conversed together in lightning-fast French. A moment later we were winding our way through the stalls again.

"What happened?" I asked.

"I bought it for a small fortune." Blackmoor shrugged. "But I'll recoup what I spent three times over the minute I put a figure on it."

He took me to a café called Chez Louisette,

where we had cassoulet and a bottle of red wine while one of the locals serenaded us with fervent but off-key Edith Piaf.

"Why are you so interested in Adrian Nadeau?" Dane asked as we walked back into the market.

"I found his name and number in Reed Corbin's apartment."

"Did you now?" The old Blackmoor sneer wreathed his lips. "Well, damn. Here I was one of Corbin's clients too, and I didn't even know he had an apartment."

I stopped short and dug my heels in. "What's your point?"

"You must've been pretty grateful to him for protecting you from that crazy fan." He started walking away.

"Are you jealous?" I jogged after him. "Because you don't have any right to be. You were the one who left, remember?"

Dane caught me by the elbows, and spun me around until we were facing each other. "That was just a matter of geography, Garner."

"What the hell does that mean?"

"You always kept me at arm's distance, anyway. It was easy to trust me when I was in the intensive care unit fighting for my life, wasn't it, Garnish? But once you figured out I was going to make it, all the old doubts started percolating in that busy mind of yours." He let go of me suddenly. "They're percolating now. I can read the question in your eyes."

"Answer it then." I took a deep breath. "Were you in love with my mother?"

"In love?" I watched the hard lines of his

face soften. "I worshiped the ground she walked on." He shrugged. "Unfortunately, though, the lady was blindly devoted to her husband."

At that moment, everything fell away—the dusty path, the barking peddlers, the hustle and bustle of the market; there was only Blackmoor and me. "So you're saying you never slept with her?"

"Somehow, Garner"—he spoke quietly, but his voice sizzled with white-hot anger—"the big picture always seems to elude you." He shoved his clenched fists into the pockets of his jacket. "The subject's closed as far as I'm concerned. You can fill in the blanks any way you want." He began walking away.

"Dane, wait." I caught up with him. "Would you believe me if I told you I didn't need to fill in the blanks?"

"I don't know." Blackmoor's sidelong glance was skeptical. "But I'll tell you one thing—if you think Adrian Nadeau had something to do with Corbin's death, you're barking up the wrong tree."

"Why's that?"

"Nadeau deals in stolen paintings, not bombs."

"Maybe," I persisted. "But obviously his name meant something to Reed or he wouldn't have written it down."

"Most likely he was trying to track down a piece of missing artwork for one of his clients," Blackmoor countered. "After my studio was robbed, Corbin's security man went through all the usual channels in the hopes that one of the stolen pieces would surface. Nadeau's gallery was on the short list of likely places."

"I hadn't thought of that." It sounded plausible, but if Adrian Nadeau was connected to a case Corbin, Inc., had worked on, how come Matthew Raice hadn't recognized his name?

It was nearly three o'clock, and the sky had turned a pearly gray. On the way back to the metro, Blackmoor stopped to browse at a bookstall, and I wandered over to a display of jewelry, looking for trinkets and souvenirs.

I was looking at an antique cameo when an old Gypsy woman grabbed my hand, and began speaking in rapid French. She was about seventy, with coarse, weathered skin, a cunning toothless grin, and a getup that was right out of Central Casting.

I tried to pull away. *"Je ne comprend pas.* I only speak—"

The woman smiled wide enough for me to see the stubs of what had once been teeth, then turned up my palm and gripped tight. With her free hand she dove into the pocket of her greasy skirt and brought out a conch shell, no bigger than the nail on my pinky. Making the sign of the cross with it, she began wailing a litany of saints.

I glanced frantically over my shoulder, trying to get Blackmoor's attention, but he was engrossed in a book, oblivious to me.

The woman ran the shell across my palm. *"L'amour."* She nodded her head. *"Vous comprenez l'amour, mademoiselle?"*

Sure, I understood love. I decided I might as well hear the old Gypsy out. *"Moins vite,"* I said. "Talk slowly."

She jabbed the pointy shell into a crease on my palm, and began to cluck. *She just found Andy,* I thought to myself. As the line curved, she began speaking faster and faster. Her words poured out in a torrent of excitement, and then she let out a low, lascivious laugh, and fanned herself. *Definitely Blackmoor.*

"Merci," I said, trying to withdraw my hand. But the Gypsy held fast, her eyes still intent on the lines of my palm. She let out a startled cry, frantically making the sign of the cross over my forehead with the shell. *"Attention, l'amour obsédé, vous comprenez? Attention—"*

Beware an obsessed lover? Or dangerous obsession of love? But who, or whose? I thought of Walter Wozniak, and Dane Blackmoor. And then, myself. Was it obsession that I felt for Dane?

Suddenly, he appeared at my side. *"Allez!"* He addressed the Gypsy sharply.

"Pardon, monsieur," she whined, retreating a little. Then the fear faded from her eyes, and she grabbed his sleeve. *"Cent francs, monsieur, pour la relique. Cent francs, s'il vous plaît."*

Dane took several bills out of his pocket and gave them to her. "Come on, Garner." Before I left, the old Gypsy pressed the shell into my hand. *"Prenez,"* she whispered in a low voice. *"Pour le nom de Sainte-Thérèse."*

"I hope you like it," Blackmoor said dryly as we walked away. "I just bought you a seashell for forty dollars."

The day had grown cooler. So had Dane. Seeing the locked-up look on his face as we rode back on the metro triggered my worst insecurities. We barely spoke until we were back at my hotel. "I have something I need to take care of," he told me. "Will you be all right on your own?"

"Of course," I replied, thinking that he had a lot of gall to even ask.

He swiveled my chin up to meet his gaze. "Meet me for dinner tonight."

"Okay."

He took out a card and scribbled down an address. "Nine o'clock," he said.

The hotel had one of those old-fashioned, glass-front European lifts. I stepped inside, and as it lurched away from the ground, I could see Blackmoor standing in the small lobby, watching me go.

THIRTY-THREE

Postcard, never mailed:

Bonjour!	
Today an old gypsy told me to beware an obsessed lover. Should we put her on as an expert witness do you think? I swear I'm being good...	MR. MAX SHRONER SHRONER LITERARY ASSOCIATES 708 THIRD AVENUE NEW YORK, NY 10017
Votre amie, Garner Q.	

Adrian Nadeau's gallery was located on the rue de Grenelle in the artsy area of the Left Bank known as St-Germain-des-Prés. I stood on the sidewalk, pretending to window-shop, summoning up the courage to go inside. Matt Raice had made me promise not to do anything that might interfere with his investigation, but I didn't see how a little browsing could do any harm. After Blackmoor dropped me back at the hotel, I'd changed into a light wool suit and heels. For all intents and purposes, I was just another well-off American looking for a painting or objet d'art to take home as a reminder of my trip to Paris.

I took a deep breath and walked through the door. The gallery turned out to be larger than it had appeared from the street. A line of velvet-covered ceiling-to-floor room dividers had been hung with dozens of lithographs and paintings, individually lit and beautifully framed. Along the side walls, glass cases displayed pen-and-ink and charcoal drawings.

Several potential customers milled about studying the art, speaking in the sort of hushed voices that are usually reserved for public libraries and the intensive care units of hospitals. They appeared to be well-dressed and law-abiding people; I wondered if they had any idea that they might be looking at stolen art.

I stopped in front of a bold line drawing of a dark-haired woman, naked except for the pair of bright red stockings she was wearing. The artist's signature caught my eye—Egon Schiele. Blackmoor had mentioned that name when we were sitting in the car. One of the sketches taken from the *hôtel* had been a Schiele.

A young man in an Armani suit took note of my interest. He said something to me in French. "I'm afraid I didn't get that," I apologized. "Do you speak English?"

"Of course," he said, giving me a perfunctory smile. "The drawing is quite spectacular, isn't it?"

"Yes, it is."

"The Nazis considered Schiele's work pornographic," the young man explained. "Many of his erotic paintings were destroyed or lost. This particular nude is as rare as it is valuable."

"I have a friend who would just love it," I told him. "Will the gallery be open tomorrow?"

"I'm afraid not." He produced a business card. "But Monsieur Nadeau often schedules private appointments for serious buyers on Monday."

"Thank you." I pocketed the card.

"Tell your friend not to wait too long," the man advised. "A Schiele of such quality comes along only once in a lifetime."

Unless it's been recycled from someone else's art collection, I thought. Out loud I said, "I'm sure he'll agree."

The restaurant where Dane and I were supposed to meet was a tiny place tucked in the shadows of Notre-Dame. I timed it so that I'd be there fifteen minutes late. "Monsieur Blackmoor?" I inquired of the maître d'.

"*Mais oui.*" He nodded. A set of stairs led down to a cavelike room with a low beamed ceiling and a white stone fireplace. I followed him to a table in the corner.

Mercedes Fields looked up and smiled. "Dane said to tell you he's running late."

The waiter was holding out my chair, so there was nothing to do but sit. "I hadn't realized this would be a threesome," I said, waving away the offer of an aperitif.

"Sorry if you're disappointed." Mercedes was already drinking champagne. "But it's my last night in Paris, so when Dane suggested it, I thought it would be nice."

"How about his other suggestion?" I hated hearing the jealousy creep into my voice. "Did you take him up on the offer to stay at the studio?" Mercedes didn't answer, and I knew at once that she had.

I looked at her, sitting across the table from me—arms folded, swelling the cleavage above the V of her Donna Karan jacket, legs crossed under the matching short, tight skirt. Our whole lives had been lived in a strange sort of counterpoint. We were sisters, in some tenuous, extended family; yet it was always push and pull with her. Ice cold and red-hot. In that way, she and Blackmoor were very much alike.

"Why did you follow me to Paris?" I asked.

Mercedes shrugged. "I'm on assignment, Garner."

"*Front Cover* didn't send you thousands of miles for the opening of some obscure French opera."

She sighed, like, *You caught me*. "I'm following the same leads you are, girl. In case
you didn't know, terrorist bombings make for
equal-opportunity stories."

"And how does Blackmoor fit in?"

"You tell me."

"I don't work that way," I said, remembering
the words of my elementary school teacher,
Sister Virginia Michaela. *Garner is a bright,
imaginative child who does not play well with others.*

"Why don't you ask him yourself?" I added.

"Garner—"

"Tell *Dane* I had a headache." I picked up
my pocketbook, tossing a parting shot. "By
the way. Love your suit."

I walked back to my hotel through streets
paved with cobblestone and a shiver of autumn
leaves. The whole way, I kept expecting to see
Blackmoor's billowing coat as he strode
toward, or after, me. It didn't happen.

It was only a little after ten when I got back
to the room, but I felt feverishly exhausted. This
time I managed to strip down to my underwear
before falling into bed. The next thing I remember was the flat, urgent pealing of the phone. I
snapped on the light and checked my watch. It
wasn't even midnight, but I felt I'd been asleep
for an eternity. It had to be Blackmoor, I
thought, calling to apologize.

"Hello?"

"Garner, it's Matt." Raice's voice sounded
crystal clear. "I hate to call you this late, but
I thought you should know. Somebody paid
Walter Wozniak's bail."

There was a short pause while he waited for a reply, but I was speechless. "We lost him, Garner," Matt said. "He's back on the street."

Wozniak was on the loose, and here I was, thousands of miles away from Cilda and Temple. "We're watching the house, of course," Matt assured me. I thanked him for that, and said I would take the next flight home.

The first thing I did was call the airlines. The earliest departure to Newark wasn't until morning. I booked a seat. My suitcase stood at attention in the open closet. With the lamp on, and the drapes drawn tightly across the windows, the room looked faded and fussy, as though it might belong to somebody's spinster aunt. I decided I'd rather wait out the night dozing in the bucket seats of a passenger gate.

When I called down to the front desk to arrange for a taxi, I asked the sleepy night clerk if there were any messages for Garner Quinn. There weren't. As I was checking out, I asked again and got the same answer. I handed the clerk a shopping bag and a handwritten card. "Could you put this in a box and send it to this address?"

The tip I slid into his hand obviously pleased him, because he said *oui*, he certainly would, and that I should have a safe trip, and please come back again.

It bothered me, returning the dress to Blackmoor without having it dry-cleaned, but it had folded nicely into the bag. You could barely tell it had been worn at all.

PART THREE

THIRTY-FOUR

I returned to a blustery Jersey November, and a home that was under siege. After his bail was paid by an anonymous benefactor, Walter Dean Wozniak had walked right out of the Freehold jail and disappeared. A letter, postmarked from Tinton Falls, arrived at my home the next day, describing, in graphic detail just how much he'd missed me. The closing read—

TILL NEXT WE MEET.
XXXXXXXXXXXXXXXXX. CHAZ

On my okay, Matt Raice directed the Protective Security Technologies team to install electric fencing around three quarters of my property; the frigid Atlantic would serve as a moat for the rest. He also suggested we move the perimeter of defense closer to the house. A team of four G&P men, working singly in eight-hour shifts, would accompany me in a duet of "Me and My Shadow" wherever I went.

Since Temple's school was closed for its annual teachers convention, I made arrangements to send her to Andy and Candace's in Manhattan for the week. Cilda Fields, however, refused to budge. "I seen a picture of Wozniak in the paper, wit' 'is jelly arms and big soft belly," she sniffed. "'E don't frighten me."

The gray weather ebbed into rain. One

morning we awoke to a wet, lacy snow, but it disintegrated when it hit the ground, leaving only a fuzzy white ribbing around the rocks in the seawall. I no longer made any pretense of going to the office. Cilda and I sat around watching television and playing cards. One of the G&P guys, a young Texan named Mitchell, joined us when he was on duty.

We got to know them all. Besides Mitchell, the poker-playing cowboy, there was Glenn, whom we secretly dubbed "the Nazi"; a tough black Vietnam vet named Dwight, who was petrified of Cilda; and Joey, the one the others referred to as "the kid." Days became delineated only by the changing of the guard. In every other way, they were more of the same.

It was a waiting game, and for me at least, each round had two levels. I waited to hear from Walter Dean. I waited to hear from Dane Blackmoor. But no long-distance calls came from Paris. Walter was clearly my more ardent pursuer. His letters began arriving daily, never postmarked twice from the same city, but all from within a radius of twenty miles.

"How's he getting around?" I asked Matt on the phone. Raice sighed, and admitted he didn't know.

Then, exactly a week after Wozniak was released from jail, we got a break. A sharp-eyed waitress reported seeing a guy matching Walter's description, driving a silver Nissan, at a traffic light in downtown Fair Haven. The light had changed before she'd been able to get the license plate number, but Raice said the woman seemed positive that it was the same man who'd been arrested for stalking Garner Quinn.

"He has a *car*?" I knew the police were still holding Wozniak's Plymouth as potential evidence. "Where the hell is he getting his money?"

"The mysterious benefactor, I suppose." Matt sounded frustrated.

Walter Dean's $500,000 bail had been paid in cash by a local bondsman who'd been given that amount plus an extra grand just for making the transaction. He described the man who'd given him the money as a well-dressed Caucasian, between the ages of thirty-five and forty, with a large build, sandy hair, and brown eyes. When the bondsman was asked whether he'd considered keeping the money for himself, he immediately shook his head and said no way. This fellow, he said, wasn't the type you'd want to screw with.

"Give me some good news, Matt," I pleaded.

He told me that when it came to Wozniak, I was a magnet. Walter wouldn't be able to keep away for long.

If that was the good news, I grumbled, I didn't want to hear the bad.

The minute I hung up from Matt Raice, the phone rang again. "Oh, Mrs. Quinn, you're back from Paris!" Peggy Boyle cried. "How does it feel to be home?"

It really sucks, I wanted to tell her. But instead I said, "Like I never left."

Peg laughed gaily. "Well, I know you're

probably busy writing one of your books, and I don't want to disturb you, but I have some good news." *Oh no,* I thought, *not you too.*

"The McCarthys are getting back together?" I ventured.

There was a pregnant pause, and I realized that she didn't even remember who the McCarthys were. When you were a Diamond Saleperson of the Year you had no room in your head for the dead-wood of yesterday's buyers. Peggy hurried on. "No, not that. We got an offer on the house, *at the full asking price—*"

"That's swell. Listen, Peg, you caught me at a bad time."

"No problem," she said, with a big smile in her voice. "You go back to your work. I'll just draw the contracts up, and get the ball rolling."

"Thanks a lot."

Cilda walked into the room. "Somebody's buying the Spring Lake house," I told her. "And Walter Wozniak has a new car."

From the way the old woman shrugged, I knew she was thinking about her daughter Mercedes, in New York, throwing all that money away on rent, without even a driver's license to show for it.

THIRTY-FIVE

The Saturday before Thanksgiving was an unusually warm day. One of the New York news stations actually sent a camera crew to Sea Bright to shoot some footage for the six o'clock weather report. It showed a bunch of diehards in shorts and windbreakers playing Frisbee, sunning themselves on the beach, even venturing into the water. "Look at them fools," chortled Cilda, "and 'ere it is, a few days until T'anksgiving."

I switched channels to avoid the sports. In the past couple of weeks, I'd become an expert channel surfer. It seemed I spent entire days with a remote in my hand, entire nights too—switching from David Letterman to Jay Leno, Tom Snyder to Conan O'Brien—a limited life, but it was all mine.

That particular night, Cilda went to her room about nine o'clock. The younger guy, Joey, had come on at eight; Mitchell would be relieving him, on the four to noon shift. Personally, I liked it better when the schedule fell the other way around, because at least then I could count on a couple of hands of cards to pass the time. Joey wasn't the type to socialize very much. You could tell he felt uncomfortable just sitting around the house, starting at every little sound, expecting something to happen. Like me.

I found him out on the porch, smoking a cigarette. "I'm turning in," I said.

"Have a good night then." He looked guilty for having lit up a smoke.

"You too."

It was still early, but I felt headachy and tired, so I didn't even bother to zap the television on. I put on a T-shirt, crawled between the sheets, and fell into one of those deep but vaguely disturbing dreams that I used to have when I was a child. When the phone rang, I had to force myself to answer it. "Hullo...?"

Cilda's son, Deon, was on the line, speaking in a voice so agitated that it took me a moment to fully comprehend. His girlfriend Gail had to go to the hospital, he said. The baby was coming early, at seven months. Kathianne had promised to watch Gail's two school-aged children, but the painters were coming to the salon early in the morning. Would his mother come take care of them, did I think?

The digital clock on my bedstand read 11:20. I'd been sleeping for less than two hours, but it felt like much more. Rubbing my eyes and struggling to sit upright, I told Deon yes, not to worry, I'd drive his mom into Brooklyn myself. Then I stumbled down the hall to tell Cilda. When she didn't respond to my knocking, I went inside the room and shook her awake.

"Gail's baby's coming," I said. "We have to hurry."

The old woman looked confused, as though she couldn't remember who Gail was. I told her about Deon's call, and watched her move wearily out of bed.

I went back to my room and put on a pair of jeans, running shoes, and a sweater. Cilda was already waiting for me downstairs, in her dress and coat, with a small suitcase at her feet. "You want coffee?" she asked.

"No. Just some aspirin." My headache was worse.

Cilda frowned. "You better let that boy know."

Except for an hourly patrol around the house, the man on duty usually stayed in the house at night. From the still-warm cup of coffee and the open newspaper in the downstairs recreation room, I guessed that Joey had just left to make his rounds. I dialed his number, but got no answer. Tucking my cellular and beeper into my bag, I scrawled out a hasty note—

Joey,
Family emergency. I took Cilda to her
daughter's in Brooklyn. We'll call you
from the road. Don't worry.
Quinn

"Maybe we should wait on 'im," Cilda faltered, torn between prudence and the desire to help out her only son.

I picked up her suitcase. "It'll be fine. Walter Dean isn't going to follow us all the way to Brooklyn."

Although it had cooled off considerably, it was still balmy for November. The black sky sparkled with a smattering of stars, but the outdoor security lights made the path look as bright as day. We walked to the garage, still logy with sleep, moving in a daze. I kept expecting Joey to jump out of the bushes, with an official-sounding warning like, *"Halt! Where do you two think you're going?"* but he didn't; most likely, he was walking from the seawall to the office, shining his flashlight into every crack and crevice.

I warmed up the car for a minute, then

put it into gear and drove slowly up the drive, and through the new security gate. It was eleven-forty. I'd had a two-hour nap but my body still felt like it had been battered by a powerful fist. Once we got out onto the road, I cranked the windows down and the radio up.

Cilda didn't speak until we were on the Turnpike; then she asked, "Do you t'ink the baby will 'ave a chance?"

I patted her hand. "Doctors can perform miracles these days," I said.

Cilda nodded, wanting to believe. "I brought two receiving blankets. The weather is bound to turn. 'E'll need somet'ing warm to come 'ome from 'ospital in," she said.

It was after one in the morning by the time we reached Kathianne's place on Utica Avenue. We found the two small offspring of Deon's hapless girlfriend sitting on the couch, watching TV in their pajamas. Kathianne was clearly at her wit's end.

"They say their mama lets them look at MTV." Kathy's husband worked the nightshift, and she was at the salon all day long; they'd never had time for children of their own. It was clear that, tonight, she didn't regret her decision one bit.

"Turn that awful noise off," ordered Cilda, "and go brush your teeth."

"We don't have our toothbrushes," said the little girl.

"Well, use your finger then. Up and down wit' the paste." The kids scampered into the bathroom.

"What about the baby?" Cilda wanted to know.

Kathianne said there'd been no news yet. "Come," she said. "I have some coffee on."

"I'll take mine for the road, Kath," I said.

"You're not staying?" She was dismayed. "I made up a bed."

"The baby-sitters don't like it when I'm out late at night." Truth was, my headache had disappeared and I figured I might as well move while I still had the energy.

Cilda said, "First you got to call the boy."

I'd telephoned Joey twice from the car without an answer. While Kathy filled up a plastic mug, I tried again. "Must be something wrong with his cellular."

"Or maybe that crazy man come and conk 'im over the 'ead," Cilda scolded. "You're not goin' back tonight, Ga'ner Quinn. Not wit'out one a them bodyguards."

"I'll keep trying him." I gave Kathy a hug, but Cilda stood fast and stubborn, warding off my kiss. "I promise I will not pass through those expensive new gates without having first made contact with one of the boys from G and P. Cross my heart."

"On your mot'er's grave," said Cilda, who knew that I frequently lied.

I sighed. "On my mother's grave."

The two kids peered into the kitchen a little fearfully. "Will you read us a story?" the little girl asked.

"At two a.m. in the morning? Heavens no!" She scooted them down the hall and into the guest bedroom.

I picked up my coffee, grinning to myself. A couple of days with Mrs. Fields and those MTV-watching children would never be the same.

THIRTY-SIX

It was three-thirty in the morning by the time I reached the outer edges of my property. The heavy air sifted through the cracks in my old Volvo, steaming up the windows. Every mile or so I used my hand to rub the moisture away. I was beginning to feel sleepy again, but my headache seemed gone for good.

Joey hadn't responded to any of my calls. It didn't seem likely that the pages hadn't gone through. I had a bad feeling, and yet here I was in a car that kept heading east, toward the house, as if it were being operated by some unseen remote control.

I'd sworn a solemn promise to Cilda that I wouldn't drive past the front gate without a sign from one of the guards to assure me that everything was all right, and I wasn't about to break my vow. But I knew that Mitchell would be coming on duty at four, and I had a vague notion of meeting up with him on the far side of the fence. Despite Mitchell's easygoing manner, he wouldn't be a man you'd want to mess with. An ex-football player, with 220 pounds of solid muscle on his frame, if there was any trouble inside, Mitch would be able to handle it. Still, as much as I liked him, I would've traded his biceps in a second to have paunchy old Mike Fedora by my side.

An apricot blush was already spreading through the pine trees. As I drove farther into the woods, the color deepened to a fiery orange. Belatedly, it hit me. *This couldn't be right. It was still hours away from sunrise.* I took out a tissue and wiped the fogged-up windshield, then craned my neck and looked upward. A plume of black smoke billowed over the treetops, blowing east toward the water.

I grabbed my cellular phone. On the leather case was a yellow sticker listing the local emergency numbers. "This is Garner Quinn, over on Peninsula Point Road," I said to the dispatcher. "There's a fire here—it looks bad...You've got to send people over quick."

"Is your house on fire, Ms. Quinn?"

"I don't know...I think so..."

"Where are you now, ma'am?"

"In the woods, outside the gate."

"Is there anyone in the house, Ms. Quinn?"

"No," I said. Then I remembered Joey. "Oh my God...there could be. My body-guard might be in there."

"Stay where you are, ma'am," the operator said. "The trucks will be arriving momentarily—" She continued to talk in her calm, kind voice, but I tossed the phone into my bag and stepped out of the car, leaving the driver's door wide open.

Night in these woods could be eerily quiet, with the ocean only a whispery roar like the air in a shell. But as I walked those last few yards to the gate, this night was filled with other sounds—the crackle-snap of wood collapsing, the slap and lick of flames. I used my security pass to open the gate. I'd sworn on my mother's grave not to do this, but she was never really a mother to me, I reasoned, and surely Cilda would let it pass, knowing that a human life might be at stake.

I could see my house, in the final throes of death by fire. Funnels of smoke blew toward the seawall. How far the devastation spread I couldn't tell—the office was too far away and great black clouds obscured the guest quarters. I wanted to run, but I kept picturing the callow young face of the guard, Joey.

Had he fallen asleep in the rec room, smoking a cigarette? Could one little spark do all this damage? If so, he was surely dead; and yet, if he hadn't been inside when it started, he might still be alive.

The easterly breeze had, up to this point, kept the garage out of the fire's path. I went toward it, shouting, "Joey! Joe—are you there?"

There was no answer. Shielding my eyes from the smoke, I staggered toward the house, continuing to call, "Joey! Joey, if you're here, please answer me!" But I knew that no one within its crumbling walls could've survived this blaze.

I changed directions, giving wide berth to the flames, moving parallel to the ocean. My peripheral vision picked up movement some fifty yards away. I turned, not believing what I saw.

A figure was crawling over the back of the seawall, having climbed up from the ocean side. On his belly, he edged sideways like a crab. Even through the sooty haze of blowing smoke, I could tell it wasn't Joey.

I watched the man lower himself on the toe-holds of the rocks. About halfway, he lost his grip, fell to the ground, and, panting heavily, raised himself to his feet. At the moment Walter Dean Wozniak saw me, I could've sworn he looked surprised.

"You—" He rushed in my direction. "You—"

I stood, frozen in horror, as Wozniak came charging, hollering my name into the fiery skies. In one crystal, freeze-frame instant, it registered—his matted hair and dirty face, the wild, half-crazed look in his eyes—how much his already tenuous sanity had deteriorated.

"Don't—" he screamed. "You've got to—"

A shot rang out through the air. Walter Wozniak's knees buckled, and he fell into a kneeling position. The next shot toppled him. Still, he edged toward me on his elbows, reaching out a hand to touch my feet.

"You—" he managed to whisper.

I looked up at the seawall, where Mitchell was standing, his gun still drawn. "I think he's dead," I called. Neither of us moved a muscle or said anything, until the loud scream of the fire engines broke the silence. Then Mitchell put his gun away, jumped off the wall.

He came to me, slinging his big, sheltering arm over my shoulder. "It's all over, Garner," he said in his soft Texas drawl. "Ain't nobody can hurt you now."

THIRTY-SEVEN

Walter Dean Wozniak had come by sea. Police discovered the silver Nissan he'd been driving parked on a side street in Sea Bright. They figured that he'd walked along the beach for miles, traveling toward the tip of the peninsula, and that he'd camped in the woods surrounding my estate for at least three days. In a tiny clearing, the security team found a nylon backpack filled with notebooks and letters, some matches, and a rain poncho. A filthy blanket, two empty sardine cans, and an Oreo cookie bag had been pushed under a log.

Matt Raice pieced together a plausible scenario which he related to me a few hours later, in the Red Bank diner where we'd stopped for breakfast. According to Matt's version of events, Joey must've spotted something suspicious on the beach when he was making his hourly rounds. He'd climbed the rickety stairs over the seawall, unaware that Wozniak waited below with a huge hunk of wood in his hand. Joey, the one everybody called "the kid," had been found lying under the rusted metal steps with his brains bashed in.

Assuming that I was asleep inside, Wozniak had then set fire to the house. "It's like in *Chasm*," Matt said, "where the demon rips his lover's heart out and burns her body. I guess, in the end, wacky Walt wanted to go out with a big symbolic bang."

"But why did he go back to the beach?"

"By that time, Mitchell had arrived," Raice explained. "He'd seen the flames from the road, and as he was coming through the gate, he got a glimpse of Walter by the guest house. Mitch actually tried to run the bastard down, but Wozniak managed to dodge him and hoist himself over the seawall. Mitchell ditched the car and started after him. He figured when Joey didn't answer his radio calls, he was on his own. He spotted Walter Dean on the sand, and he went tearing after him. Wozniak must've known there was no way he'd be able to outrun a human freight train, so he tried scaling the wall again. You know the rest."

Yes, I did. It wasn't easy to forget the sight of a man crawling on his belly to die at your feet. "The important thing," Matt said, "is that this whole nightmare has finally come to an end."

"Then why doesn't it feel finished to me?"

Matt leaned across the table and patted my hand. "Your house just burned down to the ground, Garner. You're still in shock."

I didn't feel like I was in shock. In fact, when I'd gone down the list of what had been destroyed by the fire, all I regretted losing were the photographs that Temple and Cilda had so lovingly assembled—although I did experience a twinge at the thought of Blackmoor's picture, on my nightstand, being engulfed by flames. Perhaps, I told myself, it was just another sign, signaling the end of a relationship.

"Excuse me, Matt," I said, getting up to use the pay phone. "I want to call Cilda again."

In the same moment that Walter Dean Wozniak had uttered his dying breath, Deon's girlfriend Gail was giving birth to a three-pound baby girl whom they named Cilda Chanté. "She's only a little t'ing," said Cilda, "but perfect from 'ead to toe."

When I'd first told my old friend about the fire, she'd taken the news matter-of-factly; now that it had finally sunk in, she started to cry. "And is not'ing left then?" Her voice quavered. "Not'ing at hall?"

"I'm afraid not, Cild," I said. "They're coming over later to bulldoze the place."

There was a jostling sound, someone taking the receiver from her. Mercedes's voice came on the line. "Where are you?" she asked sharply.

"At a diner, having breakfast with Matthew Raice," I said.

"Good. Now listen, Garner. Ask your friend Matt to drive you into the city. You're staying with me until you get your head on straight." I started to protest, but Mercedes was adamant. "I won't take no for an answer. You don't show up by this afternoon, I'll hunt you down and drag you back myself. Girl, you know that I will."

THIRTY-EIGHT

It was two o'clock in the afternoon when Matt Raice dropped me off in front of Mercedes's prewar building at Ninety-sixth and Central Park West. I expected the doorman to hand me an envelope with a key, but he buzzed the apartment, and I heard Mercedes say, "Send her up."

She was standing in the doorway when I stepped off the elevator. "I thought you'd be at work," I said, following her inside.

"It's not very often a family has a house burn down and a baby being born on the same day." Mercedes shrugged.

It occurred to me that Matt might be right. I probably was in shock. At least I wasn't hearing clearly, because I could've sworn that in a roundabout, assbackward way, Mercedes Fields had just called me family. I started to cry.

"Besides," she said gruffly, "it's Sunday." She went over to the kitchen counter, poured a cup of green tea, and handed it to me. "You look like you could use a shower. There's a robe hanging on the hook in the bathroom."

Mercedes sat down on the stool next to me. "By the way, I finally reached Temple in Florida." Andy and Candace had whisked my daughter off on a little Palm Beach getaway. "That ex-husband of yours is a piece of work." She shook her head. "He actually asked me if the fire had destroyed your wedding pictures."

"You should've told him not to worry," I said, sipping the tea. "I burned them a long time ago. How did Temple take the news?"

"Once she knew you and Mama were okay, the only thing she wanted to know was whether she'd be getting all new clothes. I told her yes."

"Thanks." I took a paper napkin from the counter and blew my nose in it.

"Oh, and Garner..." Mercedes stopped me as I headed for the bathroom. "While you're here, you should stay in my bedroom. I keep odd hours. It'll be easier this way."

I nodded, knowing it was useless to argue.

Mercedes's bed looked like the litter that had carried the Queen of Sheba in the mural on Dane Blackmoor's walls. Her sheets, of course, were slippery satin. She'd put down the blinds and drawn the drapes, so that I could almost imagine it was night. I closed my eyes and immediately fell asleep.

I was still in la-la land when Mercedes went to work the next morning. She left an extremely detailed letter as to what was in the refrigerator and freezer, and how her various kitchen appliances operated. My jeans, sweater, underwear, and socks had been laundered and folded neatly on the arm of the couch. I could swear my running shoes looked cleaner too. It really pissed me off. I warmed up some soup ("beef lentil in the orange microwavable bowl"), had a dish of ice cream ("low-fat but delicious"), and went back to bed.

Eight hours later, I was still there. "Rise and shine." Mercedes snapped on the light. "You're about to wear out my sheets."

As I struggled to sit up on my elbows, she swung four big shopping bags onto the bed. "What's all this?"

"I went to Bloomingdale's after work.

Picked you up some clothes." Mercedes began removing things from the bags—bright-colored shirts and dresses, a pair of velvet jeans, a white blouse with a jabot of frilly pleats, Calvin Klein underwear, a bunch of stockings, two pairs of shoes. She tossed me a paper bag, only six inches long but heavy.

"What's this?"

"White-girl makeup," Mercedes laughed, "and Caucasian shampoo."

My blood boiled, fired by an irrational but absolute anger. I wanted to throw the clothes onto the floor and stomp on them. But I stopped myself.

For the first time in my life, I realized what it must've been like for Mercedes—opening up all those birthday gifts and Christmas presents, care packages from her mama's thoughtful young charge; and later, the casual favors and last-minute rescues, the easily opened doors.

Mercedes and I were really two of a kind. We didn't easily take to being on the receiving end; we felt much better holding the reins of kindness tightly in our own very capable hands.

"Thank you, Mercedes," I said, with the same sullen graciousness that I'd often heard in her voice.

"You're welcome, Garner," she replied.

Temple called from Florida three times in one night. It was the phenomenon that I called "the progression of the voice"—in which her tone went from bright and chipper, to wistful and sad, and ended in whispered desperation.

"Daddy said I'm going home with Candace and him when we get back from Florida tomorrow. He wants me to enroll in school in Manhattan until you get us settled in another house, but I don't want to." She brought the volume down another notch. "They're driving me *crazy*, Mom. They bought me a set of *golf clubs*. With this leather carrying case that has all *Minnie Mouses* on it, wearing little golf shoes with big red *bows.*"

I stifled a laugh, while Temple went on. "Can't I come to Auntie Merce's with you? She already said it would be okay."

"Well, if Auntie Merce *said* so"—I shot a look toward Mercedes, who was innocently eating pretzels out of a bag—"it's fine with me. Let me talk to your father."

Andy got on the phone, primed for a fight, but at least he had the sense to snap his fingers and send Temple out of the room first. "This is way out of line even for you, Garner. For all intents and purposes, you're homeless. What are you going to do—drag our daughter around like a nomad, from camp to camp, visiting the hired help?"

I opened my mouth, but for a split second nothing but white-hot rage poured out. Mercedes sat across the room, midpretzel, watching me like I was the television set. "Tell Temple I'll pick her up as soon as you get back from the airport," I snarled.

"This isn't over, Garner," Andy warned. "You may have won the battle, but if you don't get your act together, be prepared to fight a war."

I slammed the receiver. "Have you noticed," I said to Mercedes, "that all the nice men get blown up by bombs on the first date?"

"No," she replied. "But then, you and I lead very different lives." She offered me the bag of pretzels.

"Besides, I can think of one"—her voice dipped into a purr—"*really* nice man you know who's alive and well and living in Paris."

"Forget him," I said, munching.

"Forget him? When he's got two of the most important qualities a man can have?"

"Let me guess." I laughed. "He's rich and handsome."

Mercedes shook her head. "He's rich," she corrected, "and the way he looks at you could soil a wench's underwear. I've been waiting my whole life for a man to look at me that way."

"Yeah, well, so have I." I felt myself blushing. "For all the good it's done."

"You give up too easy, sugar. Take that last tango in Paris, for example. You should've had your sights set on closing the deal, but no, you get all bent out of shape because Dane— thinking he's doing something *nice*—asks me to dinner. So you end up all hurt and frustrated, and instead of spending an unforgettable evening kicking in all the Parisian hot spots, I get stuck staying up half the night, listening to Blackmoor rant and rail about you."

"I'm sorry I acted like such a bitch in the restaurant."

Mercedes snatched the pretzel bag. "You showed your true colors," she said, with a sly, wide smile. "I like it when you get angry, Garner. All the icky sweetness drops out of your voice and you stop talking down to me."

THIRTY-NINE

The next morning I called Matthew Raice. "I'm thinking about renting a car and driving up to Forked Brook. Any chance you can squeeze me in between crises?"

"I've got a hell of day scheduled." He sounded tired. "What's up?"

"Just a crazy thought," I said. "Another connection with Annie and Reed."

Matt sighed. "I might be able to juggle some things between eleven-thirty and noon, but I'm not at the training facility today, I'm in Manhattan."

"Even better," I said.

The corporate offices of Corbin, Incorporated, which specialized in security issues on the federal and international levels, were located on Park Avenue in the Fifties, not far from the Waldorf-Astoria. I put on one of Mercedes's new purchases—a houndstooth check suit, black stockings, black shoes—and borrowed her raincoat.

It had been a couple of days since I'd been outside. The air hit me like a splash of cold water. I'd given myself enough time to walk the entire way, but now that I was on the street, my legs felt like rubber. When the doorman asked if I wanted a taxi, I said yes.

It had been only eleven when the cab dropped me off in front of Matt's building. I considered hiking over to Madison to look for a coffee shop, but after the inactivity of the last weeks, even a couple of blocks seemed daunting. I headed for the lobby and took the elevator to the thirty-first floor.

When the doors opened, I stepped into an impressive carpeted entranceway. *Corbin, Inc.,* was engraved on the brass nameplate. I rang the bell, gave my name, and waited to be buzzed inside. A heavily tanned woman in her forties, with a perky gym rat physique, stood up to greet me.

"Nice to meet you, Ms. Quinn. I'm Matthew's assisant, Linda Forrest. I'm afraid he wasn't expecting you until later." When she smiled, her bronze skin crinkled in a million places. "Would you like something? Coffee? Tea?"

"No, thanks," I said. "I'm fine."

"I know you were a friend of Reed's." Forrest patted my arm sympathetically. "We all miss him terribly. Although, to be honest, in the four years I've worked here, I probably only saw him a dozen times. Matt handles all of our international clients."

"So I've heard," although there was no one else in the waiting room, I lowered my voice. "How's the Adrian Nadeau investigation progressing?"

Forrest looked puzzled. "Gosh, that name doesn't ring a bell," she said. "You'll have to ask Matthew." *That I will,* I thought to myself. I also reminded myself to tell Matt about the Egon Schiele drawing I'd seen in Nadeau's gallery. It shouldn't be too hard for him to run a check on it and see if it could be traced back to Dane Blackmoor. If it weren't for the fact that with each passing day, I'd become more and more pissed off by Dane's silence, I would've done it myself.

The phone rang and Forrest answered it, "Corbin and Raice, International." I drifted over to a chair, wondering at the recent addition of Matt's name to the firm.

The reading material stacked on the end table was news- and business-oriented, sprinkled with some slick, shiny European lifestyle magazines. I picked one of the British glossies and began to thumb through it. On the back pages, there was a listing of fine properties for sale, which I scanned, thinking, *Hmm...could I be happy on these four rambling acres of riverfront gardens? Or perhaps in the charming 1830s cottage, completely furnished with antiques?* I tried to imagine Temple, Cilda, and myself living in a foreign place full of strangers, like Dane Blackmoor, or in another part of this country—Montana, or Missouri, or Maine. The possibilities were endless. And yet, I couldn't quite picture it.

"Matthew will see you now," Linda Forrest said.

She led me down a fluorescent-lit corridor. The space was typical of many New York offices. One side was an open maze of cubicles; the other had been divided into conference rooms. Matt Raice held the prized corner office, with the best view. The furnishings here were a little more plush than the ones at Forked Brook, but the only decorative touch was a bright, dappled watercolor showing a naked man leaning over, drinking from a pool of water.

"It's a John Singer Sargent." Raice followed my gaze. "My mother always said if I had a choice between a huge painting—finished, but mediocre—and a few small but perfect brushstrokes, I should always go for the good stuff."

"I wanted to thank you for being there for me," I said. "After the fire."

"Don't mention it. How're you holding up?"

"Pretty well. What about you?" He looked as though he hadn't slept for days.

"You don't want to know." Raice sighed and pointed to a seat.

"Sure I do."

His blue eyes narrowed, as though he was deciding whether to trust me or not. "This can't go beyond these walls," he warned.

"I promise."

"There's been a threat. They say they're going to set off another bomb in New York City within the next forty-eight hours."

My stomach lurched. "The Fourth Freedom?"

Matt nodded. "We're working closely with the FBI, of course, tracking every Middle Eastern political cell known in the area."

He leaned forward. "You can't breathe a word of this, Garner. Not to anyone."

"I won't."

He broke into a battered smile. "That's

the bad news. Now give me some good. What's the lastest crazy notion you've got into your head?"

"It seems even crazier after what you just told me," I admitted. "But I've been thinking a lot about Reed's brother."

"Mark?"

"I know he's into drugs. Do you think he might've had a motive for wanting Reed dead?"

"He was left some money in the will." Matt sounded dubious. "But backtrack a second. You mentioned something about a possible connection to your friend Annie?"

"It's slender at best." I plunged ahead. "Annie had a friend—a co-worker named Roberto, who recently left Dane Blackmoor's studio to go live with some man in Amsterdam."

"And you think that man might've been Mark?" He wasn't buying. "That's really—" The phone rang. Although I couldn't hear what was being said on the other end, I could tell by Raice's expression that something big had happened. Before he'd even hung up, he was grabbing his jacket.

"I have to go," he panted. "The FBI's got a bead on Abdul Amer."

"Well, what're you waiting for?"

"Sorry about this, Garn. Mind if I run ahead?" He bolted down the corridor, leaving me with a harried promise to keep in touch.

I continued walking past the cubicles, surprised when I heard a familiar voice call out my name. Mike Fedora was using a desk as leverage, trying to heave himself out of his chair. He'd lost some weight, and one hand was still bandaged. "Mike!" I jogged over to him. "Sit down, please."

"Na, if I don't keep movin' this damn leg, it gets stiff as a board. The surgeon couldn't get all the shrapnel out." Fedora's face darkened. "I heard about your house, Garner. I shoulda put a bullet in that SOB when I had the chance, but I guess you never know about these things."

"No," I agreed, "you never do. What brings you to these parts, Mike?"

"Paperwork." He shrugged sheepishly. "They offered me a nice early-retirement package, and I'm gonna take it. Do some traveling, maybe learn how to fish."

"Well, that's good," I said, not really knowing whether it was or not. "But it's a big loss to the firm."

"Yeah, well, something like this happens..." His eyes misted. "It's tough, comin' back."

"I know." I pressed his hand. "Looks like the two of us are starting over from scratch, Mr. Fedora, like the hat."

He gave me a big bear hug. "Knowin' you, Garner, you'll be pushin' the envelope again in no time."

"Say, Mike," I said, on a hunch, "remember that phone call I asked you about, the one Reed was expecting that night? It wouldn't have been from a man named Adrian Nadeau, would it?"

"Nah." Fedora didn't skip a beat. "We were waitin' to hear back from the doc." He read the confusion on my face. "Dr. Raice. Apparently there was some kinda mix-up with the invitations. The doc's wife didn't realize the book thing was that night."

"They'd been planning to come down from Boston for the party?"

"Oh, they don't live up there no more," Mike said. "After Doc retired from Harvard, they moved into one of those big high-rises over by Lincoln Center."

"Are you sure that was the call Reed was so anxious about? When I asked you about it in the hospital, you said you couldn't remember."

"It took a while for it all to come back," Mike said. "Some parts I wish I could forget." The old tough guy was on the verge of tears. "Every night in my sleep that damn bomb goes off, Garner. Hell of a thing." He shook his head. "Hell of a thing."

FORTY

When I thought about it, it made perfect sense. Gerald Raice had been Reed's mentor. Naturally, he would've wanted the old man to be present at a book party celebrating the publication of *The Fear Factor*—especially since the book had been dedicated to him.

> *To Professor Gerald Raice,*
> *For telling me I could,*
> *and for always listening.*

Just minutes before he was killed, Reed had said he felt as though he'd been going around in circles. I wondered now if, during those last days, he'd sought the counsel of his friend and benefactor. It was another long-shot, but I had hours to pass before I picked up Temple at Andy's, and the Raices' apartment building in Lincoln Plaza was only a short cab ride away.

When I spoke to her on the phone, Mary Raice told me that the professor took his nap after lunch, but I was welcome to call on them at two o'clock. I got a quick bite at a café on Amsterdam Avenue; then, in a gesture of calculated kindness, I stopped by an Asian grocer's and bought a bouquet of autumn flowers. From the two brief conversations I'd had with Mrs. Raice, one thing was clear—whether her taciturn husband would open up, or retreat farther into his shell, would be completely up to her.

"Gerberas!" she cried, taking the flowers from me. "And such a beautiful shade too! How did you know they were my favorite?" *And Garner Quinn scores the first point.*

"Come, my dear." I followed Mary Raice into the small apartment. "We were just about to have some tea."

The living room, which was only the size of my old bedroom, had been crammed with art objects and collectibles, a wealth of possessions accrued over the course of two lives, which had at one time probably fit very neatly into the Raices' Boston home. Here, in this beige box of a room, they were almost overwhelming. Oriental carpets overlapped each other, forming quiltlike patterns over the hardwood floor. The shelves of the bookcases did double duty, displaying an array of antique ivory and Limoges boxes. *This is what the fire saved you from,* my inner self whispered, and the thought was strangely exhilerating.

Dr. Raice sat in a worn morris chair in one corner. In his younger days, he'd probably been a tall man, but he appeared to have shrunk to fit the proportions of the room. An old boxer curled up lazily at the professor's feet. The dog's ears pricked up and he whimpered at the sight of me.

"Gerald," said his wife, "this is the young lady we met at poor Reed's funeral. Garner Quinn. One of Mattie's clients?"

"Please don't get up," I told him. But only the boxer was on his feet.

"Sit, Shadow," commanded Dr. Raice; then, gesturing to a sofa, he said to me, "You too."

"Well, if you'll excuse me for a moment," Mary Raice said, "I'm going to put these exquisite flowers in some water, and bring in the tea."

After she left the room, the only sounds were the asthmatic breathing of the boxer and the ticking from an ormolu clock. I knew the old woman wouldn't be long in the kitchen, so I decided to take the direct approach. "You don't know me, Dr. Raice," I said, "but your son Matt thinks I'm a bit of a pain in the ass."

Had a flicker of a smile really passed over his lips, or was it just the play of lamplight and shadow? I went on: "Pain in the ass or not, I really liked Reed Corbin, and I won't know a day's peace until I find out who killed him."

I waited for the old man to say something, but he didn't. "Your son," I told him, "and the FBI agents working the case think a group of terrorists are responsible. I don't know why, but I'm not so sure. Something was bothering Reed before he died. Now, besides Matt, you were probably the person closest to him. Did he say anything to you—anything at all—about what was on his mind?"

Dr. Raice leaned forward in his chair, causing the boxer to lift his jowly face and whine. "I didn't go to the party that night," he said.

"I know."

"I was invited," the old man said, "but there was a mix-up. I can't recall the details. You'd have to ask my wife."

That's when it hit me, like a ton of bricks. *Holy shit. Gerald Raice was senile.*

I saw it now, in his slack jaw, and the unblinking, opacity of his stare. "Have you ever been to the Metropolitan Opera?" he asked suddenly. "It's only two blocks away. My wife and I used to go frequently, but somehow we don't anymore. Funny too, because I believe that's why we moved here."

"It's a lovely apartment," I said, at a loss.

"Lemon or milk?" Mary Raice's voice sang out from the kitchen.

"Milk," I called back. I began edging out of the room, desperate to escape from the claustrophobic clutter. "But please don't fuss."

Mrs. Raice set down the tea service on the

dining room table. "Oh, my dear, I'm afraid fussing is out of the question these days."

Our eyes met, and I realized that under her bone-thin elegance was a frail, tired woman. "Teatime, Professor!" she managed to sing merrily. "Time for tea!"

Gerald Raice shuffled into the room, the old boxer tagging after him. "Tea," he said. "Tea and cookies."

The table and chairs were contemporary Pottery Barn, probably purchased because they could fit in such a confining space. A corner cabinet angled awkwardly against one wall. On the mahogany sideboard a dozen photographs, mostly of Matt, were proudly displayed.

I picked one up. "You two certainly have a handsome son."

The breezy compliment blew up in my face. "That's not my son," the professor thundered. His face turned beet red and contorted with rage. *"My son is dead!"* Under the table, the boxer stirred nervously.

Mary Raice compressed her lips together, bleeding neatly applied lipstick over the thin line of her mouth. "Now, Gerald," she said. "Calm down. Garner wasn't talking about Reed. She meant Mattie, Gerald. Our Matt."

"I've lost my boy," the old man wailed. "He's gone...blown into pieces..." He hammered his big fists down onto the table so hard that the silver chattered and the dog whined. "Dead—do you hear me? MY-SON-IS-DEAD!"

"I'm so sorry," I said to Mary.

She smiled sadly and shook her head. "He gets this way sometimes. It's been much worse recently."

Dr. Raice began muttering incoherently, rocking back and forth in his chair so frenetically that the room seemed to shake with aftershocks. "Look, Daddy, see what I have," Mrs. Raice said soothingly, going over to the corner cabinet. "Your bestest thing in all the world."

She brought a beautiful enameled Easter egg back to the table. Her husband reached for it greedily, but she held it away from him, saying, "Shh. You know the rule—you have to be perfectly still."

The old man sputtered and sighed. I heard but did not watch him. My eyes were fastened on the egg. Its color—a particularly vibrant shade of red known as vermilion—seemed not quite of this earth. Gold lattice fretwork, studded with diamonds, added to its gemlike splendor.

Dr. Raice stared, silent, enthralled. "Are you ready, Gerald?" his wife asked. "This is his favorite part," she explained. "The surprise inside, the beautiful surprise."

Her slender fingers worked the tiny clasp. "*Ta-da*," she sang. The egg opened to reveal an exquisite miniature of a palace, fashioned out of precious metals and encrusted with diamonds and pearls.

Gerald Raice's dead eyes lit up, and he smiled. "Again," he said, watching in delight as his wife closed and opened the delicate shell.

It took me a while to find my voice. "It's a Fabergé, isn't it?" I whispered.

"Bless your heart, dear." Mary Raice smiled. "A genuine Fabergé egg would cost upward of a million dollars, I imagine. Mattie gave this to me for my birthday last year—although I told him, I said, it's just the most amazingly detailed replica I've ever seen."

"Yes," I agreed. "Yes, it is."

A few minutes later I said my goodbyes. Gerald Raice was still sitting at the small dining room table, lost in the splendor of the vermilion egg.

"I hope you'll forgive the professor's outburst," Mary said as we walked to the door. "And I'd appreciate it if you didn't mention anything to Matt. Poor Mattie." She sighed. "He and his father always had such a hard time of it together. Not like Reed, of course. Reed Corbin was the apple of my husband's eye."

FORTY-ONE

That night, we all went out to one of the noisy Columbus Avenue bistros for dinner. Temple and Mercedes slid into the upholstered bench across from me. They checked out men, finished each other's sentences, and had at least three separate attacks of the giggles. When Auntie Merce spoke, my daughter listened, with an expression of rapt adoration on her face.

It made the knot in my chest feel almost like a heart again, just to watch them.

. . .

Temple got clingy around bedtime, so I tucked her inside a fleecy blanket, as insulation from the satin sheets, and we cuddled, and cried together about the house. "What's going to happen to us, Mom?" she asked in a groggy voice.

"We'll be fine." I kissed her forehead, while the knot moved up to my throat.

When she finally drifted off to sleep, I walked out into the living room. "I need a favor," I said. "Could Temple hang out with you at work tomorrow?"

Mercedes looked surprised. "Sure. But remember, it's Inflation Eve."

On the Upper West Side of New York, "Inflation Eve" referred to the night before Thanksgiving, when the famous Macy's parade balloons were taken out of storage and inflated with helium. The residents along Central Park West groused about the noise, the crowds, the inconvenience of having all that hubbub on their doorsteps, but the sight of those huge crumpled, flat canvases unfurling and taking shape drew even the most jaded New Yorkers out to the street. Wrapped in stadium blankets, they sat in portable lawn chairs and sipped champagne, watching the sleeping giants spring to life. The annual ritual had become as much of a tradition as Thanksgiving itself. Mercedes was planning to do a feature for *Front Cover*.

"The later you keep her out," I said, "the better."

319

Mercedes frowned. "What's this about, Garner?"

I sat on the counter stool next to her. "I'm not sure," I said. "I'm just not sure."

FORTY-TWO

The call I'd been waiting for came at noon the following day. Matt Raice apologized for cutting our meeting short and asked if I could meet him for dinner. I told him there was nothing I'd like more. "Why don't you stop by the office around eight-fifteen," he suggested. "There's something I've been meaning to give you."

By late afternoon, it had started to drizzle. The forecasters were calling for light precipitation through the evening, and then a clear but breezy Thanksgiving Day. Before they left this morning, Mercedes had made Temple swap her short skirt and platform shoes for jeans, a warm sweater, and low-heeled boots. I wondered if my daughter would think being a television reporter was so glamorous after she spent a few hours tramping around in the rain.

The day passed slowly. Sleep had eluded me the night before, but instead of being tired I felt edgy and nauseated. I put on the coat I'd borrowed from Mercedes, a camel-colored jacket with a hood, and then took it off— twice—to run to the bathroom. When I finally managed to make it down to the street, a cab was waiting at the curb. I cracked the rear window, hoping the cold, rainy air would revive me.

I ran into Linda Forrest in front of the polished mahogany doors of Corbin, Incorporated. "Oh, Ms. Quinn, I was just locking up. Matt's waiting inside." She glanced at my wet coat. "It's raining? Shoot. I better go get my umbrella." She pronounced it "*um*-brella" like people did down south.

We walked into the office together. I shook off my jacket, and Forrest fished a portable Totes out of a cubby of her desk. "Would you like me to tell Matt you're here?"

"No, go ahead." I waved her off. "I know the way."

Once she was gone, I headed down the hall to Raice's office. The cubicles were empty now, lit only by the building's security lights. In one of the conference rooms, a cleaning lady emptied trash into a large bag on a metal trolley. She smiled when she saw me, and I smiled back.

Matt was working at his computer. I knocked on the doorjamb. "Guess who?"

"I hope to hell it's my dinner date," Matt said, glancing over his shoulder. Then he shut off his monitor, sighing, "Goddamn, I'm tired."

"That makes two of us." I sat down in the chair across from him. "Where are we going, anyway?"

Raice swung his feet onto the desk. "I didn't even make a reservation yet. I figured the night before Thanksgiving, all the normal people would be home, stuffing their turkeys."

"What does that say about us?"

"I don't know." He laughed. "How about a quick drink for the road? Take off your coat. Relax."

I shivered. "I'll pass. My stomach's been doing a number on me all day."

"Really. It must be going around." Matt crossed to the cabinet, took out a bottle of Dewar's, and poured himself a shot.

"So what's the surprise?" I asked. When his eyebrows shot up, I reminded him, "You said on the phone you had something to give me."

"Oh, right." Matt picked up a shopping bag from under his desk, and slid it toward me. "I thought you might want these."

Inside the bag were the Batman bookends that I'd given Corbin to celebrate the publication of *The Fear Factor.* "Poor Reed." His name caught in my throat. "He really wanted to save the world."

"Yeah." Matt took a long swig of his drink.

The phone rang. "Raice," he said. His face tensed. "Are you sure?"

I heard muffled words from the other end. Matt checked his watch. "Thanks," he said. "I'm on my way." He slammed down the phone, and picked up his jacket. "Sorry, Garner. This is getting to be a habit."

"What is it now?"

"That was Barrow. The FBI got an anonymous tip. The Fourth Freedom's planted another bomb. It's going off tonight."

"Where?"

"The Upper West Side, over where they're setting up for the parade."

I'd been running down the hall, trying hard to keep up, but Raice's words sent me reeling into a wall, *God, no.*

"Garner?" Matt turned around.

I said, "It's just...all those people—"

"Tell me about it," he said, grimly.

We walked through the dark reception area. "I want to go with you," I said.

"Forget it. It's out of the question."

"Please." I clutched his sleeve. "I promise I won't get in the way." Then I added, "It's a public place, you know. I can go there, with or without you."

"Jesus Christ, Garner," Raice muttered in frustration; then he sighed. "I don't know why I let you talk me into these things."

FORTY-THREE

I sat in the front seat, holding the bag with Reed's bookends on my lap, while Raice expertly wove his Corvette in and out of the lanes of preholiday traffic. The FBI, he told me, keeping his eyes on the road as he spoke, had been on alert for the past forty-eight hours. Yesterday they investigated a claim that a man fitting Abdul Amer's description had been seen hanging around in front of the Hoboken warehouse where the balloons for the Thanksgiving parade were stored.

"That was the call that came in when I was in your office?"

"Yes. Unfortunately, we got there too late to catch him." Matt sighed. "It would be disastrous if that happened tonight."

"Where did Barrow tell you to meet him?"

"Over at the site," Matt said vaguely. He'd put the windshield wipers on the mist setting, and every time they clacked across the window it made me jump.

"Why don't the police just evacuate the entire area?"

"They're hoping to close in on the terrorists before that becomes necessary," Raice said. "It's a large target. Barrow's got shooters along the rooftops, all the way from Seventy-seventh to Eighty-first, and a team of men circulating in the crowd."

A million variables ran through my mind. "What about us—how will we even get through to them? Where will we park?"

"There's a cordoned area for vehicles with security clearance." Matt dug into his glove compartment and brought out two official passes. "Which we have."

I glanced at the digital clock on the dashboard. "Nine-fourteen," I said.

Matt reached over and touched my shoulder. "Follow my lead, Garner. Act natural. We're just another couple taking a stroll, checking out the parade balloons, okay?"

I clutched the shopping bag close to my chest, afraid I might have to use it as a barf bag. "Yeah, sure."

"The main thing is, you do what I tell you, when I tell you. Agreed?"

"What about Barrow? How do we communicate with him?"

"By radio." Matt patted his jacket. "But let me worry about that."

I looked at the clock again. "Nine-sixteen," I said.

We turned on Seventy-seventh Street. Raice flashed his pass and a city cop motioned us ahead. We pulled behind a line of network news vans and television remote trucks. I wanted to pound on their doors, until I found someone who could tell me where *Front Cover* was shooting. "At least they should evacuate the children, don't you think?" I said, asking no one in particular. "There'll be a lot of kids here. They shouldn't put their lives in danger."

"It's not our decision, Garner," Matt said. He shut off the engine and pocketed the keys. "You ready?"

"Yep." I gave Batman and Bruce Wayne a little squeeze and put the bag down on the floor mat. Then I opened up the door.

The fine spray of rain felt good on my face. Matt linked his arm through mine, and we started up the sidewalk, heading east, against the wind. Visibility was poor. I pulled my hood up over my head. Between the apartment buildings, I caught a fuzzy glimpse of Central Park, green-black and swathed in mist.

Then, all at once, I saw the most strange and wonderful sight. A huge purple mushroom cloud surged into the sky. It twisted spasmodically, buoyed by the breeze. There was the sound of rushing air, and it blossomed further, sprouting a purple head, arms, and feet, and a long purple tail.

"Look." My laughter had a brittle, hysterical edge to it. "Barney!"

Matt quickened the pace. When we reached the end of the block, I stopped short. Up and down Central Park West, as far as the eye could see, the Inflation Eve sideshow was being played out under a big tent of rain. Gigantic balloon characters crouched in the middle of the road, in various stages of being born. Others—giddy with the infusion of pure helium—strained against their ropes, causing panic among the jumpsuited parade workers trying to tether them with sandbags and nets.

Police barricades had already been set up along the length of the parade route. There must've been about a thousand people sitting in chairs or leaning on the wooden horses on either side of this four-block stretch. *Get out of here,* I wanted to scream. *Something awful is going to happen tonight. Run!* But of course, I was really only warning myself.

Uniformed officers stood at regular intervals. Their presence comforted me about as much as the flotation devices did in airplanes. If things went bad, I knew it would be too little, too late. I scanned the block, trying to spot Mercedes's television crew. Would Temple be with her? I didn't want to think of it. "What do we do now?" I asked Raice.

"It's going to be like trying to find a needle

in a haystack." He reached into his pocket, took out a radio, and handed it to me. "Know how to use one?"

"I think so."

"We'd better split up. I'll head up toward Eighty-first, you go downtown. Work your way through the crowd. And keep your eyes on the parade people too, while you're at it."

"How do you expect me to do that?" I protested. "They all look alike in those jumpsuits, especially at night, in this rain."

"Is this going to be too much for you?" Matt asked sharply. "Because you can always go back, you know, wait for me in the car."

"No, no," I said. "I'm fine."

His face relaxed. "Go balloon by balloon. Study body types and faces," he said. "If you see anybody who looks like Amer, radio me his position."

"Will do."

Matt kissed me on the cheek and whispered, "Good luck, Garner."

I watched him disappear into the crowd. All I could think of was that among these carefree, festive faces, there was at least one individual here with murder on his mind. And, too close to him for comfort, were a couple of people I loved—my daughter, and my friend, Mercedes Fields. *You're my friend, Mercedes,* I whispered fiercely to myelf, *you hear that? No matter what happens, you're my friend.*

I moved along the barricades, focusing my attention on the balloon handlers. You could tell just by looking at them the ones who'd done this before; the ones who'd signed up as a lark, not knowing how much work it would entail; the ones whose arms hurt, who wanted to get out of the damn rain.

A group of them were trying to maneuver a flaccid Spider-Man. Next to me, a kid of about ten or eleven started singing, *"Spider-Man, Spider-Man, does whatever a spider can..."* and it made me wonder what it was about boys and comics—Reed and *Batman,* Walter Dean and *Chasm.* "Go home," I said. He told me to fuck off.

Halfway down the block, I finally pinpointed Mercedes Fields in a pale yellow raincoat, working the crowd with her microphone. Temple wasn't anywhere in sight. *Stay away, baby,* I whispered to myself. *Go sit with the guys in the truck.*

I passed another balloon lying, flat as a pancake, on the ground.

"See there, Tommy? There's the Cat in the Hat!" cried an enthusiastic young father.

Tommy, who was only a toddler, made a raspberry sound. "Is not," he told his dad.

Just then, the wind billowed the flat cat a few feet into the air. "Here he comes," said the daddy. The little child clung to him, wailing in fear. I wanted to tell the man to take his son and get away from here, to grab a taxi and drive toward another part of town, but I knew he'd just think I was crazy, so I continued to walk.

Then I stopped.

A few feet ahead of me—watching intently as the Dr. Seuss balloon struggled to take form—stood the waiter I'd seen with Annie Houghton on the night of Reed's book party. Abdul Amer, aka Alex Haver. My stomach lurched. I took a few steps away from the barricade, and put the radio to my lips. "I see him, Matt," I said. "He's standing just south of Seventy-ninth. Near the Cat in the Hat."

"Copy. I've got the area in sight," Raice's voice said. "Now listen. I want you to clear out. *Clear out,* you hear? See the bleachers on the other side of the street?" I answered yes. "Walk over there as fast as you can. Go around back. Hide under the steps until I come for you. Do you copy?" I told him I did.

Before I crossed the street, I went back to young the father. The little boy was curled up, on his shoulder. "He looks pretty tuckered out," I commented in a strange voice, that sounded nothing like my own. "I'd take him home if I were you."

The man stared at me for a moment, then he said, "You know, I think you're right." And I thought, *Hallelujah.*

The bleachers had been cordoned off. Tomorrow, during the big parade, they would be filled with VIPs, Macy's execs and their families. Tonight, their flat metal benches glinted in the rain. Following Matt's directions, I walked around to the rear.

God, I prayed to myself, *please don't let anything bad happen to these people. And let it all be over soon. Amen.*

I ducked under the stairs, entering the dusty, dark area under the metal seats. Almost immediately the rope hooked around my neck, yanking tighter and tighter, forcing the air out, until I could no longer breathe.

I stayed completely still, with the rope around my neck, fighting nausea and the encroaching dark. After what seemed like an eternity, I heard the sound of footsteps. The metal rungs of the bleachers pinged as someone leaned into the crawl space. Through my closed eyes I could feel a flashlight roaming over me.

The man stepped under the bleachers, keeping the beam trained on me. "Mitch?" he whispered.

They came at him from all directions. Six FBI men, heavily armed.

"Barrow," Matthew Raice cried. "Thank God you're here. I saw Amer running away. He must've attacked Garner—"

I sat up straight, relishing the look of surprise on Raice's face.

Barrow said, "Don't worry about Amer. One of my men picked him up the second you crossed the street. He's sitting in a patrol car right now, along with your pal Mitchell— minus the backpack of explosives that were set to go off in an hour."

"I don't understand." Raice looked from Barrow to me.

"You didn't expect the FBI to be here, did you, Matt?" I asked softly. "Bad news for you, huh? Good news for me."

FORTY-FOUR

Once again, it had been my idea to use myself as bait. Barrow hadn't liked my proposal, and Hogan was adamantly opposed to it. Only after Raice's call was patched through to the FBI office where we were meeting did it dawn on them that I was right. The only way to get Matthew Raice—and at the same time capture the bomber—was to throw me into the thick of it.

Still, if Mercedes hadn't insisted that I call the FBI in the first place, it would've been a completely different ending for me. "Call your pal Hogan," she'd urged when I confided in her after Temple went to bed that night. "Didn't you say he'd been working on the Fourth Freedom case? See if the FBI knows anything about a new bomb threat."

"What do you mean?" I'd scoffed. "Of course the FBI knows. I was there when Matt got the call."

"You were there when Matt got *a* call," Mercedes corrected.

When she was right, she was right. Neither Hogan nor Barrow knew anything about a bomb threat. They'd listened with interest, however, while I rambled through my list of suspicions. I admitted that I didn't yet know the why or wherefore. All I had was a disjointed succession of damning images—Reed's face, so drawn and preoccupied; the mysterious benefactor who'd bailed Walter Wozniak out of jail; a shady art dealer in Paris, whom no one at Corbin, Inc., claimed to know; a half-crazed man dying at my feet. And a vermilion Easter egg that opened to reveal the tsar's palace.

It wasn't until I got to Matthew Raice's office that the scope of his deception really hit me. By then, I realized the Jordanian terrorist Abdul Amer hadn't been spotted hanging around a Hoboken warehouse. There was no anonymous tip about a bombing. The FBI wasn't staking out the preparations to the Thanksgiving parade. These developments had been staged, solely for my benefit.

But Matt Raice hadn't counted on my friends at the Bureau, or the team of technicians who'd wired me and wrapped me up in Kevlar. Of course, none of *them* had counted on Raice's pal Mitchell trying to choke the daylights out of me under the bleachers either. Luckily, Mercedes—who never missed a trick, and who was also wearing a wire—had reported seeing a man waiting underneath the metal seats.

I don't know who pounced on Mitchell, but my pal Hogan was the one who reached me first. "Sing to me Hoge," I'd managed to croak.

"I can't." As far as I knew, it was the first time he'd ever turned down a song. "My fucking balls are still up my throat."

After it was over, though, I sat in the back seat of an unmarked car with Temple and Mercedes, when Hogan began to croon, *"I love you. You love me. We're a happy family—"* He glanced over his shoulder and said, "Christ,

Quinn. Did you really say, 'Look. Barney!' to the guy who's been trying to off you for months?"

"Yes, she did," Mercedes said. "I got it on tape and I'm putting it in my story."

"Nice to know you all were listening," I said, leaning on my daughter's shoulder. "While I was out there risking my life."

I met with Matt Raice in a glassed-in interview room in an administrative area of Riker's Island. It was Thanksgiving. Normal people were at home, eating the turkeys they'd stuffed the night before.

Matt's face looked milk white and the trendy stubble on his chin seemed to have gone gray overnight. "I can't get rid of you, can I?" he asked.

"No," I told him. "But you earned points for trying."

He laughed. "Don't take it personally, Garner. You were a major stumbling block, but in some ways, I actually liked you."

"I'm touched." I leaned forward. "How many times did you try to kill me, Matt? There was Reed's book party, only I went and messed things up by giving my seat away. But that wasn't your first attempt, was it? You sent Wozniak the tape from my answering machine—which you'd had in your possession ever since you changed the outgoing message. You must've felt like you'd hit the jackpot when you heard that old message from Temple telling me to come pick her up.

"What was it Wozniak told those detectives? *A little bird gave it to me*—something about an American eagle flying through the red roof and leaving it, special delivery. Of course, everybody knew he was crazy. But even crazy men, holed up at the Red Roof Motel in Eatontown, occasionally get express mail, don't they, Mattie?"

"You're the storyteller, Garner." Raice's eyes were ice cold. "You tell me."

"When I picked up on Adrian Nadeau—one of the dealers you'd been using to fence your stolen treasures—you must've panicked," I said. "You had to get me back from Paris, so you arranged to bail Walter Wozniak out of jail."

"Old dumbass Walt," Matt muttered.

"Yeah." I nodded. "He was a tad too nuts to do your bidding by then. You had to cook up another plan."

I'd already figured out the scenario. Mitchell, the cowboy bodyguard, had fiddled with our gas lines, leaking enough carbon monoxide into the house to make Cilda and me sleepy. Then he'd waited for Joey to make his rounds, lured the poor boy onto the beach, and bashed in his head.

Mitch knew Walter Dean had been camped out in the woods for days. The only thing left for him to do was set the house on fire, wait until his four a.m. shift, and then report it. At that point, I'd be char-grilled and Wozniak the stalker would be neatly taken into custody. But the premature birth of Cilda's granddaughter had put a snag in the plan.

I realized now that if I hadn't called the fire department when I did, Mitch would've put a bullet in my head and blamed it on Walter. But with the trucks halfway down the drive, he hadn't dared to take the chance. Instead he'd put his arm around me, and cooed in his soft Texas drawl, *Ain't nobody can hurt you now.*

"That must've been the final straw," I said to Matt. "You must've nearly gone berserk when you got the call saying I was alive."

"Tell me about it." His face darkened. "You've been a pain in my ass from the very beginning."

"I used to think you were kidding when you said that." I shook my head at my own naïveté. "Guess eventually you figured out a way to use my persistence to your advantage, huh? You knew if you set it up right, I'd insist on going to Central Park.

"You had Amer stationed in the crowd, and Mitchell under the bleachers. By taking me out in such a public place, you were killing two birds with one stone. You could play the part of the hero, finding my body, then later you could shoot the fleeing terrorist. I imagine Abdul was becoming too much of a liability, anyway."

Raice nibbled the cuticle of one nail. "I was just so tired of you nosing around," he said softly.

"You know, I can almost understand," I told him. "I posed a threat. You wanted me gone— like you said, it wasn't personal. But killing Reed, killing your *best friend*…What makes a person do something like that?"

Raice shifted his weight in the chair. Even now, I could tell by his face; he wanted me dead in the worst way. I glanced at the guard outside the door. "They never took me seriously. Reed and my old man."

Matt folded his arms petulantly across his chest. In that moment I saw the angry little boy, still looking for his father's approval. Then his expression darkened. "You think Reed would've gotten all those big-name clients if it wasn't for me?"

I didn't answer. Hogan and Barrow had spent the previous twelve hours piecing it all together, aided by Mitchell's confession and the testimony of several bewildered innocents at Corbin, including Mike Fedora, Bill Mallet, and Tamara Ma. It appeared that Matt Raice had been double-dealing his partner for years. Using Corbin's PREDICT system as a data base, he'd assembled a portfolio of men and women who fit a certain profile—cold-blooded assassins; cat burglars and thieves; loners who could be manipulated by the promise of easy money; terrorists with causes to proclaim; sociopaths who enjoyed living life at the edge.

Raice had them all at his fingertips. In the words of his best friend—*nobody understood the criminal mind better.* The scheme was simple, but brilliant. Raice would set his sights on a wealthy target, then decide how best to proceed. Most often a robbery would be enough to convince a target they needed to hire a security firm. Sometimes they had to be hit on a more psychological level, threatened or stalked.

Matt contracted these jobs out to the

experts—the ones who not only knew how to break into houses, or scare the wits out of someone, but actually got a rush from it. Then he'd sit back and wait for the frantic new client to apply to Corbin, Inc., for protection.

It was the ruse he'd pulled on Dane Blackmoor, the same one he'd used on Warren Petty fifteen years before. But after overbilling and siphoning money from Petty's account for so long, Raice got sloppy. He had an eye for beautiful things, and often he couldn't bring himself to part with them. Petty became suspicious when he noticed a painting hanging on Raice's wall, a rare watercolor that had been stolen from one of the billionaire's wealthy friends a few years before.

Realizing his mistake, Matt had been forced to act swiftly and terribly. He engaged the services of Abdul Amer, a Muslim fanatic, who'd been more than willing to set the bomb in Petty's jet in order to gain a platform for his beliefs. So that it would appear the act had been orchestrated by a splinter terrorist organization, Matt invented "The Fourth Freedom"—a name that had puzzled Dane Blackmoor for its undeniably American ring.

The fourth freedom, as outlined by Franklin Roosevelt, was the freedom from fear. In an act of childish arrogance, Matt Raice had named the phony terrorist group after a Norman Rockwell painting.

"What about Annie?" I'd asked him. "How was she involved?"

Matt only shook his head. Annie, he said,

had the misfortune of being in the wrong place at the wrong time. They'd hooked up together in Paris, and later spent a week in the south of France. She was a nice girl, aggressive in the bedroom and out, which he rather enjoyed, although according to him, it had proven her undoing.

"If she hadn't chased me all the way to New York"—Matt sighed—"she'd still be alive today." He said this as if he really believed Annie's headstrong nature had more to do with her death than the bomb he'd set, which ultimately killed her.

"But how did she recognize Amer?" I persisted.

That was a fluke, Matt said. He'd made the mistake of showing her how the PREDICT system worked. Annie had just happened to see the wrong face.

"You know, I'm not what you think I am," he told me.

"What do I think you are?"

"Some *psychopath.*" The word clearly disgusted him. "I don't have a mental condition. I simply made choices. Some of them were damn hard.

"You think I wanted to kill Reed?" Matt laughed off the preposterous idea. "It was either him or me, babe. He knew something was wrong with the Petty case. Another day and he would've made the connection with Nadeau. But I never killed anyone indiscriminately. I made sure my old man wasn't on stage, didn't I? I could've gotten rid of him at the same time as Reed, if I'd wanted to."

Raice sat up straight and stared coldly into my eyes. "It was the fucking Fabergé egg that turned you onto me, wasn't it, Garner?" I remained silent. "The minute my mother said you'd stopped by to see them, I thought, *Oh shit.*

"You want to hear something really funny?" he went on. "My mother never liked that egg. It offended her sensibilities because she thought it was a knockoff, a fake. But old Gerald, the absentminded professor, he *knew* all right. Deep down in that vague, senile mind of his, he probably even suspected how I got it, but he's so addled, so fried, he's past all caring."

Matt leered at me. "That egg was just so fucking exquisite he wanted it. And he owed it all to me. Ironic, isn't it?"

The day after Thanksgiving a jubilant Peggy Boyle called me at Mercedes's apartment. "I drew up the contracts," she said. "The buyer is extremely motivated, Mrs. Quinn. He suggested we meet at the house to get the papers signed."

"When?"

"Well, of course it's up to you," she deferred, "but generally speaking, sooner's better than later."

Boyle was right; there was no use in putting this off. "I could make it down there by three," I told her.

Temple had been listening in on the conversation. Now she turned to me. "Are you really going through with it, Mom?"

"Yes," I said. "I really am."

My trusty old Volvo had been sitting in Ben Snow's garage ever since the fire, so that afternoon we headed down the shore in a rented Jeep Cherokee. Cilda, who'd taken the day off from playing grandma to her namesake, sat in the back, knitting something pink.

"Where will we live?" Temple asked.

"I don't know, kiddo. But we'll probably know it when we see it."

The temperature had dropped considerably over the past two days, and the sky looked like snow. We took the long route, down Ocean Avenue, marveling at the waves as though they were old friends who'd grown since the last time we'd met. At the Spring Lake gate, I put

340

the Jeep in park, and turned off the radio. "I can't do this," I said.

Temple clapped, and Cilda stopped knitting. I put the car in drive again, continuing down the road until I reached the big old house. "Stay here," I told them. "I'll handle this myself." I got out of the Jeep, walked over to the big For Sale sign, and pulled it out by its muddy prongs.

It wasn't until I reached the front door that I realized all the windows in the house were wide open. Peggy Boyle appeared on the threshold, looking flushed and nervous. "What's going on?" I demanded. "It's freezing in here."

"The buyer said he wanted to air the place out." Peg wrung her hands.

"Tell the buyer the deal's off." I tossed the sign down in a corner of the empty foyer. "I've decided not to sell."

"But Mrs. Quinn—"

I walked past her, into what had once been the drawing room, but was now just a room with no name. The open windows were causing the long chiffon drapes to billow like sails. Dane Blackmoor stood near the piano.

"It's amazing," he said, "what a little fresh air can do."

I swallowed hard, and looked right at him. "I've decided not to sell the house."

Blackmoor took a step toward me. "I thought you said it never felt like a home." He brushed a few little snowflakes from my hair. "That it was missing something."

"Not anymore," I said, walking into his arms.